CONTENTS

This story was written for my family. My mom and dad who, if they were still here, would be proud of me. Donnie, the little brother I miss dearly, and Jay and Roxanne, the brother and sister who remain supportive.

My thanks goes out to all the those friends who encouraged me to write—Tim, Harry, Michelle, Linda, Mike and Connie—thank you so much, and most importantly Anne Hill. A special thanks to Julie Richardson who without your help I would not have finished.

PREFACE

Leslie Phillips, RIP

Leslie Phillips felt her world collapsing as the life drained from her body. The struggle to remain conscious was surrendering to the grip and pressure of her attacker, an attacker with a vise-like grip that prevented her from twisting or turning to free herself. Only her mind remained alert, filled with questions of why and how this had come to happen to her? She was fully aware that her attacker was someone she had come to know and occupied a position that would evoke trust.

The proceeding day and evening had been no different than many of her days or evenings during this time of year. It had been a day of flitting from one private party to another on the last day of one of the largest barbecue competitions in the world. The parking lot of the massive Dome complex had been transformed from parking squares to avenues and promenades with names and number separating the placement of large tented structures housing the three hundred-plus teams who participated in the competition. Each team had brought high-tech barbecue pits so large they were carried on wheeled trailers. Elaborate faux fronts lined the avenues reflecting the name of each team and many of their corporate sponsors. Each tent was strictly for team participants and guests; wooden and wire fences constructed on the outer edges of their assigned spaces discouraged the casual passerby or the uninvited from entering.

Leslie had spent the day in the company of some of the rich and infamous members of the largest charity rodeo and livestock show in the world. She had parlayed her companions and the inescapable fact that she was an attractive young woman into assuring her entrance into even the most selective of venues. As the evening wore on she and the entourage she followed had retired to the VIP club, housed in the new stadium, to complete their day with a final couple of nightcaps. One of the men had been very attentive to her all night and, in her state of inebriation, she had let her morals slide and had sex with the man in the bathroom. It had been only a momentray tryst, but it was way outside her normal upright character. A liaison that left her both unsatisfied and regretful of her slip in morals and decency, but nevertheless it had been part of the role she played as a Badge Bunny.

"Badge Bunnies" or "Buckle Bunnies" were the local slang terms for girls who hung around outside the contestant facilities at rodeos seeking to meet the daring young men who rode the rough stock in the bull and horse events. The term had morphed into "Badge Bunnies" as a phrase to characterize those girls who hung around and offered themselves to generally older and married men who made up the hierarchy of this particular charity soiree.

Subsequent to her sexual adventure in the bathroom with her quick-firing admirer, she had returned to the club only to find that he and his accomplices in debauchery were fixin' to leave for another of their frequented watering holes. The young ladies were not to be included in their company. Leslie had passed tipsy a long time ago, but she didn't think she was too impaired to find her car and drive herself home. An offer of a ride home was made by a staff member of the club and politely turned down; after all, she reasoned, I'm a capable young woman and home is close.

At the moment of the attack she had tried to scream, but her pleading had been choked off and the only sound she could hear was the gurgling and the gush of air from her lungs. Her once shining eyes were growing dim, like someone was using a candle snuffer to extinguish the flickering flames, one by one. Her body weakened and she slumped against her attacker—a person she had once thought of as an ally.

Just as Leslie gasped to breathe her last breath, she realized her world was ending. Images of lost family flooded her mind and her face took on a mask of serenity. *I'll soon be joining Mom and Dad....*

It was in this moment the killer always found the intrigue of a victim's death both surreal and satisfying. Still holding the victim tightly, the killer could feel the calm wash over her and the prevailing silence that accompanied the beautiful young woman's last moments of life. These last seconds sent shivers of ecstasy through the killer's mind and body like the afterglow of passionate lovemaking. This final surrender of the victim and the killer's acknowledgement of total control of this lovely person's death brought back to mind the memory of the first kill. That wondrous adventure and the reasons for starting down this path oh, so many years ago. Not a one of the killer's victims had any idea why this was happening to them or how they had been selected. That was a secret only the killer could answer and didn't share with the innocent; only the diary the killer kept would chronicle the passion.

Teetering on the brink of darkness, sinking into unconsciousness, Leslie was spared the knowledge of what the killer had in mind for the climax of the demented act. Her final seconds of life were filled with the smell of honeysuckle and the caress of soft lips on hers. Then she heard her nemesis whisper, "My sweet darling, you are going to join your sisters of sin where you belong."

CHAPTER ONE

Death at the Dome

Storm rolled over, hoping it was a dream, but he soon knew it wasn't. It was his mandatory office cell phone playing that god-awful "Stormy Weather" ring tone the guys at work had programmed into it just to annoy him. Done as a bad joke and play on his name, Storm was not technically savvy enough to change it, so over time he had come to accept and hate that maddening electronic version of a tune he had once liked. Sundays were the only days he could sleep in—although sleeping was rarely what he did; rather, tossing and turning was usually how he spent those extra morning hours. A few hours rest here and a few hours there were all he had been able to get since Angie, his wife, had been murdered. Her memory and the fact that no one had ever been caught for the crime gave him dreams, nightmares really, that had awakened him in the middle of almost every night since he had found her lying across the threshold of the door to the home they shared. He would find himself kicking off the blankets and sweating as if he was back in college persevering through the miserably hot two-a-days at Texas Tech fall football camp. He had tried to ignore the dreams and train his conscious mind to forget them, but the unconscious emotions they left behind were quite another matter.

He picked up the ever-present cell phone from the nightstand, quickly looking at the clock display illuminated on its face. It was 6:30 AM, way earlier than he normally arose on Sunday. As he had feared, the office was calling him. His office was not your normal Houstonian's office. Storm was a Houston Police homicide detective and if they were calling him it meant someone had died the night before and he had to go look for a bad guy.

Though Houston had been like a small town when Storm became a cop, a town struggling with its growth and population expansion, now it had become a metropolis like any other large city, where someone always dies on a Saturday night. Death could find anyone but not all of the homicides are cases that require the expertise of a detective, especially one on his only day off. Most Saturday night fracases fell into the category of gang hits or they involved some incorrigibles in a bar fight that ended in a death. These murders were usually easily solved and seldom required a detective's expertise.

Storm shook his head trying to clear the cobwebs and hoping to sound a little more awake when he called the number back.

"Dispatch."

"This is Storm. What's up?"

"Hey, Detective; Lt. Flynn passed this one to you. A body's been found at the Dome."

Storm knew immediately where he needed to go. Many Houstonians still called the area "the Dome" even though the old domed stadium itself had become dormant since being replaced with a new stadium and convention center complex that now almost blocked it's view from the street.

"Got any details?"

"Nope. Only you're to see Sergeant Hebert when you get there. The officers at the gate will tell you where to find him."

Storm groaned. "Thanks." He hung up the phone, rolled over, and put his feet on the old wood floor of his bedroom. The highly polished oak surface was cold in late February and it sent a shiver up his legs that ended in the base of his neck. Storm's six-foot-three two-hundred-forty pound frame struggled to free itself of the bed. The years of physical abuse he had put his body through had left its toll. Years of sports in high school and college and years of pick-up games in the park had weakened the knees and caused his lower back to spasm as if held in a vice. Add the last few years of wallowing in self-imposed depression and alcohol, he knew he would never again be the same man he had once been. He hesitated to look in the mirror, because when he did, he saw the refection of his father looking back at him. The once black hair had grey flecks throughout the temples. The once bright brown eyes now appeared somewhat duller, and even his mustache had wild unruly whiskers of gray running through it.

As children, Storm and his little brother had always been told how much they looked like their mother. Her native American heritage and perpetually tanned skin and dark black hair repeated itself in the boys' complexions and hair. What people often failed to notice was that their features were more angular and Anglo, more reflective of their father's western European linage. As Angie had always said; he was a contrast in nature, a true American mutt.

The house where he now lived in lonely silence had been a celebratory purchase after Angie had gotten her promotion. Angela Storm had been the love of his life, his wife and his best friend. She had been named the vice president of sales for a large oil field supply company. Although her income dwarfed Storm's, she never gloated or was the least bit flagrant with her earning power; they were partners so the total always outweighed their individuality. With their combination of incomes and Angie's desire to own a home, they could now afford to buy a house in the neighborhood she wanted, and that was the old historic Houston Heights. Always the eternal optimist, Angie convinced him that the close-in neighborhood would rebound and their investment would grow. Storm thought of her as a Mary Poppins, who always saw the future ahead as brighter than he did and in spite of his hesitation, he agreed and went along for the ride.

The Heights is an old community adjacent to downtown Houston, with classical wood Victorian houses built in the 1920s and '30s. Constructed before Houston's meteoric expansion, the Heights had been the part of town where the working class had lived. They rode trolley cars and horse drawn carriages downtown to work and in the evening families sat on the porches hoping to catch any cooling breeze that might blow down the tree-lined streets. They waved and greeted their neighbors. Children played in the front yards, as was the custom in early Houston, before retiring to bedrooms with screened windows and oscillating ceiling fans.

The neighborhood had been idyllic in the '20s and '30s, but as the city began its development to the suburbs west, east, south and north, it had lost its appeal to most Houston natives. Houston became a boomtown attracting people from around the world seeking their fortunes, but in the '60s and '70s, Houstonians seemed to all want new homes with big yards and with nice new schools built nearby. Even the oil companies were moving out of downtown to the upscale Galleria area and modern developments further north and west. With the addition of the new interstates and four lane highways the commute downtown became easily accessible for the newly rich and growing middle class. Many of these Houstonians worked in the growing oil patch or the growing medical field and wanted to stake their claim to a piece of the American dream.

Following these Houstonians' exodus to the suburbs, the Heights became a low cost housing area, which meant it was an area where oppressed immigrants coming across the border to seek a better way of life could find cheap places to live. Four or five families would move in together and they could save their money to send home to the families they had left behind.

In the 1980s the yuppie movement started in Houston, and the Heights began to make a resurgence. Oil companies, engineering firms, and banking institutions built giant skyscrapers as paeans to their success and more people were again working downtown. The super highways of the 1950s were becoming congested and could not keep up with the growing traffic. Some of the advantages the suburbs had offered in the early days were now gone, replaced with hour-long commutes or trips on the express buses, which meant leaving the Houstonian's ever valued personal car at home. In Houston the idea of leaving your car at home was akin to not being able to drink a cold "tall boy" on the drive home—it was just not done in Texas. Eager young couples began to buy up the dilapidated Heights properties and remodel them or replace them with updated three-thousand-square-feet contemporary two and three story homes; most were replicas of the original homes with the advantages of modern innovations.

Angie had always been the one who had the solid judgment for investments—even her ventures into the stock market had paid dividends. She had seen this trend coming and had pushed Storm to buy a stately two-story three-bedroom, pier and beam house, built circa 1930s with shuttered windows and porches that ran the length of the house.

Although he put up a good fight, Storm's plea to buy a new house in the west part of town had fallen on deaf ears. Shortly after college when he was still single, he had lived

9

in the Galleria area of town and loved it. It was a great place to see and be seen, with country dance clubs, upscale restaurants, and other frequented haunts, life was good. But Angie stuck to her guns about the Heights, as she always did, and like she always did, she got Storm to accept her plan. It was always a war he couldn't win and mostly didn't care to. She would giggle and smile at him and he knew his goose was cooked. When it came to Angie, he had always been out of his league; that was another thought that always made him smile. Storm had been a college football player when they met. He had never had a problem meeting cute girls, but not the type of girl you would marry or take home to Mom. When he met Angie he knew that intrigue was over. She was not only beautiful, but she was smart. She used to tell him she was smart enough to marry him.

They had fixed up the house, turning it into a three-bedroom home with two-and-one-half baths and a large family/party room, which opened onto the kitchen. Over the years the house had been a great place for their friends to gather and have fall-down, party-your-butt-off barbecues.

Angie, though, had always wanted children. She was of Italian descent, tall and slender with those magazine model good looks. Blended with Storm's rugged athletic features, a bright gorgeous child would have been a natural outcome. Storm continually wanted to give Angie everything she required. Unfortunately, the extra bedroom went unfinished along with their hopes of picking the paint colors for a son or a daughter. Children seemed not be something he could give her, and as yet, adoption had not been a consideration.

* * * *

Sunday was usually Storm's day to rest; it was also the day that left him with unfilled time to dwell on memories. While flooded with thoughts of the past, he also knew he had things to do and a place to be. Storm dragged himself to the shower and began his routine. He was out of the house in less than twenty minutes, not that the body was going anywhere, but time is always critical when you investigate a murder.

The trip from Storm's house to the Dome took no time at all. He used service roads and the back streets, arriving only forty minutes after he had received the phone call from the dispatcher. The Dome complex had changed immensely in the past two years with the addition of a new stadium and the demolition of the old convention hall. There were even rumors that the Dome itself would be torn down, but Storm had never heard anything confirming that those innuendos were anything more than gossip. He felt they came from people with too much time on their hands who tried to guess the future, however he also knew you could never totally discount rumors, as many times, fiction did become fact.

The main entrance to the Dome complex hadn't changed, at least not yet, and he turned in between the banners advertising the Lone Star Livestock Show and Rodeo. Why didn't I remember it's that time of year? He asked himself.

Lone Star time was when Houstonians dusted off their hats and shined their boots in hopes of recapturing the days of cowboys and the cattle herds that had once thrived on the land that surrounded the city of Houston. That storied past, with its free grazing land where cowboys slept under the stars was long gone, replaced with oil company offices and new housing developments. But once a year the city donned its Western garb and cowboy attitudes of the old days in the guise of raising scholarship money. Houston was proud of its Lone Star Livestock Show and Rodeo and the contributions it had made to youth of the city and surrounding rural South Texas, but Storm was also always amused at the trappings of the event. Women wore leather outfits adorned with feathers and fur and the men wore their cowboy hats and expensive exotic skinned boots, talking of horses and cattle, when again, Storm was sure the closest

11

most of them had been to a horse was the local racetrack on the north side of Houston.

Storm was waved through the north Kirby gate by one of parking lot attendants working the early shift. He noted how the new stadium's sign, its big bright red letters announcing its new name and sponsor, reflected the change from the old Dome days. The stadium, only a year old, sat directly on Kirby Street; the rest of the complex's sixty-five acres was bounded by Fannin, Old Spanish Trail, and Interstate 610. The new stadium was grand—actually, so big it almost blocked out the view of the old Dome from the street. Like many native Houstonians, Storm was resistant to change. The thought that the "Eighth Wonder of World", as it was once called, had been diminished to a supporting player gnawed at him like the loss of an old friend.

The huge new convention center surrounded the Dome on its north side, and the sheer size and scope of the place was overwhelming, so Storm had not yet been able to locate the flashing lights or police presence of the murder scene.

"Where they at?" he asked the guard, showing him his badge.

"The cops? Boss, you will need to go ahead on and turn around and pull in at the south Kirby gate," the guard directed him. "That's where I seen the other police cars go in." Storm backtracked and turned left so that he could enter at the south side of the stadium.

So far, this morning had not been one of Storm's best: he had lost sleep, wrestled with memories of Angie, been faced with changes he wanted to ignore to a place he had known and enjoyed most of his life, and as yet, had not even had his first cup of coffee. What else did this morning have in store for him? Only the murder scene would to tell him that.

After entering the southern gate he saw the cars and crime scene tape around the site of the discovery of the body. He parked, got out, and immediately saw Sergeant Ralph Hebert holding court as the officer in charge of the scene. Sergeant Hebert saw him too and motioned him over to where he was regaling his troops with stories of the old days...

"Well, Detective, nice to see you could join us this morning." His snide tone registered his disapproval.

Sergeant Hebert was a thirty-year veteran cop and had been around the department most of his adult life. He made it clear to anyone who would listen that anyone but a street cop was an overpaid, pampered pencil pusher. Born and raised in southeast Texas, Hebert was more Cajun than Texan and was obviously proud of it. He was known to be hard headed and contrary, but in all their dealings Storm had always felt that, although cantankerous, he was always fair.

"Nice to see you too, 'Hee-bert.'" Storm knew that to pronounce Hebert's name with an "e" sound rather the "a" sound (most Cajuns used the "a" sound) would piss him off. One good verbal jab deserved another. "What have we got?"

Hebert, glowering at him, spat out, "Dead girl found at around 5:00 AM this morning, nude. She fell out of a trash dumpster over there." He pointed to a row of dumpsters placed in the parking lot for use during the three-day Livestock Show Barbecue Cook-off, which was a precursor to the three-week long show that would begin tomorrow.

"Who found her?" Asked Storm.

Hebert just pointed to a man wearing what looked like a cleaning crew uniform standing with a group of other police officers and dismissed Storm by saying, "You're the big detective, you figure it out."

The medical examiner had not yet arrived so the body was still lying where it had been discovered. Storm could tell even from a distance that the girl was young, brunette, and had ash-colored skin due to blood loss. As he got closer he saw that her features looked almost serene. She had been a pretty girl and way too young to have come to this awful end in this cold place. She was naked and no one had covered her up, probably waiting for the M.E. and the crime scene people to arrive to officially pronounce her dead. Although the M. E. would establish an official cause of death later, Storm could see her throat had been cut, slit from ear to ear, he also noticed there didn't seem to be much blood around. If this young girl had died here and bled out, there would have much more blood, but there was no sign of any. The poor girl was lying there exposed to the prurient interest of the onlookers.

The policemen standing around the girl's body were talking to the man in the cleaning crew uniform when Storm walked over.

"I'm Detective Storm of HPD. Your name, sir?"

"Ernie—Earnest—Underwood."

Storm noted the name on his notepad. "Occupation?"

"I works for Manpower doin' cleanup for the livestock show."

Storm knew Manpower provided temporary help to the Livestock Show. They contracted for cleanup of the facility in the early hours of the morning before the crowds arrived. Manpower's employees were mostly men on hard times who needed work and would do so for minimum wage. The livestock show had always been about helping the community in one way or another since its inception in the late 1930s and hiring these men qualified as one way to help.

"OK, Ernie, how did you find her? What made you look in here?" Asked Storm.

Ernie said eagerly, "Well, Boss, I comes out here to throw out the garbage bags from the stadium. We carry them bags down to the loading docks of the stadium and when the dumpsters there are full we start to bringing dem out here. This is loose," Ernie motioned to the hinges that held the doors to the dumpster open, "and when I pulled on it, the door fell open like it is now. Kinda like it's broke or something, so I hadta be careful not to tump everything inside out, ya know? Well, I was making sure it didn't tump all over on ground when this arm fell out. Boss, it scaid the hell outta me, so I jumped back and that's when that white girl came a-tumblin' outta that thing. I ran back inside and got the boss and he was the one who called the police. I been out chere ever since talking to all the policemen."

Ernie hesitated a little looking at Storm with frightened eyes. "Boss, that girl is a white girl."

"Yes, I see that," Storm replied dryly.

"Well, Boss, I just found her, nothing else. I been workin' inside 'til I found her. You can ask everyone they will tell ya, I was inside till I found her."

Ernie sounded scared. Storm didn't blame him. Like a lot of big cities, the HPD's record with minorities wasn't sterling. In the midst of jotting his notes, Storm stopped and looked at Ernie. "Don't worry; I am sure you did the right thing. We will just double-check with your boss before we leave. Now what time was it when you found her?"

"Well, we got to work about midnight and by the time we were done with the stadium it was about four in the morning. I was down on the docks for awhile, then started to carry things out here where I filled up that one first," pointing to the dumpster next to one where the young girl lay. So I guess it was about 4:30 when I found her."

"Have you touched or moved her since you found her?" asked Storm.

"No, Boss, I don't. I told you it scaid me and when I came back down here I brought the boss. I didn't want to be alone with her 'til you police showed up." After a momentary pause and a sideways glance, he continued, "But, Boss, them policemen did pick her up and move her some, not much, but some." Ernie quickly darted his eyes toward a group of police still standing near the girl's naked body, ogling her.

"What do you mean they 'picked her up?'" Storm asked.

"Well, Boss, when she came out of that thing she fell out face down, and well, they rolled her over to look at her," Ernie said nervously.

15

Beat cops ignoring procedure was nothing new to Storm. In his experience with HPD, what cops did or didn't do didn't surprise him anymore. More than once he had seen policemen on the scene move or roll a body, especially if it was a young woman, so they could see her exposed breasts or some other exposed part of her body. Storm never ceased to be amazed by the perverted behavior of the human race, but most especially, the police. When he asked the policemen who had moved the body no one took credit.

"Who moved this girl?" Stormed directed his questions to the cops standing closest to girl still looking at her.

Sheepishly the men turned their heads as if they didn't hear his questions. "I said, 'who turned this girl over?' Did you?" Storm stood in the face of a big black officer standing next to the dumpster.

"No, didn't touch that white girl, none of us did." The patrolman was visibly angered at being spoken to this way, but Storm wasn't backing down.

"Then who did? How long you been here?" Storm's voice was getting louder and his face showed his distaste for the men.

"Me?" asked the officer.

"Yes, you dumb ass, were you first on scene?" asked Storm.

"No, I just got here a few minutes ago," answered the patrolman.

"But you felt you needed to come over and look at a naked dead girl?" Storm was barely able to control his anger. The black patrolman and other officers slowly turned, lowered their heads and began to walk away. Storm was pretty sure he had made his point.

Hebert had heard the conversation and started to voice his objections to Storm talking that way to his men, but before he could Storm got in his face. "If I ever come to another crime scene where your officers have gotten their jollies off looking at a dead girl and I find out they have moved the body I am going to arrest them for interfering with an investigation and since you are in charge of them I might just file charges against you, too."

All Hebert could do was sputter; he knew his men had turned the girl over; he knew they had been looking at her, but that was what cops did. "OK, Detective, OK. My people were wrong, but you yelling at them ain't gonna do any good. We are at your direction now."

From the lack of blood in the area it was obvious to Storm the girl had bled out somewhere else. It didn't really hinder the investigation that her body had been moved, but the fact they had stood there ogling her pissed Storm off. This girl was a human being and she deserved some final respect and dignity in death. Storm removed his jacket and covered the girl's naked torso until the forensics team could arrive.

After calming down Storm turned and asked Hebert "You found any clothing, shoes, panties, anything else?"

"Nope. We've looked through the dumpster. Nothing, zip."

The morbid interest of the loitering police officers was over but they still had to wait for the M.E. to declare a preliminary cause of death and move the young woman's body from its resting place. Storm would retrieve his jacket then.

Charity Kills

CHAPTER TWO

A Slip of the Tongue

By the time the crime lab folks and M.E. showed up, it was almost 8:00 AM. This morning was already dragging by and Storm had still not had coffee. Hunger was setting in, causing his stomach to rumble, it crossed his mind. *I could eat the north end of a south-going skunk.* Storm shook off the hunger pangs and the growing desire for coffee, finding it, as he always did, amazing he could still think of food after seeing a young pretty girl lying dead in a heap of garbage with her throat cut, but he did.

The M.E. and crime lab crew didn't take long to pronounce the girl dead and report they had found no clothing or ID in the dumpster where her body had been discovered.

"All right, we'll have to look for her personal effects." At that point Storm summoned the same cops he had chewed out. "Now, listen up," Storm directed the policemen waiting for instruction. "Search the grounds around all entries and exits and all other dumpsters in the area. Be looking for girl's clothing or a purse or wallet with some type of identification so we can give this unfortunate girl a name. Keep your eyes peeled for a possible bloody crime scene where the attack might have actually taken place. Bag anything you find and keep the evidence pristine. Got it?"

Storm left the killing field to drive downtown to police headquarters and check in with whatever superior was working the shift today. Sundays were normally days off for many of the force, but those responsible for overseeing the workings of a police division took turns rotating once a month to handle the weekend shift. Even if not physically onsite, they were on call twenty-four hours a day over that time period.

I also need to pay a visit to the M.E.'s office, Storm decided. I'll go after I'm sure she's received the body. Maybe the staff will be able to shed more light on the events leading up to the girl's death.

On the way downtown there was going to have to be the obligatory stop at a new Starbucks in the West University area for his much required and overdue cup of coffee. Although it was still early when he made the stop, the coffee bar was already full with a long waiting line that stretched to the front door. Storm despised lines and couldn't imagine why so many people would get up so early to get a cup of very expensive coffee with steamed cream in it. However there he was, too, begrudging the wait to get his "Grande" and head on to his office.

The extra large cup of specialized coffee did satisfy a small portion of his void but his stomach wanted more—hopefully he'd find a few of the much maligned donuts in the coffee room at Homicide Headquarters. If he really got lucky he might find someone had brought in *kolaches*, baked rolls of dough filled with meat or fruit, a local breakfast treat that probably originated in Slovakia and his personal favorite. The consumption of coffee and thoughts of kolaches at least momentarily diverted his mind from the image in his mind of the dead girl lying there with her throat cut.

He parked and headed for the entry of "59 Reisner Street," Houston police headquarters and office for his division of the homicide department. Ever since 9/11, procedures for entering a city, county, state, or federal building had changed. All entries and exits were now miniature mazes that would allow the guards at the door the ability to handle one person at a time. Non-law enforcement personnel entered the maze waiting their turn to unload any objects that might set off the metal detectors and to open for the guard's scrutiny any briefcases or file boxes they might be carrying. Law enforcement personnel entered through another opening where they had to display credentials indicating they were allowed to carry weapons on their bodies without unloading personal side arms and ammunition magazines. They, too, would be scrutinized and often requested to open any container they might be carrying.

Storm pulled his ID and badge and slid them across the table at the guard. The guard nodded his head. "OK, sir, proceed," he said, handing the credentials back. Storm crossed the lobby to the elevators and rode up to the third floor of headquarters to check in.

His immediate boss, the man who would have normally not been in on a Sunday , was sitting in his office waiting for Storm and motioned him in with a wave of his hand. Call it respect or old-fashioned manners, but Storm always stood in the boss's office and never sat unless invited to. The boss might have been younger than Storm but protocol prevailed. Storm was one of those who believed that in the presence of a superior you didn't sit or relax slumping in a chair.

His boss, Lt. Ralph Flynn, was a young black police lieutenant who had made grade faster than most. He was almost ten years younger than Storm and rumor suggested him to be very attached to the mayor's office. Lieutenant Flynn, well educated in Eastern schools, had worked on

Richard Lemay's staff in New York City when he was chief of police there and had followed Lemay to Houston when Lemay had returned and become mayor.

Flynn had only been lieutenant for a year now, but he had made it clear to Storm he was aware of the detective's reputation. He had made it no secret to Storm about what would happen if he screwed up again. Storm merely shrugged it off—he knew he had made his own bed and there was nothing to do now but lie in it. His only other option was to retire, but he was too young and he wasn't ready for that yet. Besides, the lieutenant was only calling it like he saw it. Flynn seemed fair so far, so Storm had no problem working mundane cases and doing follow-up work.

When Storm's wife Angie had been killed and the sparse leads had gone nowhere, Storm had gone off the deep end. Angie had been coming home from one of her numerous trips out of town, this time to Latin America. She had been negotiating a deal for oil tools manufactured by her company with Latin American offshore drillers. Her plane had arrived back to Bush International Airport around 5:00 PM but by the time she had retrieved her bags and cleared Customs it was closer to 6:00 PM and already dark in the Bayou City. As a company executive Angie knew she had the clearance to use a limousine service to pick her up and take her to the airport. Similarly, on her return she could call the service, and by the time she cleared Customs, a driver would be waiting to carry her home.

Storm had worked late that night on a murder/suicide, a case involving a husband who had accused his wife of cheating and then killed her and himself out of remorse. Excited to see his wife after her trip, Storm cleaned up the paperwork related to the homicide and hurried home, hopeful of finding his wife waiting for him.

He found her, all right—lying just inside the front door in a pool of her own blood, shot twice in the back of the head by what appeared to be a small caliber gun. From the looks of things he could not have been more than thirty minutes behind her. She was dead and her blood was soaking the foyer.

In a state of panic he called 911 and then Russell, his best friend, but there was nothing anyone could do for Angie. Arriving patrol cars and the emergency ambulance personnel found Storm sitting in the doorway holding Angie's bloody head in his lap, sobbing like a baby. Russell, his staunch ally for so many years, arrived shortly after the police; all Russell could do was comfort his friend, who went from shock and depression to outright rage. "I will kill whoever killed my Angie," he swore to Russell. "I will hunt him down. And I will kill him."

As in any homicide, the first person you look at is the spouse, but Storm's alibi was air tight. He had been working on the night's murder/suicide with other detectives at the time that Angie had been murdered. Angie had no known enemies, and even with Storm and her employers racking their brains, no possible scenario except for robbery could be deduced.

Since her purse and money had been found with her, the motive of robbery was out of the question. No leads were uncovered and the investigation stalled, although it was never out of the minds of Storm's friends or fellow police officers. It downright haunted him, but nothing had turned up to implicate anyone.

Angie's murder was sent to the unsolved cases file, and only a fluke would ever reopen it again. After her death Storm often didn't show up for work at all, or if he did, he would be drunk or drinking. He developed a penchant for screwing up some high profile murder cases and was replaced on them. His drinking and wallowing in self-pity made it necessary he be put on administrative leave for a period of time to sober up or lose his job. When Storm would drink, if one drink was good, then a bottle was better. That approach to his depression left him aimlessly lost in a fog of regret and doubt. Administrative leave and the threat of losing his job was the only thing that brought him back to reality; he had to stay on the force if he wanted to pursue Angie's killer.

Storm's mentor and old boss, Lieutenant Bob Smith, had gone to bat for him. "I know you're not handling Angie's death well," he had told his former protégé. He and Smith had known each other since Storm had entered the police academy. The lieutenant had been an instructor when Storm had entered the academy and he had recognized Storm's true potential. As he had watched his former student sink deeper and deeper into depression, he had warned him, "I don't want the force to lose you, David, but you gotta get a grip."

When Storm got out of the academy years earlier he was like any other new uniformed patrolman in some ways, full of piss and vinegar, out to save the world from bad guys. But he was also smart, a lot smarter than most, and had a way about him that let him work with anyone, in any ward (a *ward* was an imaginary geographical line that divided neighborhoods laid out years ago in Houston). In addition, Storm was half Cherokee, tall, athletic, and handsome, all traits that worked for him with the Hispanics in town. It also made him not totally "white" when he was working with black citizens who lived in the inner city.

Being an ex-jock in the "Great State of Texas" had not hurt him, either. Many of the people from the community remembered when he played high school and college football. "Oh, yeah. He's that Indian kid who played linebacker for Yates High School in Houston and later went on to play for the Texas Tech Red Raiders," they'd say to each other. He had been good enough to play in college but wasn't big enough or mean enough to play pro ball.

He had met Angie in college, the woman who had forever changed his life. They became an official couple after both found being together was infinitely better than living as singles. Angie, like his mom, always told him he was more than a football player and he could amount to be more than some ex-jock always living on his past accomplishments. Lieutenant Smith had been there on their wedding day. "I saw in your eyes that day how much you loved and depended on her," he told Storm at Angie's funeral. When she was killed, Lieutenant Smith, along with Storm's best friend Russell, had stepped up to support Storm through those empty, lost weeks and months.

Too bad it's Flynn, not Bob, who's on duty today, Storm thought, as he went and stood in the lieutenant's door.

"What have you got?" Flynn asked quickly.

"Looks like a young girl was murdered out at the Dome last night. She was found by a cleaning man in a dumpster early this morning, nude, with her throat cut. I'm pretty sure the body had been dumped since there wasn't enough blood evidence around the dumpster for the killing to have happened there." Storm was trying to keep what he said to the point and not speculate or waste time.

"So what are you waiting for now?"

"For the M.E. reports on how she died and an ID."

"Nothing at the scene to ID her?"

"Not that we found so far."

"Who did you leave in charge to canvas the area?"

"Sergeant Hebert was there with some of his patrolmen. Hopefully they will find the clothes or some ID—a picture would be good—so we can put a name on her rather than another Jane Doe."

"Speaking of Sergeant Hebert, I just got a call you chewed out some of his men for moving the dead girl's body and that you threatened them to file charges for hampering a murder investigation.' Is that right?"

"Yes, sir, they had rolled the body over just so they could look at the girl's naked body. It pissed me off."

"Did you tell Sergeant Hebert you would file charges on him and his men?"

"I told him if I had another scene where they had moved the body I just might."

"You do know you could never make that stick, don't you?"

"Probably." Storm knew he was being dressed down, but politely.

"Where you going next?"

"Down to medical examiner's office as soon as I know they have the body."

"After you've seen the M.E. I want you back out there helping that search. You do know we don't need a media circus out there. The mayor has already called me this morning to tell me the Livestock Show officials have offered to help with our investigation any way they can. The mayor doesn't want this blown up in the papers and media. The Show has a lot of very influential people involved out there and it is an organization that doesn't need any black eyes over a girl found murdered on the grounds. From what you've said, this could have happened anywhere in town, so let's keep it low profile. And Storm, one other thing: Remember those officers are there to help. They're not your enemy." The look on the lieutenant's face made it clear to Storm he had better understand his meaning.

With that, Storm was dismissed with another wave of the hand.

As he headed down the hall, he couldn't help but reflect on his conversation with the boss. No wonder Lieutenant Flynn was in the office. The mayor had called him and put the pressure on. *I wonder who's putting pressure on the mayor?* The thought flashed through his mind as quickly as the hunger pangs returned to his stomach.

Storm still had had nothing to eat and when he walked by the coffee room, and he checked for something to tide him over. Spying donuts and bagels, he walked in to grab something to "soothe the beast."

Sergeant Julio Hernandez was in the room and saw Storm coming.

"Hey, Dave. I hear you caught the murder at the Dome last night."

"Yea, I am Mr. Lucky, pard," said Storm. "Anything left in here to eat? I'm starving."

"There's some donuts left and these bagels, but I don't know why anyone would want to eat 'em, no frosting or anything," Hernandez grinned.

"Hernandez, you wouldn't like anything without sugar or salsa on it. You damn Messicans are all alike, no hot sauce or sugar on it and you don't like it," Storm said laughing.

"So, another dead girl out at the Dome?" Hernandez asked matter of factly.

"Huh, what do you mean 'another dead girl'?" The sergeant's question stopped Storm dead in his tracks.

"Oh hell, Detective, this one's not the first. Where you been, Storm? There have been others."

"What are you talking about? I hadn't heard of any other girls being found out there." Storm was still trying to clear his head.

Hernandez pulled himself up. Storm quickly analyzed the sergeant's body language. *He realizes he misspoke. This must not be common knowledge, and maybe there's a reason.*

Hernandez guffawed, "Hell, Storm, you know me; I'm talking out of my ass again. I don't know where I come up with this shit. Forget it."

Hmm—does sound like he's trying to cover his ass, Storm acknowledged to himself.

"Well, if anyone can find a killer, you da man, Storm," Hernandez said, and left the room as fast as his one-and-a-half legs would carry him.

Storm watched Hernandez limp out of the room. He knew Sergeant Hernandez's history—everyone did. Julio "Pancho" Hernandez, a decorated police veteran, had been wounded and his partner killed years earlier in a drug bust gone bad. Hernandez and his trainee, Jesus Ortiz, had come upon a parked car with a load of bad guys exchanging money for drugs near Texas and San Jacinto streets in downtown Houston. Officer Ortiz had only been out of the academy for two months and was riding with Sergeant Hernandez as his training officer when they came upon the car parked in a manufacturing section in South Houston. Suspicious of what a car was doing sitting idling at that time of morning and in that section of town, they went to investigate.

To give Ortiz some experience and not expecting any real trouble, Hernandez told Ortiz to exit the blue-and-white and approach the driver's side of the suspicious vehicle, (normally, one officer stays behind to protect the other, but this was a teaching ride). They approached the car, one on each side, and told the two men in the car to put their hands out the windows of the car and slowly get out. The man on the driver's side did as he was told, but the passenger got out a split second later, brandishing a sawed-off shot gun. He shot Ortiz in the face and Hernandez in the legs.

The perps escaped, leaving Ortiz and Hernandez lying in the street in a pool of their own blood. Ortiz had been struck dead but Officer Hernandez dragged himself to the blue-and-white and pushed the panic button on his radio, giving the dispatcher the "officer down" distress call and their exact location.

The perps' car was found abandoned near the ship channel a few days later, but neither of the bad guys involved in their shooting were ever caught. Sgt Hernandez was given a medal of commendation and Ortiz was honored posthumously by the HPD as one of seven officers slain in the line of duty that year. HPD officer Ortiz's name was added to a special memorial built beside Buffalo Bayou and his name was etched with the names of fallen HPD heroes.

After months of physical recuperation and fitted with a prosthetic leg, Officer Julio Hernandez had been assigned to a desk. Storm knew he was just marking time, occupying space 'til he could retire with full benefits and medical leave.

He had now been on the homicide desk for five years and like any good cop, he hated it.

Hernandez was a real cop, not a desk jockey, but he had a quick mind. Storm knew about Hernandez's legendary memory for details. He remembered everything that came into the homicide department. Storm also knew Hernandez recognized the desk job was HPD's way of taking care of their own, so nothing to do but wait out his remaining time.

Storm's head again filled with questions. What had Hernandez meant by "another Dome murder?" Who were these others? How many murders had there really been involving young women at the Dome? Could he have been in such a fog that he somehow missed hearing about the other ones? Now Storm had even more questions and even fewer answers.

Storm tried to clear his mind as he headed for the M. E's office. It was located out on Old Spanish Trail not far from where the girl had been found. For some unknown reason Houston City Government had relocated the morgue and the medical examiner's office away from downtown. It would take him about twenty minutes to get back out there but the drive would give him some time to think about Hernandez's slip and about multiple murders at the Dome.

Charity Kills

CHAPTER THREE

No Longer Jane Doe

Detective Storm decided to stop off at the crime scene again before going to the M.E.'s office. This time he knew where to enter. Even though he was back for the second time that day, he again felt the pangs of melancholy about the changes to the complex.

Sergeant Hebert had remained onsite watching over his troops like the mother hen he was. Seeing Storm returning he yelled out, "Hey, Chief, we found her clothes." Hebert often made jabs that played on Storm's name and heritage.

"Are you sure they're hers?"

"Yes I am sure, and we found a purse with some ID in it that is a, pardon my rudest, a dead ringer for the dead girl." Hebert growled like someone had just kicked his dog.

"Where did you find her things?" Storm let the growl roll off his back. Who cared what this old fart called or thought of him?

"In that other dumpster, over there, at the bottom of stairs just when you leave the first floor of the stadium near the docks." Hebert motioned toward where the body had been found.

"What did you do with the clothes and purse or has it gone to the M.E. already?"

"Bagged it for forensics and no, everything is in those evidence bags over there," he answered, pointing to a box laying on top of a nearby patrol car.

"Can I see it?" requested Storm.

"Sure, just don't go digging around in those bags; I am not having a homicide get kicked because some dumb assed detective fucked up the evidence. If you open it and corrupt it, it is all on you, Office Boy." Hebert gave Storm a scornful look like the ones Storm remembered getting from his mother when he had done something wrong as a kid.

The clothes and other found articles would be shipped to the M.E. and forensics to find any trace evidence of anything that might be incriminating to a suspect, but the purse and ID would be another matter. Storm wanted to see them; he wanted to see the picture ID so the girl had a name. *This girl deserves to have a name—we need to respect her that much.*

When he looked at the evidence bags he saw the purse had been bagged separately, so he put on a pair of sterile gloves and took it out, making sure not to smear any fingerprints that might remain intact. He looked at the driver's license and sure enough, the picture looked just like the dead girl. She was no longer a Jane Doe—she had a name, and her name was Leslie Phillips. He put the purse back into the evidence bag and motioned for Hebert to come over as he took off his gloves.

"When did you find this and did you find the murder scene?" Storm asked as the latex gloves made a popping sound coming off his hands

"About 8:00 this morning, right after you left to go downtown, and no, just the bloody clothes and purse."

"Nothing else? No blood soaked ground, no bloody weapon. How the hell can a girl bleed out and we can't find where it happened?" Storm's tone registered his disgust with this turn of events, but the question was crucial: How can a young woman bleed to death and you can't find a blood pool or at least splatter left somewhere?

"Nope, just the clothes and purse they were found in another dumpster and after walking every inch of every entry and exit to this place, no bloody scene and no weapon." Hebert seemed somewhat irritated he had to repeat himself.

If the girl had bled to death on site, there had to be a mess somewhere; lots of blood—the human body holds five quarts. Since none had been found, it created another question: Had the murderer been focused enough and ballsy enough to take the time to clean it up? If he had cleaned it up, had he been smart enough to eliminate all the evidence? Storm's mind was whirling. Too little information and too many questions.

"Thanks Sergeant. When will this stuff get to the M.E.?" he asked.

"In the next twenty minutes," said Sergeant Hebert, still sounding put off by the way the detective had spoken to him.

"OK, talk to you later. By the way, are you still in charge of the cops working the show?"

"Yep, all three hundred of them," replied Sergeant Hebert.

"Thanks. See ya."

As he prepared to leave the crime scene another question came to Storm's mind. If Sergeant Hebert was in charge of the cops working the show, he would know about the other deaths, if there were other deaths. Even though the relationship between Storm and Hebert was tenuous at best, Storm needed to talk to him about them, but that would have to wait 'til later.

He needed to go see the M.E. now.

* * * *

Storm pulled into the parking lot of the Sharps Building, home of the Houston medical examiner. The Sharps Building had been built in the 1970s and was run down and in need of repairs, but as long as there was a city office in it and the rent was paid, not many would care about its condition.

The city had built the Sharps Building and then sold it to a rental agency so the city could not be accused of rent fixing. The rental agency bought the building for a dime on the dollar and rented the space back to the city. This gave the bureaucrat in charge at the time a new building and a way to pad his income and not get caught by city oversight officials looking for internal graft.

In Houston it was well known that the real estate scam was the best scam someone could pull off; if a prominent official did get caught participating in such a scam it was easy to cover up unless that official was not part of the controlling political party. Hell, one ex-mayor of Houston had done a deal with the cable TV people when cable television was new to the city. He had gotten caught taking millions of dollars in kickbacks and his only punishment had been the loss of the job the next time he came up for election. The mayorette, who had uncovered the shady dealings, was the person who replaced him. Shortly after her election she herself was suspected in taking kickbacks from a company who was hired to do a study on an overhead light rail system for Houston. She took over $3 million in kickbacks from a contractor. A contractor who had the dubious honor of being indicted in every state in the union on RICO charges and bid fixing, and, as usual in politics, no wrongdoing was ever prosecuted. To top it off, she came back to Houston to attend a dinner thrown in her honor as a "great citizen of the city of Houston!"

Graft in a fast-growing city is nothing new, Storm said to himself, as he reflected on the building's history. The medical examiner's offices were located on the first floor, as most Houston buildings don't have basements due to the proximity of sea level. To say it was not a bright and cheery place was an understatement and Storm always hated coming here. He had seen lots of dead bodies in his years on the force, but coming to the M.E.'s office was the pinnacle on his list of things not to do. It was cold, metallic, smelled of chemicals, and the sight of the dissection of bodies always made him queasy.

Dr. Alisha Johnson was the Assistant M.E. in charge on weekends. Her boss was another politico, appointed by the mayor who never worked late or on weekends. He was a motivated ladder climber, so he had to stay in front of the people who got him his job to make sure he was bound for greater glory. He and the mayor's office had been through the ringer lately for all the errors coming out of the forensic labs, but both were good at smoke screens and so far had deflected any innuendo of blame.

Dr. Johnson, on the other hand, was a different story, and she was one of the best. She knew how to run her traps and what to look for while at the same time following exacting procedural protocol. In her favor also was the fact her name hadn't been associated with any of the problems discovered with shoddy work; so far, her documentation and procedures had been above reproach. Simply, she was just damn good at her job.

Dr. Alisha Johnson had come from the one of the toughest neighborhoods in Houston. She had worked her entire life to become a doctor and when she did, she found she liked studying the dead more than curing the living. She loved the mystery of solving the cause of death and finding the clues that could catch a killer. The medical examiner's office has been the perfect place for her. She had grown up in the Houston's Third Ward and had seen her share of dead bodies even before she had entered high school. The Third Ward was a very unpleasant place to grow up; it was an area where surviving was a daily struggle. Because she was smart and good at science, she had earned a scholarship to

Texas Southern University. After graduating with honors she attended Texas Baylor School of Medicine. Being black had never deterred her from her goals and no one ever accused her of exploiting it, either; if they did, Storm was pretty sure he wasn't the only one who had heard her give that unlucky person an ear full of expletives describing their own family background.

A clerk met Storm at the door and told him that the girl had been picked up and was in Exam Room 2 with Dr. Johnson. As Storm walked down the hall, he was reminded why he hated this place; it was full of bodies waiting to be autopsied. Every questionable death required an autopsy before the body could be released to the family to bury. The idea that people were kept waiting to end their suffering over someone's death always made him uneasy. Angie's body had been here, and he, too, had been made to wait.

He vividly remembered her lifeless form lying on a cold metal table covered with a sheet and how he had had to offer positive identification of her for the M.E. He had been made to wait in a sterile waiting room until her exam had been finished, the reports written, before he could claim her body and make arrangements for a religious service, a ritual meant to comfort the living but that did little to release the demons in his mind.

He didn't know yet if this girl Leslie had any family to grieve for her, but he knew a funeral would not satisfy them anymore than it had him. Finding a killer and hopefully discovering a motive would be the only thing to answer those unanswered "why?"s.

Storm found Room 2 and went in. He found Dr. Johnson looking at the body of the girl he had seen earlier. The girl was even prettier than Storm remembered and she looked so much better lying on this steel table than lying amongst the garbage.

"Hey, Alisha, what do you think?"

Alisha turned around, saw Storm standing there and motioned him over. Storm hated looking at dead bodies this way; it was not right, the dead had rights, too. They deserved dignity. But he looked. He had to.

Alisha had split the girl open from the base of her neck to her pelvis and laid most of her insides out on the table. A slit had been made in her stomach and the contents removed. They would need to be analyzed to see what she had eaten in the last few hours of her life, in hopes of discovering a clue as who might have seen her last.

"She bled to death, Storm. Her throat was cut and her carotid artery was slashed. She would have bled to death in less than a minute. Whoever did this also knew to make the cut so it would stop any kind of noise from his victim. He cut the windpipe in half. The only sound she would have made is the exhaust of air from her lungs."

"Did you find anything else?"

"Yes, she had sex in the last twelve hours."

"How do you know that?"

"We did the rape kit; you probably know it's routine in a case like this. I found her vaginal opening had been bruised and semen had been left. She also had spermicidal left in her vagina and sexual lubricant in her anus."

"What does that mean? Do you mean she had anal sex before she died?" said Storm, shocked by this new revelation.

"No, I think someone sodomized her after she was dead. As I said, there is some bruising in her vagina but none in her anus. The vaginal bruising could be from consensual sex."

"So she had sex with the perp and then after he killed her, he sodomized her?" This was over the edge even for Storm. Nothing should surprise him anymore, but sexual crimes did, and he knew he had to come to terms quickly with this one.

"Well, I can only tell you what I found. I will do a DNA test on semen in her vagina to see if I can get a verifiable donor. I will then run it through all the data bases I have access to and see if we get a hit.

"Thanks, Alisha. I am on my way back out to the crime scene. Let me know what you find." Damn, the asshole did her, then killed her, then sodomized her. *This is one sick bastard.*

Alisha went back to the examination with the same methodical precision she always did.

Storm called back over his shoulder, "Oh, by the way, her name is Leslie Phillips."

"I will put that on her toe tag, I always like a real name better than 'Jane Doe.'" Alisha, already absorbed in her work, acknowledged this new bit of information.

* * * *

Across town Leslie Phillip's killer sat admiring the trophy from the morning's kill—an almost new pair of Tony Llama cowboy, or in this case, cowgirl, boots. The killer was still swooning in the delight of the rush that came when the girl's life slowly ebbed. Each girl's death was such ecstasy to the killer, as the victim's eyes stared pleadingly ahead, the light in them slowly fading, while warm blood crawled across their skin.

Raping her had been done for the police's benefit; it was not really part of the rapture, just something to throw the cops off. *I'm so much smarter than the cops.* "Rape" is such a strong word. An insinuation of rape will send law enforcement in a totally wrong direction; these girls were all whores, anyway. They all cheated. They didn't care who loved them. They all deserted the one who really loved them.

When the evening news came on, the killer finally got the confirmation. The news had just broken that a girl had been found dead in the vicinity of the Dome. There wasn't much else in the report, just that she was found naked and dead in a dumpster outside the new stadium.

The killer knew the political cover-up had begun. It would be just like the others; the killer was the only one who had really cared about them. There might be more in tomorrow's paper, but for now all that was mentioned was that police investigators would be looking into it. The killer knew nothing would be found—the killer was too good for that. Everything had been cleaned up: no blood trail, no bloody crime scene, just bloody clothes tossed somewhere else near where the girl had been found. There was not a sign of anything left behind belonging to the killer. It was a good thing the county didn't have an open burning prohibition; the fifty gallon burn barrel in the backyard had taken care of any trace that might lead detectives to figure out who the killer was. The killer was sure no clues had been left, but if the cops found something, the killer would be close enough to the investigation to know.

The first girl had been a true love, but had betrayed the killer, leaving for a different way of life. The first murder had been out of rage and torment toward someone the developing serial killer had once loved, someone the killer had shared a life with. It had been sloppy and the killer had gotten lucky that no evidence was left to point to who had taken part in the girl's disappearance. But the thoughts and memories of the total control over another person's life and death had lingered. *Ah, the exquisite pleasure I felt as the life left her eyes. And the feel of the warm blood covering my hands as it ran down her neck.* That body had disappeared and would with luck never be found.

It was during these hours of lucid thought and sexual perversity after the first kill, that the thoughts about how to commit another murder began to develop. It was then the killer meticulously formulated the plan. The killer picked out the target and the execution date and then became the predator.

During the past nine years the ever-more-efficient killer had acquired increasing expertise with each murder.

Disposing of the bodies in hopes they would never be found was out of the question—the killer had discovered not only how to never leave any clues behind but how to leave behind red herrings that would lead law enforcement to the wrong conclusions. The killer learned to be purposeful and patient in everything: the target selection, the timing, the method of the kill, and the clues left behind. When a chance opportunity to be involved in the largest high dollar charitable event in town each year presented itself, it became the perfect hunting ground. The killer knew that such an event could not allow negative public awareness, and if the victims were correctly chosen, there would be no one left behind to push for a solution to the girls' deaths. The entire thing would simply disappear after a period of time and the loss of one more young nobody would be forgotten.

While sitting in the spotless trophy room, the killer with eyes closed visualized the scene once again, feeling the blood, seeing the plea in the dying girl's eyes, which brought with it the magical orgasm of untold pleasure. Then the killer opened the diary and began to write. In the future someone would read the pages that described this death and the others, and relive vicariously the consuming passion it brought back to life.

CHAPTER FOUR

Friendship Cost

Storm called Russell Hildebrant, his lifelong friend and trusted confidant, to see if he was up yet. Russell had never been good at getting up early and it was only 9:30 Sunday morning. After rasslin' with the receiver, Russell answered the phone in his customary Sunday morning guttural drawl and Storm was sure he had had another of his infamous late night tutorials. A "tutorial" was what Russell called his late night rendezvous with one of his many female admirers.

Russell was a local television celebrity doing the work week's nightly weather at 6:00 and 10:00 p.m. On weekends he spent time playing golf and hanging out at the country club where he had belonged since his parents had first taken him there when he was a boy. He, too, was a Houston native born and raised, but on a different side of the tracks from Storm. They had met in college when they had become roommates and for a short time played on their college football team.

Storm figured the Saturday night before had been no different than many of Russell's Saturday nights. He had probably participated in a charity gathering with initials for a name—there had been so many of these over the years one set of letters began to resemble all the others. Many times at these functions Russell acted as the master of ceremonies and reveled in the limelight. He would schmooze with the powerful and wannabe famous who contributed to charities in hopes of getting their pictures in the society section of the local papers. Most times these events were also attended by social-climbing young women looking for the man who would sweep them off their feet, marry them, and give them the life they felt they deserved.

Russell fit exactly the bill. Storm understood that the only problem with Russell was that he was a confirmed bachelor. Marriage had never entered his mind, and he still had a plethora of women to keep him busy. Whether at a bar or a charity dinner, his mind was on one thing, his enjoying life. If he didn't have someone au courant accompanying him, he would simply cast his net to meet a new evening companion. The night would consist of drinking 'til he couldn't drive, calling a cab, taking the girl home to his house, popping a little blue pill, and trying to have sex till he passed out, which was probably before it was mutually satisfactory. More than once Russell had awakened to find some of his stuff missing, but that didn't seem to bother him—he wrote the missing items off to "meeting Miss Wrong." Being a trust fund baby meant money and possessions had never held too much deference to him. Things were replaceable; it was the people in his life, friends like Storm, Russell could never replace.

"You up?"

"No," groaned Russell. "How far away are you?" Storm could tell Russell understood the drill—calling this early meant his old college friend was on his way over.

"About fifteen minutes. Time for you to get rid of the floozy," snickered Storm.

Storm knew Russell's modus operandi. If a girl did happen to be there, a cab would be out front before Storm could get to the building. If the girl had not yet made her departure by the time Storm got to Russell's condominium building she would be down by the door with the doorman waiting for her ride. The doorman knew Storm and usually just waved him in, giving Storm a wink if the woman standing with him was the one Russell had just pushed out. Today was no different; a young brunette with a bad case of bed head and rumpled clothes stood next to the doorman and tried to not make eye contact with anyone. Although she looked irritated, she just stood patiently waited for her ride to wherever she had to go.

Hildebrandt lived in a high-rise condo overlooking Memorial Park near Loop 610 and the Galleria. His monthly maintenance fees were higher than Storm's entire mortgage payment, but Russell didn't seem to care. There was a doorman, a pool, tennis courts, and even an on-site dry cleaner. Russell lived on the eighteenth floor and the view from the huge picture windows was awesome. He had lived there for ten years and Storm and Angie had spent enough time there to feel at home. One of their favorite times was watching the downtown Fourth of July fireworks from the wraparound shatterproof windows that offered a view east toward downtown and overlooked the park.

Russell and Storm had always been at home with one another and always had each other's backs. Lately it had been Russell's turn to stand by Storm. Although physically different—Storm was dark, Russell was fair—they were both taller than average and athletic. Russell's blonde hair and blue eyes made him and Storm look like different sides of the same coin. Even their personalities were different but complementary: Russell was gregarious and outgoing, where Storm was more serious and soft-spoken. The friendship had developed as easy as bees take to honey.

With the loss of Storm's brother in college and Russell being an only child, they had filled a void in each of their lives and their friendship grew through the years of both bad times and good.

Storm pushed the doorbell and waited, and a rode-hard-put-up-wet Russell answered the door, dressed only in knee length shorts and with a serious case of pillow creases across his face.

"Well, Baretta, what made you wake me up so early?" asked Russell as he wiped the sleep from his eyes.

Storm didn't care for the nickname, but Russell had used it since he had made detective. So he had learned to live with it.

"I am your wakeup-and-vanquish-your-latest-floozy service. Didn't I tell you? It's my new vocation in life." Storm grinned because this has been his typical answer for more than twenty years.

"Fine. But really, to what do I owe this early morning intrusion into my otherwise exciting and devil-may-care life?"

"I'll tell you, if you make me some coffee, or did your latest road whore steal your coffeemaker this time?"

"I don't know, check the kitchen. If it is still there she didn't steal it, and who told you she was a road whore?" Russell chuckled, well aware of his own reputation.

Russell went to work making himself a Bloody Mary, a habit that had been part of his Sunday morning ritual since his parents used to take him to the country club for brunch since the age of twelve. He once told Storm that he and the other children of prosperity could always get the wait staff to bring lightly made drinks while their parents weren't looking. As he listened to the tinkle of ice in the glass, Russell asked again what had brought Storm over so early on a Sunday.

Storm snickered and said, "Oh, I was up and the thought crossed my mind, who is a bigger pain the ass in the morning than I am? Poof, your name sprang to mind. I know you love getting up early for breakfast, although it be liquid, not to mention I wanted to make sure you got off to church on time."

Russell walked into the kitchen in time to watch Storm fumble with the coffeemaker. Storm's big hands did not do minor things well and a "tablespoon" of coffee per cup meant Storm adding ten spoons in an eight-cup coffee maker.

"Are you going to be at that long?" Russell asked as he watched Storm.

"Might be. You never know. Had a murder at the Dome last night," Storm said, almost as a second thought.

That got Russell's attention. "OK, Baretta. Talk to me. Who got murdered? I hope one of those dickhead big wheels down there."

"Nope, a young girl. Found her this morning in a dumpster with her throat cut"

"Young girl, huh? Was she cute and do we know her?" asked Russell.

"Her name was Leslie Phillips according to the ID they found along with some clothes they think are hers. Those were also found in another dumpster outside the stadium."

"The new stadium?"

"Yep."

"Who found her?"

"One of the guys on the cleanup crew."

"Wow, so you have already had an intriguing morning. But, why come see me so early? Did she have my wallet or anything of mine on her?" Russell said, smiling, his way of trying to lighten the mood that had suddenly turned somber.

"You know why I'm here, Russell," Storm answered. He had turned his friend into his sounding board for more than half their lives. They had met on their first day at football camp at Texas Tech and had ended up being roommates throughout college. He was there when Storm had met Angie and was their best man when they got married. He was there shortly after Storm found Angie dead and had consoled his friend for hours, knowing it was all he could do.

Russell was from a wealthy family and had gone to Bellaire high school. He had played against Storm when they were in high school and the rich kids were sent home not just beaten but bloodied. Being from a wealthy family had always given Russell his perks. His dad was a Texas Tech grad and from the time Russell had made the high school football team, Tech was the only place for him to go to school. His dad pulled some strings and made sure his son had gotten a shot at the big time in college ball.

Although Russell had some talent, he was basically lazy. In his sophomore year at Tech he quit football and took up what he really enjoyed, which was women and booze, and from then on he had more fun than most college students are allowed to have. It had disappointed his dad greatly but he had persevered through it. Russell was a good student, so he got to stay at Tech and room with Storm. He took communications classes, which was basically television broadcasting and basket-weaving. They were easy for Russell, who kept saying he liked the idea of being on TV someday. He might not have been too good at football, but he was charming, and he had everyone on campus watching to see what stunt he would pull next while doing a live broadcast on Tech's college station. The camera loved him and he was a more than adequate storyteller, so he ended up being a reporter and writing for the college newspaper.

When they graduated, Russell, Storm, and Angie had all come back to Houston to make their fortunes. He was picked up on one of the local TV stations doing news reports and later being the nightly anchor before becoming the nightly weather man; again his charm worked and he became one of the most recognizable television personalities in the Houston area. He did numerous charity events like golf tournaments and local fund raisers, which added to his notoriety. Unlike his friend Storm, for Russell monogamy with a single woman had never entered his mind. The world he viewed was his playground, and a variety of female partners only added to the fun.

Storm turned to Russell. "You've been in Houston all your life just like I have and you've been with the TV station for more years then either of us wants to remember. Have you ever heard of a girl being killed at the barbecue before?"

"Not that I remember, Rain Man, but that doesn't mean it didn't happen. Why do you ask?"

Storm knew that anything he told Russell was between the two of them. "When I was at the precinct this morning Hernandez said something like, 'So you got the Dome murder.' Then he insinuated that there had been others, but when I pressed him about what he said he clammed up and said—" Storm paused. "He said nothing. He just made up some flimsy excuses and scurried off to his desk."

"Hernandez—he's that guy who lost a leg a few years ago, right?"

"Yeah, he is the sergeant on the homicide desk now at headquarters."

"Well, he probably hears everything that comes in and hears things you probably wouldn't or you might have forgotten when you were in, well, let's say, 'when you were not operating at full function,' right?"

"You're right, but I'm surprised something like that didn't stick in my mind."

"Are you going to ask him more about it?'

"Yeah, but that will have to wait until later," Storm growled, still struggling with the coffee pot.

"Well, I could ask the old time news guys at the station if you want. Do some digging around."

"Would you?" Storm had hoped Russell would volunteer to do so.

"Sure. Now, about this coffee you're making." Russell looked at the coffeemaker and just shook his head and stepped into the operation. If he didn't take over, the coffee would never get made and even if Storm had gotten it to perk, the coffee would taste like road tar.

"So, you going out to the Dome to talk to the show people?" asked Russell.

"Yeah. Lieutenant Flynn said that the mayor had already talked to them and they were going to help in any way they can." Storm looked at Russell as if it made sense that the mayor was already talking to the show.

"Look, Storm. That doesn't set with me. The mayor already knows about this?" asked Russell.

Storm could see the question marks appear in his friend's' eyes. *He's thinking, "why is the mayor involved in this?"* Storm just shook his head "yes."

"What else did your lieutenant tell you?" pressed Russell.

"That the Livestock Show was going to help to keep it quiet." Again Storm looked to Russell for comment. "You know better than I do how much influence those people have with the mayor and his cronies."

Storm knew Russell's dad had been a big wheel at the Livestock Show and Russell had grown up around it. Even if disillusioned with the whole kit and caboodle of the Show, he still retained his perks and kept up on who was running things out there. He had seen and been around all the shenanigans that had gone on out there for years; stuff that most outsiders didn't know about. He knew about the girls and why there were rules against cameras in the VIP clubs. Russell still had access to his privileges, his badge, and his passes to the event and the VIP clubs, although he seldom used them. Even with his inactivity at the charity, his dad remained much too much a man of consequence for Russell to lose his benefits. Not that Russell wanted to pay for something he could get for free, but he would rather buy tickets than use the assets in the special club levels reserved for those esteemed charitable benefactors. So, yeah, Russell knows all the ins and outs of the Show.

"Where are you going next, Storm?"

"Back out to the Livestock Show offices, meet with the staff."

"OK. Call me later to let me know how it went. I'll go in and check with my old buddies at the station to see what they know and hey, by the way, us insiders just refer to it as the "Show" or the "Rodeo," not by its full name."

Russell smiled like the proverbial cat that ate the canary as he poured cups of coffee into clunky ceramic mugs for each of them.

After three more cups of coffee at Russell's house Storm needed to pee real bad, but he hurried and controlled the desire till he could get back to the Dome. In a place that big he figured he could find at least one men's room to get rid of the coffee overflow.

Charity Kills

CHAPTER FIVE

Country Dog in the City

By the time Storm left Russell's condo it was past midmorning and traffic on the 610 Loop had increased to a paralytic crawl consisting of both churchgoers and people heading to the trendy bistros in the Galleria for brunch. With expansion and growth in the city it was always repairing some main thoroughfare or building an extra lane and that always made the Loop an even bigger maelstrom of hindrances. The longstanding joke was that if you started to work on a road in Houston when you were eighteen, you could retire at age sixty-five from a road crew that's working within ten miles of where you started. This seemed more fact then fiction.

At the Dome complex, Storm was directed back to the first entry he had tried that morning. The offices for the rodeo were in the new giant sparkling contemporary center on the north side of the new stadium. This time, after he showed his police credentials he was told where to park, with emphasis that he not park in any spaces reserved for members of Houston's new football team—and one of those spaces was exactly where he pulled in. He put his police tag in the window in case someone had a problem; his police tag trumped jock parking.

The new center was huge. When you entered the massive hallway on the west end, you couldn't see the east end—it was at least a quarter of mile long. To the left of the main hall was the exhibition area that ran the length of the building. The front of the exhibition area was occupied by vendors selling everything from Western clothing to artwork or farm equipment; you could get a turkey leg or sign up for college. Further back were the stalls and judging arenas for 4H and FFA animals to be exhibited: cattle, pigs, sheep, goats, turkeys, rabbits and chickens.

Storm took an escalator up to the second floor of the building some fifty feet above the entry floor, which was composed of myriads of meeting rooms and offices for the Livestock Show, the National Football League, and the complex management company. Many of the rooms in the upper level were huge expanses of space that had sliding walls that could be configured as smaller rooms for meetings or large temporary members-only bars that dotted the entire complex during special events.

Storm walked halfway down the long hallway till he saw the Rodeo offices on his left with its elegant mahogany double-doored entrance that opened into an opulent reception area. He remembered the simple offices in the now razed old convention center, which would have fit into the foyer of this place. "Nice digs," he said to himself, his eyes moving over the magnificent Western art and sculptures. The lobby of these offices showed the Rodeo had arrived. This was no longer "a small town goat ropin'"; it was the biggest charity in the state and the largest indoor rodeo in the United States.

Behind the huge mahogany reception desk sat a gray-haired lady gatekeeper. She asked his business and he explained who he was and that he was to meet someone from the rodeo staff.

"You're expected. Miss Taylor will be available to see you shortly," she announced. "Please take a seat. Any seat is fine. Miss Taylor will be right out."

Storm sat on one end of one of the overstuffed leather sofa and continued to study the art and memorabilia in the lobby. There were gorgeous paintings of Western scenes, handsome bronze sculptures, replicas of Remington's and cases of Show memorabilia, along with 18' X 24' framed photographs of past Rodeo presidents. Things had changed considerably, as most things change with huge increases of revenue; where the old offices were understated and belied the amounts of money that were accumulated and disseminated, the new offices were opulent. There was no doubt that this was an institution with financial strength and grandeur.

Since this was the active season of the rodeo (the business was year round) people scurried back and forth and in and out, some already looking frazzled, while others appeared preoccupied with their radios and cell phones next to their ears. Activity would now be twenty-four hours a day; this was the beginning of the three-week period when the preparations of the previous year came to fruition, entertaining the throngs of patrons and garnering money for the scholarship fund. Storm didn't envy these people or what they had to put up with over the next three weeks. The work of collecting donations for scholarships for Texas' future leaders included soothing the never-ending complaints of spoiled patrons and members, covering up dropped balls that the public never saw, currying favors to keep donors happy, staving off various and sundry potential problems— and that was on a good day. No thank you, Storm smiled to himself. He didn't like people that much, anyway, so God bless those who did, or could at least abide them without giving away their real thoughts.

Storm had not been waiting long when a very attractive blonde woman with impeccable hair and a cute figure hidden by a suave business suit appeared. She was followed by a tall man in a rumpled corporate suit of armor that gave him that slept-in look. The receptionist pointed out Storm, sitting on the overstuffed leather couch, next to a display case containing countless belt buckles, trophies and pictures from past decades of rodeos. He stood as they approached (his momma had always taught him good manners and Angie would never have forgiven him if he hadn't—"You stand in the presence of a lady!"), the blond extended her hand and said, "Hello, I'm Dakota Taylor, head of marketing and the assistant general manager of Show, and I'm sure you've met Mr. Vern Nagel from the mayor's office."

Storm introduced himself, shook hands with Miss Taylor, and said, "No, I haven't had the pleasure of meeting Mr. Nagel."

Nagel nodded and grunted, held out his hand for Storm to take and said, "Detective Storm, Vern Nagel, assistant to the mayor."

Storm looked quickly at Nagel's business card: "Second assistant to Mayor Richard Lemay," it read. He must think "assistant" sounds better than "second assistant," Storm reckoned.

Nagel looked like he had been pulled out of his nice warm bed early that morning by the mayor, probably given the lowdown, and told to report to the rodeo offices. Storm figured he was with Miss Taylor to be the eyes and ears of the mayor.

A flashing thought sped through Storm's mind. Who the hell is this guy, really, and why does the mayor already have someone staked out with this Miss Taylor? Another question nagged at him: Why would the Show assign a marketing person to be the liaison in a murder case?

The reception area was cavernous and Storm was sure he would not be overheard when he asked, "I take it you've both heard about the girl that was found on the grounds this morning?"

Dakota Taylor responded, "Yes, it is a tragedy. How could anything like this have happened? Do you know who killed her or how she ended up in one of our dumpsters yet?"

Dakota took Storm's elbow and directed him to a private glass conference room just off the reception area. She closed the massive door and they each took a seat around a small round table secure from any eavesdropping ears that might have wandered into the reception area. "Detective, I do not want us to be overheard," she said.

"No, ma'am. We do have her name from her driver's license. Her name is Leslie Phillips. Does that ring any bells for you?" asked Storm.

"The poor girl. No, Detective, it doesn't. But I'll be sure to make inquiries to see if any of the staff or management know of her." Dakota added that promise almost as if an afterthought.

"Do you know where she was killed, Detective Storm?" asked Nagel, sounding as if he was trying to get his two cents in.

"No, sir." Storm turned to face Nagel. "She was found in the dumpster outside the new stadium next to the exits leading away from the stadium and her clothing and purse were found near the loading docks in another."

"Do you think she was dumped here because we have so many dumpsters on site this time of year?" Asked Dakota.

Storm's mind focused for a second or two on the implications of her question. What does she mean "dumped here"? Why doesn't this woman think she could have been killed here? What the hell is going on? And why is this guy from the mayor's office getting involved?

"Miss Taylor, why would you think she was dumped here? Have there been previous incidents of this kind?" Storm asked, trying to see if Miss Taylor would admit to any other incidents of found dead girls on the grounds.

Storm noted the shock in Miss Taylor's face, the frown, and a tightening of the lips before she answered. "Well, yes, there have been a few robberies and muggings, but I don't believe we have ever had a *murder*." Dakota stressed the last word and smiled, though the smile looked artificial, or maybe just practiced, to the detective.

"Will you be the information "go-to person" from Show for this investigation, Miss Taylor?" asked Storm.

"Yes. Please contact me first if we can be of any assistance," said Dakota, still with the stiff smile creasing her lips.

"I will be back if I have more questions when we have more information." Extending his hand, he ended his visit. "Thank you, Miss Taylor. I am sure I will be seeing you again."

With that said, Storm rose from the table and turned to leave. Damn, this broad was as cold as a well digger's ass— and why the hell was Nagel here? He asked himself. Again he had more questions than answers and he was beginning to feel a little like the line from *Best Little Whorehouse in Texas* about the country dog in the city: "If I stand still they fuck me ... if I run, they bite me in the ass." It seemed to fit in this situation.

CHAPTER SIX

"I Know Nothing"

As Storm left the offices he realized again how big this place was. It was at least three hundred yards just to get to the escalators, then a two-story ride down and another one hundred yards to the doors to the parking lot. Then another two hundred yards past the stadium, a structure big enough to house half dozen Goodyear blimps or the 70,000 spectators watching a game. It dwarfed the Dome, which stood sadly empty, looking forlorn and falling apart.

After hurriedly walking across the expanse of the complex he was almost out of steam and needed a second to catch his breath when he got to where Hebert remained, still holding court over his minions.

"Well, office boy, I see you are back again. Did the boss send you back to see how real cops do their jobs?" Hebert asked with his usual coonass smirk. Storm was annoyed by Hebert's attitude toward him but he checked his emotions and let the stones of verbal abuse roll off his back. Hebert would never get used to the fact that a cop didn't have to wear a uniform to be a good cop. He was an old-school street cop and nobody was ever better then a street cop, not that Storm had ever insinuated he was.

Hebert pushed on. "I got some copies of the picture from the dead girl's driver's license and gave them to my officers so they can canvas the grounds and ask if anyone knew her or saw her last night. Did you know the kid was only twenty-five years old?"

This was a piece of the puzzle that had escaped Storm till Hebert said it. What had someone so young been mixed up in that would get her killed? Who the hell was she mixed up with?

"Didn't know that, He-ee-bert," he answered. "If any of the guys come up with something you let me know. I'm gonna talk to the cleaning crew supervisor. Maybe he can shed some light on what went down here."

Storm found Ernie's boss still there, timing out the men who had to stay late to clean up after the M.E. and forensics teams had finally left the scene. Henry Dillon had started out working for Manpower as a part-time worker himself not so many years ago. After proving himself a steady hand, he had been hired full-time as a work crew supervisor. He, too, had been a drunk with one or two felonies against him, but he had turned his life around and was now considered a responsible and respected man who could supervise others like himself. Dillon saw Storm coming and turned to meet him. He seemed to know who Storm was before Storm introduced himself.

"Hello, I am Detective David Storm. I'm in charge of investigating the murder of the girl who was found here this morning."

"Yes, I know, Ernie told me who you were."

"Good, then I would like to ask you some questions about last night. What time did your crew come on last night?"

"Actually, we had people here at 10:00 pm last night, but I didn't come out until midnight. I was running another job across town and the men out here know what is to be done and what is expected of them. This group is pretty good at self supervision."

"What were your people doing last night?"

"This time of year, during the rodeo, we make sure the stadium is cleaned up before the events of the next day begin. Sometimes that's easy, sometimes it's hard, depends on the function and circumstances."

"What was it like last night?"

"Last night should have been easy. The only people allowed in the stadium during barbecue are the big wheels from the rodeo and security persons. The VIP club is open and they can go in to drink and party. But we also handle cleaning up the dumpsters from the barbecue. So, I have to spread my guys a little thinner and all over the tented area."

"When you say the "big wheels" are allowed in the stadium, who would that consist of?"

"The people with the badges that say things like, 'Vice President,' 'Director,' etc. The cops working the gates keep an eye on who gets in or not."

"Do they bring in husbands, wives, dates, or whatever with them?"

"Yeah, sure. Sometimes they bring both. There are always lots of girls that come in with them. You see it more often when the rodeo actually starts."

"Did you see this girl last night?" Storm held out a copy of Leslie's picture from her driver's license that Hebert had given him.

Dillon looked at the copy of the picture and said, "No, never saw her 'til this morning when Ernie came running up and said he found a body. Scared the beJesus out of him."

"When you saw her this morning did you think you had seen her before?"

"No." Dillon shook his head in the negative.

"The dumpster she was found in, could it have been one from the barbecue?"

"No, those dumpsters are only used for trash we take from the stadium. The dumpsters for the barbecue are mixed around the area inside the fences that cordon off the midway, the carnival and barbecue tents."

Storm put the picture away and said "OK, thanks. If you think of anything else after I have gone, here is my card. Call me."

With that Storm left and headed back to his car to go to the M.E.'s office to see if Alisha knew anything more about the exact cause of death.

* * * *

During his trip to the murder scene another meeting was taking place in the Show offices. Dakota Taylor had wasted no time in calling together the persons who needed to jump in to control the public spin. Seated around the ornate conference room besides Dakota were Vern Nagel; Leon Powers, the president and CEO of the Show; and the eleven-member executive committee. The late arriving HPD Sergeant Hebert appeared at the meeting as soon as he was free to leave the site of discovery of the dead girl.

Leon Powers started it off looking at Dakota, "OK, Dakota, what do we know?"

Inwardly checking her heart rate and composure and making sure to appear in control in front of the others, Dakota responded, "We know a young woman was found dead early this morning in a dumpster outside of the stadium. We know the manner in which she died from information supplied by Sergeant Hebert. Her throat was cut, severing her windpipe, and she bled to death. Further than that we only know she was found by one of the Manpower workers cleaning the stadium. I have already met with the HPD detective in charge of the case; his name is David Storm."

She saw Leon was taking notes. "When we met with him earlier today he didn't seem to know much, only that a young girl, Leslie Phillips was her name, was found murdered on the grounds."

Powers asked, "Who else met with him besides you?"

Dakota quickly pointed to Vern sitting in the middle of table opposite herself. "Vern Nagel from the mayor's office and I met with him, and of course, offered any help we can in the investigation. In the meeting with the detective, Vern and I both suggested that she could have been possibly dumped here because of the number of dumpsters we have on the property."

Powers smiled at Dakota. He knows what I mean, she thought. The Show would not impede the investigation, but on the other hand, would also do nothing that would put the Show in a bad light.

Then Powell grunted, "What do we know about this Storm? What type of man is he?"

Sergeant Hebert took that question. "He's a twice decorated officer, been on the force about twenty-five years. About five years ago his wife was murdered. Nobody was ever caught and he went off the deep end. He is a drunk and of late his friends in the department have covered for him, trying to keep him out of trouble until it's time for him to retire. Given the last five years, he's perfect for our needs. He will spin his wheels, file reports, and this will most likely become another of those unsolved cases that disappear after a few months."

"Will he buy the proposition that the girl could have been dumped here?" asked Powers.

"In the old days, no, but now I think he is just counting days and doesn't want to rock the boat," answered Hebert.

Nagel then spoke up. "The mayor's office and the chief of police are aware of the situation and are in agreement that the public's attention should not be focused on this tragic event, as this is nothing more than a random incident."

Powers questioned, "What about the press, have we heard from them yet?"

Dakota replied, "No news vans have shown up and nothing has been released at this time, as I was waiting for your permission to give out a statement of regret for this unfortunate young woman's death and how the Show wishes her family our deepest sympathies for their loss. The good news is it's Sunday, so when it is picked up, it will make only the evening news and Sundays are the least watched."

Powers looked again at Dakota. "Do you have a meeting set up with the Show committee chairs, to make sure their committee members understand they don't talk to anyone, press, cops, anyone, and they redirect any inquiry they may get to the Show management offices?"

"I'll do it later this morning, sir. It will be like the cow charging through the kids' incident sir a few years ago, it will be reinforced to them that if asked what happened they should be like Schultz on *Hogan's Heroes* and say, 'I know nothing.'" Dakota smiled as she mimicked the inept POW camp sergeant from the old television show.

Powers then focused on Sergeant Hebert. "How about your cops?"

"Leadership is on board, Leon," Sergeant Hebert said. "Her picture is being passed around to all the officers who worked last night. They won't withhold information, but they work for me or at least most of them do, so like me, they don't really have much regard for office boys." His well-known dislike of the police in suits was obvious in his tone.

Powers turned to look at Dakota and Nagel. "Does Detective Storm know anything about the others?"

Dakota didn't reply, except to shake her head no.

"OK. Keep me informed of anything that comes up that could tarnish the Show."

As if an afterthought, he asked, "Do any of you know this Leslie Phillips or have you ever seen her before?" He threw the copy of the picture Hebert had brought onto the middle of the table. None of the eleven executive committee members answered. They sat silently, merely looking at the dead girl's picture.

* * * *

Powers looked quietly at the face of each of them, one by one, trying to read body language. He knew someone at this table had seen the girl and possibly knew her, but none would answer now, not in front of so many of their cohorts. One of them might even know who the killer was, but would never admit it. It was time to circle the wagons. He suspected they all wondered if this murder could be tied to the other killings of young women found in or around the vicinity of the Show over the last seven years. He had to depend on their discretion. This was a closed group, a society within a society; too much was at stake for this to become anything more than the tragic death of a young woman with no ties to the Show.

Charity Kills

CHAPTER SEVEN

Russell Finds an Ally

Channel 5 News had been Russell's home since returning to Houston from college. He had started as a rookie reporter making less money a month then a city street sweeper, but it wasn't the money that pushed him. It was news: the finding a story and pursuing it 'til the facts came out. In the twenty-five years he had spent at Channel 5 he had risen up the ladder of success, becoming the nightly anchor for the 6:00 and 10:00 pm wrap-ups at the age of thirty.

After five years on the anchor desk he found he was bored. He looked at the jobs afforded him and he discovered being the weatherman better fit his work ethic, which had reverted back to his apathetic, unconcerned approach to life. He found he was good at doing the weather; it didn't take much preparation and it afforded him the same notoriety as being an anchor.

As he pushed open the station entry doors that Sunday after his conversation with Storm, he glanced at the foyer and reflected that not much had changed in the almost twenty-five years he had been there, with the exception of the arrival from time to time of fresh new energetic faces. These new people were mostly young and always looking to make their mark and to step up to a bigger market stations or the chance to get to go to the "Show," which is how they referred to a chance to go to the network. Many of them secretly and some not so secretly harbored the idea they were the next great investigative reporter or the next anchor for the network morning news, but just as in all professions, many aspire but few are chosen.

Russell had never had those kinds of aspirations. Although in his first years the thrill of a good story had inspired him, rarely if at all did he fantasize about leaving Houston. This was his comfort zone and here he planned to stay. Doing the weather required little real work on his part unless there was an anomaly like a hurricane. In those instances he was required to perform a 24/7 operation until the threat passed, but those situations were rare and far between.

He usually arrived at work no later than 2:00 PM and went home or to the bar by no later than 11:00 PM He had grown up in Houston and was well-known but at the same time thought of by many to be somewhat infamous, so he was also the perfect guy to send out for "meet and greets." This homegrown personality was perceived by his viewers as their neighbor, just one of them.

Russell enjoyed the exposure and attention. He played golf in local charity tournaments and often acted as the M.C. for them, but what he truly liked about this part of his job was the chance to stay in front of the local beauties. As he looked at all the fresh faced beautiful girls around the station he knew why he was here—he loved women.

But today was different. First, he didn't work Sundays, and second, he was on a mission. He had purpose again, and it brought back the memories of past glory. He had to find someone who could answer the riddles Storm had given him.

Like any typical local television station, there were a few cameramen, producers, and stage managers who had been around since "Shep was a pup" and these were the guys he needed to talk to. They were cameramen or sound guys or producers who were still around putting in their time before mandatory retirement and being relegated to an existence of daily golf or fishing. For active people such as they were, these days usually meant long hours of excruciating boredom.

Russell understood and appreciated them, although reluctantly Russell accepted the fact that in a few years he would be one of them. These old guys knew where all the bodies were buried, but that knowledge they wouldn't share with just anyone. A newbie, for instance, would never get anything out of them; respect was earned, not given lightly. Russell, on the other hand, was one of them. He knew that if any of them could solve a mystery about girls being found dead at the Dome, they would share it with him and probably even help him narrow his search for the information.

That was when he spied Grady Anderson, sitting alone at a coffee room table seemingly lost in his Sunday paper. Grady was just one such guy. Grady had been a cameraman at the station for over thirty-five years and only had a few more months to go to reach age sixty-five and retirement. Grady had long since stopped doing location work. Now he shot the 6:00 PM and 10:00 PM evening news and stayed inside where the air conditioning worked. He was in early most days because the station was home to him; he lived alone and the people here were his family. Grady had been divorced for years. His wife had since remarried and his kids were long grown and now had families of their own, all living in cities around the USA. Grady was a fixture at the station and had been instrumental in teaching Russell about camera presence and telling a good story.

"Damn, a big storm must be coming for you to be here on a Sunday! And little early in the day for you, isn't it?"

Grady remarked, peering over his paper as he saw Russell approaching.

"Why do you say that, Grady—and by the way, screw you, you old fart!" Russell just grinned—he could give as well as receive.

"Why else would you be here on a Sunday and at an hour a little too early in the day for you?"

Russell got himself a cup of coffee and sat down. "Yep, you're right, it's way too early for me, but sometimes a guy has to make an exception." Carrying the coffee pot, Russell refilled Grady's cup as he continued. "You remember that pard of mine, Dave Storm?"

"Yep, sure do. Indian kid who was one helluva football player back in the day. He's the cop whose wife was murdered a few years ago ain't he?"

"That's him."

"What did he do that got you up and made you come to the station this early on a Sunday? He a medicine man now or something and have a premonition about a hurricane and ask you to come check?" Grady laughed at his own joke. Grady and Russell had shared a lot over the past twenty-five years—drinks, stories, good natured ribbing, but most importantly, respect. Not many still existed in their world with the history they had.

"Nope. He had a question about something I couldn't answer and he asked if I would do some research for him."

"Something to do with the station?" Grady knew Storm was a homicide detective, and Russell could tell the implication bothered him.

"No, just a question about history."

"Maybe I can help." Grady had probably forgotten more than most people remembered, Russell figured.

"What I was hoping for when I saw you. Did you know a girl was found dead at the Dome this morning?"

"Yeah, it just broke. Why?" Russell could see the questions begin to flicker in the older man's eyes.

"Storm caught the case. He will be the detective in charge of the investigation"

"Really?! You gonna tell Sweet Britches about it?" "Sweet Britches" was what they dubbed any new self-important female reporter who thought she was going to be the next Connie Chung. At the station now that person was Christine Chu, a beautiful Vietnamese girl just out of the University of Texas who was already charging headlong into the fray to move up the ladder as fast as her gorgeous legs would carry her.

"No, let her find out on her own," Russell scoffed. "But have you heard anything?"

"Nothing much, just that they found a body. Chu jumped on it and ran out with her infatuated camera boy to find out what she could. They haven't broadcast anything back yet. I am sure the Show will release their normal bullshit statement like 'it is unfortunate and our deepest sympathies go out the victim's family, but as yet we have no further information. When we get an update from local law enforcement we will be of any help we can be to the investigation.' Blah, blah, blah."

"Storm know anything about it yet?" Grady asked, now looking to Russell for clues.

"Storm said they found her name off a picture identification in her purse, and they found some clothing thrown somewhere nearby. He told me someone had slit her throat, but she was moved to a dumpster after she bled out. Early this morning they had found her body in a dumpster outside the new stadium but still hadn't found a bloody crime scene."

"What did he think you could do? Check your datebook for girls the right age?" Grady smiled, obviously tickled at his question, as he waited for Russell to tell him why he was really here.

"No, smart ass, he heard something that puzzled him and he asked me to look into it. You remember Hernandez, the

69

cop that lost his leg a few years ago when his partner was killed in that drug bust gone bad?"

"Yeah, that was a shame. The kid that died was young, just out of the academy, wasn't he?"

"Yep, the same guy, and yes, the kid was young only like twenty-three, I think. Anyway, he's working the homicide desk downtown and said something to Storm about his having caught 'another murder' at the Dome." Russell looked over at Grady. "Do you know anything about any other murders that have taken place around the Dome area during this time of year?"

"Yeah, seems like I did hear something about something like that, but I don't remember it having anything to do with the Show, just some unknown girl found dead near the Dome. I don't think the case was ever solved, in fact, I think the coverage died out fairly fast, almost as soon as it happened."

"So you don't remember anything about the Show being tied to it?"

"Not that I remember, but I could be wrong," admitted Grady, watching Russell's face as if trying to find what his friend could be looking for.

"You think there's anything in the archives about it?' asked Russell. "Or you got any idea where we would start to look?" Grady's interest was piqued now, and like anyone who works in the news media, his curiosity would get the better of him. Unanswered questions irritated newsies.

"Let's go look," said Grady, as he rose from his seat. "We should start about a year ago; I think there was one about then. Let's see what we find." Russell accompanied him as they found their way to the climate-controlled storage area that held many of the news reports and investigations from the past ten years.

During the last couple of years most of the archives had been moved to a computer data base, making it easier to retrieve and do a search. However, since Houston had a significant number of murders every year, it would take awhile to wade through them all to find similar cases. After about an hour of looking through the archives and researching old press releases, they found a case that appeared to be very similar. The naked body of a young girl named Stephanie Gilmore had been found by a cabby in a vacant lot just across Old Spanish Trail from the Dome complex. Her throat had been cut and her clothing tossed aside with her purse and identification. She was from Huntsville, Texas (only about fifty miles from Houston) and had worked for a law firm downtown. They found nothing more about her or her murder, but both Grady and Russell thought they had found something that might lead Storm to more killings.

Russell looked at Grady. "I'd appreciate it if you wouldn't say anything to anyone about what we are doing and hide our research. Right now I need to report what we've found to Storm. I will be back as quick as I can and we'll see if we can find more." With that, Russell left and Grady printed the material, put it in an envelope in his backpack, and deleted their searches. If there was a story here, it would be his and Russell's; breaking a story like this would be a great way for an old guy to go out.

Russell called Storm's cell phone to tell him what they had found. He got Storm's voice mail so he left a message and went back to Grady.

Charity Kills

CHAPTER EIGHT

Just the Facts

The M.E.'s office always had that combination of cleaning solutions and chemicals in the examining theaters that created an aroma that permeated even the cement walls and stainless steel examination tables of the rooms. Storm would often don a surgical mask, not that he worried about germs, but to stifle the smell. But today he put aside his normal aversion for the place and found Alisha still examining the body of Leslie Phillips.

"Any news?" asked Storm, bringing Alisha back from her concentration on the girl's body.

"Well, I can tell you she died of exsanguinations, and from the bruising on her neck, she was asphyxiated before she died." Turning to look at Storm, the plastic face mask covering her head, she then put it in layman's terms for his benefit. "Someone simply choked her till she almost passed out and then cut her throat and she bled to death."

"She died before her throat was cut?" Storm was confused, but then, everything else about this case was confusing— why not the way she died? he reasoned.

"No, not what I said, she lost too much blood for that, anyway, but she was probably closer to unconscious then dead. See the bruises on her neck? Whoever did this had their hands around her throat, thumbs in the back, attacking her from behind. The instrument used to cut her throat was sharp, no jagged edges. It was clean and swift like a razor or a scalpel. The killer cut the arteries while holding her head down, knowing it is easier to cut the throat with the windpipe directly in front of the blade. It also eliminates any chance she might scream or make a sound. Our killer simply choked her as a way of gaining control of her."

"Then you're telling me they knew what they were doing and we could possibly be looking for a doctor or someone in the medical field?"

"That or a professional assassin; somebody trained in how to kill someone easily and most importantly, quietly," agreed Alisha.

Storm asked a rhetorical question, more to himself then Alisha. "Why would someone hire an assassin to kill this girl?"

Alisha just shook her head, showing the same bewilderment as Storm.

"When will the final report be done?"

"You will have it tomorrow."

* * * *

Alisha frowned and resumed the grizzly duty of autopsying the young beautiful girl. The killer was good; nothing much had been left behind to assist her in determining the killer's identity. She had preformed a rape kit on the girl and found semen and a spermicidal. Someone, maybe the killer, maybe not, had had sex with her using a condom, but it must have broken. Alisha had combed the pubic hair to see if she could find any hairs not belonging to the girl. She found a couple, so if they were lucky and found a suspect, they could match the DNA samples.

There was some bruising, but that could come from consensual sex. It was the anal abuse that was the most troubling. Alisha had removed the paper bags on the girl's hands used to preserve any evidence on the hands and took scrapings from under the girl's nails, but found no skin or other trace. This meant the victim hadn't inflicted any damage to her assailant, and there were no defensive wounds on her arms or legs, which indicated she hadn't fought back.

Alisha bagged the evidence, recorded it, and passed it on to the property room for them to hold till someone would need it, and then sat down to write her report from the notes she had made and the audio tape she had recorded while doing the autopsy. When the report was completed, she would drag her tired butt home after another long day. It seemed to her it would be nice if once in a while Houston would have a day without a killing, but she knew that was too much to hope for in a city its size.

* * * *

Storm drove back to the office to check in with the lieutenant one more time, hoping to snag Hernandez before he left. Sunset came early this time of year and by the time he got to Reisner Street he had to turn on the lights to see inside the dark parking garage. He never understood why they couldn't change the hours for the garage lights when daylight saving time switched back to regular time, but they couldn't seem to get it right. He didn't fear the lack of light, but darkness depressed him. With darkness came too many hours for idle thoughts, too many hours to think of Angie, and now, too many hours to think about Leslie Phillips. In both cases he wanted answers to the how and why they had died.

As he entered the division offices he saw Sgt. Hernandez and was reminded that he needed to talk to him again. Hernandez's earlier comment was still bothering him and he hadn't heard back from Russell as of yet. The shift change was happening and Hernandez would be getting off, so this would be a good time to ask him more about what he had said

"Sergeant," Storm waved Hernandez over. "How are things on the desk, Sergeant?"

"SOS, but keeps me off the streets and gets me another day closer to retirement."

"This morning you said something that's been bothering me all day. What did you mean by 'another murder at the Show'?"

"Listen, Detective, I shouldn't have said anything. I really don't want to get into this and besides that, it's not my place."

"You mean you won't tell me what you meant or you don't want to?" Storm's eyes burrowed into Hernandez's face.

Hernandez looked around and over his shoulder before speaking. "OK, but you didn't get this from me." It was clear what he was about to tell Storm was not a mere rumor, but something someone wanted well hidden. "There have been other murders at the Dome. I think today's may be the seventh."

"How come I never heard about them?"

Looking Storm in the eyes he said, "Sorry, Detective, for the way I have to put this. They started when you were, let's say, 'not doing so well.'"

"You mean when I was drinking?" Storm acknowledged what Hernandez meant.

"Yes, Detective. Right after I was put on the homicide desk five years ago, a young girl was murdered down there. No one was ever found for it; in fact, no one was ever really a suspect. It ended up as one of the unsolved cases. Like this one, the mayor's office and some pretty big people from the community put pressure on us to bury it."

Storm felt a throb beginning in his temples. At least now he had an explanation as to why Nagel from the mayor's office had been at the Show offices with Dakota Taylor that morning. He looked at Hernandez. "You said there were more?"

"Yes, Detective. Like I said, I know there were others, I think seven, including yours."

"Were they all young like this girl?"

"As I remember it, yes."

"They were all found at the Dome?"

"Yes, I think they were all found somewhere on or around the grounds."

"Are there any official records of the murders or anything that will tell us more?" asked Storm

"I'm sure there is, tucked away somewhere probably in the unsolved case files in the file morgue."

Storm knew he had pushed Hernandez as much as he could for the moment. "Thanks, Sergeant. You can be sure this will remain between us, but if I think of something else, can we talk again?" He wanted Hernandez to know he wouldn't betray his confidence but also wanted to make sure the sergeant knew it wasn't over.

"Sure, Detective. I am close enough to retirement now and what with being wounded, what are they gonna do to me?" Hernandez snickered. "I had a hunch you'd be back again. I've been itching to solve a case like this for a long time. And maybe we can find something from other cases that might help solve your wife's homicide. Hey, I'm in."

"By the way, Sergeant, the girl's name is Leslie Phillips and she worked for Tejas Petroleum downtown. Tomorrow morning will you get hold of personnel at Tejas Petroleum and find out who were her next of kin and notify them that their baby girl won't be home for Easter?" Although Storm realized he sounded more than a little sarcastic, he also knew Hernandez understood and would take care of the notification Monday morning first thing. He would check with him later that day to see if anything came out of the phone calls.

Storm moved on down the hall; it was time to face the lieutenant.

The lieutenant was waiting for an update, and outside of the girl's name and the possibility she might have been killed by a professional, Storm didn't have a lot more to tell him. She had had sex prior to her murder but that could have been consensual. They still hadn't found the crime scene and if the killer was as good as Storm was beginning to think, they might not ever find it. Seeming satisfied with the progress of the day's work the lieutenant dismissed Storm and wished him a good night.

* * * *

Storm had one more stop to make before calling it a night. It was one he made any time he was feeling he might be getting closer to that old friend "the Edge," and now was not the time to fall off it. His next stop was the cemetery where Angie, his little brother, and his parents were all buried.

It was almost sunset then and the grounds were quiet. He always stopped and bought roses to put on each of their graves. He picked up red ones for his dad, who had always been there to watch out for him, and for his little brother, who had died way too early. His father had been a disciplinarian; spanking his sons was always on the table, and he was tough, but he was a fair man and proud of his sons. It wasn't until Storm's brother died that he saw the grief his father expressed and how it indicated his dad's deep love for them all.

Storm's younger brother's death had been the result of a head-on collision with a drunk who had escaped without a scratch. The loss haunted him even when he was drinking, and though he knew he was a drunk at the time, he had enough sense to never drive while in his cups.

He brought yellow roses for his mom because of her love for Texas. She used to say Texas had changed her life and made her the best person she had become. It was her strength that convinced her boys they could do anything they set their minds to. Lastly, he brought white roses for Angie, the love of his life, who had been his strength after he lost his parents.

When he got to their graves, he arranged the flowers in the vases attached to the headstones and said his hellos to each of them. He cleaned the outer edges of each brass marker, making sure the grass didn't cover their names or the words of sentiment inscribed on the face. Previously, when he had been trying to quit drinking, being here had made him calmer and eased the heartache, replacing for awhile the desire for a drink. It was here he could draw the courage to battle the demons in his mind and feel closer to those who had given him strength when they were alive. He knew their souls were with God, but he felt their support was still here for him in this place.

His visit today was different. He was there to tell them about Leslie Phillips and the possibility of other deaths like hers. He explained, telling them about her senseless death and what Hernandez had told him, wondering out loud if there were more related murders. He told them about his visit to Russell and how Russell had jumped in to help as they would all have expected him to do. Smiling at Angie's headstone, he told her how Russell still had a revolving door on his condo. He also asked them silently all to help him in any way they could, and he said a prayer over them. Finally, as always, he promised Angie that someday he would find the person or persons who had taken her away from him.

Charity Kills

CHAPTER NINE

Leslie was Not Alone

Nights had always been the worst for Storm after Angie had been murdered; it was this time of year when the darkness came early and along with it the damp and cold of a rainy Houston winter. This was the season when Houston had a lot of slow miserable rain storms and those added to the lower temperatures made the city seem even colder and more inhospitable.

Storm remembered that as a kid he had never liked the cold; the uncomfortable damp of a winter rain seemed to penetrate the skin and settle all the way to the bone. As he got older, the achiness seemed to intensify. He had turned off the lights and turned down the heat when he left that morning, so the dark cold house was not a welcome sight when he returned.

When he got in he noticed that his cell phone had registered that he had missed a call earlier, and he had a message from Russell. Eager to hear it, he hit the voice mail button and began listening to Russell's report that he might have some news for Storm, some information on the other girls that had died mysteriously and their bodies found near the grounds of the Dome, and all during the same time of year. He got his friend on the first ring.

"Hey, Baretta."

"What you got?" Storm asked. The anxiety was nearly killing him.

"I might have something on the other girls. Meet me for dinner and I'll fill you in."

"Where?" was all Storm asked.

"Meet me at the Brownstone."

The Brownstone, located inside the 610 loop, was an upscale eatery that Russell frequented. It had been a fixture in the River Oaks neighborhood for years and was frequented by local people and those in the know around Houston. It was an old home with a brick wall running along the street and lush gardens on the grounds. The dining rooms were semiprivate and would give them a chance to talk without disturbing other diners and without being overheard.

Walking through the door, Storm saw Phillip, the manager. Phillip knew them both and directed Storm to a room where Russell was already seated with his favorite cocktail in hand.

"What did you find?" Storm hurriedly pulled his jacket off and grabbed a chair opposite Russell, waiting to hear the news.

"Hey what's this, no 'hello, honey, how was your day'?" Russell grinned, trying to lighten Storm's sour mood.

Storm jibed back. "OK, fine, hi, sweetikins, how was your day? Now what did you find out?"

"I went to the office, as you asked, and acted like I was there to check on the weekenders to see if they were busy while I pulled the latest sheets from weather bureau. Chu was running around trying to find someone to scoop, with her hopelessly smitten little camera guy following the next Emmy award winning journalist around like a puppy with a shit eating grin on his face. No big things happening so I went to the coffee room. The good news is, in there I ran into Grady Anderson, you remember him, been around the station for years."

"Yeah, I remember him. Isn't he retired yet?"

"Marking time but still sharp. You know at one time he ran that place. My first day on the job he was the floor director. Anyway, I recruited him to help me."

"What did you tell him?" Storm demanded, hoping Russell hadn't let too much out of the bag.

"The truth, he is to sharp for me to lie to, so yes, I told him what this was about and no, he won't share with anyone else." Russell looked at Storm as if his friend had just called him a red-headed stepchild.

"OK, so what did you tell him?" Storm pushed for more information.

"That you had a case and you had heard a rumor about other killings that might be similar, maybe even related. I asked if he remembered anything about anything."

"Well?" snorted Storm, frustrated with the time Russell was taking getting to the point.

"He did. It took us about an hour to find it, but we found the murder of a girl named Stephanie Gilmore from Huntsville. She was found near the stadium about a year ago naked and her throat cut."

"Was there anything in what you found about anyone ever getting caught for it?"

"Records from the station didn't show that anyone was ever caught or convicted. In fact, from what we could find, it seemed the entire case seemed to just disappear."

"Did you find any more mysterious killings of girls this time of year or around the Dome?"

"In fact, Baretta, you won't believe this. We found five more news items that suggest five more girls over five years that were found just like the one you got this morning. And you ready for this, *hombre de mio?*"

"Yeah, come on, give it to me," Storm answered impatiently.

"The circumstances seem eerily similar in every case!"

As the waiter approached to ask Storm if he wanted a drink the conversation fell silent. Storm ordered water and Russell ordered another Jack and Coke.

After the waiter was dismissed Storm asked, "Was there any information about them; names, addresses, family, anything?"

"Yes, I have a list of their names here for you. They all had their throats cut, they were all found in the neighborhood around the Dome or on the grounds of the Dome, they were all about the same age, similar in appearance, and nobody was ever charged with their murders." Russell hesitated, pausing over his drink, his brow furrowed. He took a slow drink. Finally he asked, "Storm, what have you gotten me into?"

"I got no idea, yet, but you've done enough. Stop digging for now and don't leave a trail at the station. I don't need some hotshot reporter looking into 'til I know what I got on my hands."

Russell shot back a wounded look. He sounded irritated. "First, this is you and me. Second, I'm in this now, and so is Grady, so if this breaks as a story it is ours and yours. You make the arrest and we get the scoop."

"Hell of a long way from the weather, Russell." Now Storm was trying to make a point. He was concerned for his friend. No one knew where this was going to lead and how dangerous it might end up being.

"Hell with you. I started as a reporter—remember that? And think of the babes I could get if this turns into 'How the Hero Weather Man Solved the Woman Killer Crime of the Decade.'" He repeated it smiling. " Hm ...'Hero Weatherman Solves Multiple Murders.' I like the sound of it."

"OK, but just keep it between you and Grady, and go ahead and keep digging. Let me know if you find something else. And for God's sake keep your head down if this goes ugly," Storm warned Russell.

Storm wasn't sure what he had gotten himself into yet, either, but it looked like Leslie Phillips was the tip of the iceberg, with five other murders before her. This case of a girl's murder might have just multiplied and the implications were almost unthinkable. He needed much more information, as there were many more questions than answers so far. They ordered and ate their dinners quietly, catching up on how Tech was doing in basketball since they had hired Bobby Knight and settling into a conversation that would get them back to some semblance of reality and relaxation.

Charity Kills

CHAPTER TEN

The Model Employee

Early Monday morning the day after Leslie Phillips' body had been discovered the invisible minions who performed the day-to-day toil, who were generally unnoticed by the general public and working members of the largest rodeo charity, began to arrive at work.

Peggy Wise was one of those unassuming employees everyone wants working for them. She was efficient and extremely capable while performing her job, no matter what the hour was. She was cute and young but on the generously proportioned side, so the office Romeos didn't hang around her desk romancing her or wasting her time. Peggy was affable, with dirty blonde hair, maybe just a smidge overweight but her personality sparkled. She could captivate most people with her good-natured attitude and warm smile, but if you judged by her physical appearance alone, you'd think of her as quite ordinary and almost invisible.

Every morning she was not just on time for work, but early. The upcoming three weeks, being early was a necessity and more than just the office ethics of doing a good job. She had worked for the Show for the past eight years, starting as a basic runner or "step'n'fetchit girl." She had worked her way up to assistant to the head of ticket sales, a promotion that she took seriously. Beginning in January and running through April, the number of employees at the Show ballooned to more than five hundred, including additional office staff, waiters, bartenders, ticket sellers and cleaning staff. During that time she managed a huge group of employees, and clients, customers, and underlings who manned the ticket window quickly discovered she was a problem solver and that she led by example.

Peggy's Monday morning routine had just started when the rumors about a girl being found dead on Sunday had begun to filter in from the temporary staff. The entire floor was abuzz with whispers and speculation. Softly spoken murmurs could be heard passing from one part time employee to another: "A young woman has been found dead, yes, on the grounds, yes, they say her throat had been slashed and she had been raped," each time the details repeated with wide frightened eyes and a shake of the head..

Eight years of employment with the Show had taught Peggy a lesson she had learned well. Negative rumors would not be tolerated. She knew she had to put a stop to them, or at least quiet them down in her department. Employees who persisted in spreading idle gossip about something that could be construed as negative would be let go.

"I will not tolerate gossip," she told her staff. "Rumors are not facts, but the public perceives them as facts, and we cannot be the source of those rumors," she explained. "Now let's quit discussing this unfortunate event and leave the settlement to the powers that be to worry about."

She reassured her female employees that there were plenty of police officers and male escorts to walk them to their cars after dark, so no one should be afraid. She laughed and said the only problem she'd had in eight years was a drunken cowboy whistling at her. With her figure, she told the girls, she had considered that a compliment, and even the temp girls in the office had giggled at her carefree attitude.

Peggy also took the opportunity to remind the staff of the rules against fraternization with Show members, committee persons, or fellow employees, a reminder that drew a large collective sigh followed by more giggles—like any of them would fess up, anyway! The Show had always been a great place for singles to meet, whether they were looking for a rich spouse or just someone nice to date. But the Show had made it perfectly clear during informal indoctrination that dating a committee member was off limits to all employees. Dating, drinking, or partying with committee persons was the fastest way to lose your job.

Peggy went back to her desk and began to work on the receipts of sales from the day before, organizing the remaining seats, calling the ticket vendors, and putting together her report, which was accurate to the last ticket. Tickets that still remained unsold for some of the upcoming underappreciated performances were noted and set aside for further work. Selling unwanted tickets was another part of her job; she enticed local businesses friendly to the Show to buy them and pass them out to employees and clients. The Show hated not being able to say a performance was sold out, or at least ninety percent sold out.

Over her eight years at the Show, Peggy had seen a lot of changes in the lineup of entertainers, with the most dramatic changes having come in the past couple of years. When she had first come to the Show it was mainly all about Country and Western acts and the Show had attracted the biggest names in the business: George Strait, Reba McIntire, Brooks & Dunn, Martina McBride, and many, many others. But that, too, had changed. When it was decided to extend the length of the Show, now almost a month long, the emphasis changed, too, adding performers from other music genres like Hilary Duff and Little Bow Wow. These performers brought in a much more diverse clientele and added a younger crowd to the mix. The annual dates of the Show had also been moved back almost a month in hopes of attracting high school and college kids on spring break. The new facility was bigger, the carnival was larger, and of course, they had the new stadium that held more people for each of the performances. So everything was changed or changing, some changes positive, some not so.

During the Show, Peggy's hours were longer, and they meant working a seven day week. It wasn't unusual for her to work fourteen-hour-days during those weeks. Many of the staff and working committee members even rented small apartments near the Dome to cut their travel time, many sharing one apartment to cut the cost. Peggy's decision to buy her home in the neighborhood she had picked had been influenced by her job and proximity to work. She now only lived twenty minutes away. She was pleased that she never had to worry about traffic; she could use back streets, avoiding major thoroughfares, to get in early. Her sleepy bedroom neighborhood was safe, and with the neighborhood watch and the proximity of a police station she never worried about her late hours.

In spite of being a proponent of the rumor rules she couldn't help herself, and that Monday morning while sitting at her desk, Peggy's mind began to wander to the murder. Who was this girl? Peggy was of the few who was aware of the others; she even knew one of them, Elaine Gage. Elaine had been a friend when they worked together at Tejas Petroleum. She too was from a small town not far from where Peggy had grown up. Elaine was a pretty girl and all the guys at Tejas had always been stumbling around her desk like flies to honey. Elaine never had a problem meeting men, even the inappropriate ones and she had dated a lot, always coming back to work after a weekend more tired than she had left for it. Elaine and Peggy were different as night and day, but that had never stopped them and they had become fast friends and had seen a lot of each other until Peggy left Tejas and went to work for the Show.

Not long after Peggy began to see Elaine at the Show, too. Elaine had joined a working Show committee and would come visit or call Peggy regularly. Many times the two of them would meet for a soft drink or sandwich when both could get away.

When Elaine joined the committee, she got the privileges that went along with it. She was able to attend social functions given by the Show as partial reward for the hours of work committee members donated to the workings of the Show. She could go to membership only clubs that provided a place where volunteers could drink and mingle without the general public. Over time she and Peggy had drifted apart. Peggy would often see her heading to one club or another with her new acquaintances to drink and flirt with the cigar store cowboys. As for Elaine, she had found a target rich environment at the Show with volumes of available and unavailable men to tempt. There were rich ones, poor ones, cute ones, single ones, and the oh- so-many men who wives were conveniently absent from activities this time of year. The advent of the term "Rodeo Wife" came from the "What happens in Vegas stays in Vegas"—or its twin "What happens in the Show stays in the Show"— attitude that persisted in the VIP Clubs and provided safe sanctuary for the event elite. The so-called Rodeo Wives are actually the young women who were constantly in company of these elite.

The year Elaine had been murdered, Peggy had seen her going and coming from the VIP Clubs. One club in particular was a watering hole for dignitaries of the Show and affluent guests. These were people who contributed large amounts of money to the Show or had personal relationships inside the "Good Ole Boy Network" to relax in a nonjudgmental environment. The "gentry" had privileges not afforded the regular committee people—their own bar, real glasses for drinks, and a four-star restaurant. They also had their own security diligently guarding the door, so the riffraff couldn't intrude. These types of clubs were no different than exclusive country clubs and restaurants in at least one way. The moneyed men who frequented them drew a bevy of cute young women vying to meet her "Cowboy Charming." The money was in the VIP Club and if these girls didn't mind letting their morals or ideals slide just a bit, they were welcome, unless they were coming to make a nuisance of themselves. Affairs and trysts were commonplace, with two rules: Just don't get possessive, and always remain discreet.

Peggy had known a few of the girls who had gained entry into this world of exclusivity and had done well; they had found someone who would leave his wife for them or been convinced to wait for the wife's demise, leaving the field open to them. But these girls were the exception rather than the rule. Most rodeo wives accepted their role as the mistress or the other woman, content with the perks bestowed on them. When Peggy saw Elaine she was always in the company of a married man, but she had nice clothes, nice jewelry, and was always invited to the right functions, as long as the wife was not there, and sometimes even if she was.

There were two VIP clubs, one in the new center and one in the new stadium, both nicer than those they had in the old Dome and old center. There were always extra badges and credentials available to the directors and vice presidents for their "guests." With these credentials, the girls could come and go without security or committeemen who worked the door asking questions.

Peggy had listened and watched many things since her friend had been found dead across Fannin Street in an abandoned car. She had talked to the policemen who worked security on the grounds, questioning them about the crime. She knew cops were all voyeurs and would know how the girl had died and if she had been violated. Peggy was revolted by the thought of these strangers looking at her naked friend lying in an abandoned car on the side of an empty city lot, but she was right; most of those working that day had gone over to see the body after it was discovered and could describe the scene in minute detail. She also knew she could ask them and they would tell anything they knew of any leads or clues. In Elaine's case all the officers knew was she had been found naked and that she had been violated.

At the time Peggy heard about Leslie's murder, she knew the police still had no leads and no apparent motive, except for rape. Peggy hated that nothing was being done, and she hated how the media had treated Elaine's murder as if Elaine had somehow been in the wrong, as if somehow her friend had gotten in with some bad people who had killed her without leaving a trace. The newspapers had carried just a small article about a girl being found dead in an abandoned car near the Dome where the new rail system would soon be built; a rail line that would connect the Dome with the Medical Center and downtown Houston. The article had seemed more concerned with how the location of the rail line would mean the demise of an old apartment project that had been an eyesore for years than with the untimely and ugly death of a pretty young girl.

The obituary, too, was small. It only told she was from Hallettsville, Texas, she was twenty-five years old, and that she was single with no family. It also mentioned she worked for Tejas Petroleum and was being buried in a cemetery near where she lived in the Westbury area of Houston.

Peggy had gone to Elaine's funeral, a sparse affair attended by only a handful of people. She saw a couple people she vaguely recognized from Tejas Petroleum, though she couldn't recall their names, and another woman who piqued Peggy's interest because she couldn't remember where she had seen the woman before. She was a tall blonde woman who looked familiar, but try as hard as she could, for her life Peggy couldn't put her finger on where. Maybe she had worked at Tejas. Maybe that was where Peggy had seen her, but she just wasn't sure so she didn't say "hello" to the woman.

Since Elaine's murder Peggy had been writing down notes and observations about things that happened at the Show, keeping an eye open to who she saw with whom. If another girl disappeared she wanted to see if she could link them to anyone in particular; someone who could possibly be a murderer. As the years passed, Peggy kept clippings from the other murders; some had pictures, most didn't. She found she liked playing "sleuth," her word for herself in this situation. She liked studying the information she found in the papers and the rumors she heard at work. Over time, she found that the cases had a few things in common; each girl was from a small town, most had no family to speak of, and the scariest thing of all was that those for whom there had been photographs, each girl had resembled Elaine.

But what did that mean? Was it just a coincidence? And what was there other than looks of the victims to tie them together, if anything?

Peggy pulled out the notebook she had been hiding in her private desk drawer, the one that required a key to open it. She opened it to the first page, on which she had taped some newspaper articles about her friend Elaine.

Peggy's notes:

My friend Elaine
*   has been found dead.*
Her body found
*   across the street from*
*   the Dome inside an old car.*
My only friend from Tejas...

We just had lunch
*   she giggly about the fun*
*   she was about to have*
*   at Rodeo.*

Gage

Elaine Marie Gage, 25
Of Houston/Hallettsville passed away February 26, 1998. Funeral services will be March 1, 1998 at 11:00 a.m. at Westbury Cemetery, Houston, Texas.

I told her I was worried,
  she had fallen in with some
  not so nice people·
Saw her with stinking
  big wheels that like younger
  women and are all married·

They found body Sunday a·m·
Cops told me someone
  had cut her throat·
She was naked and they
  were sure she had been abused
Her funeral was in town,
  she didn't have any family left·

The funeral was simple
  not too many there,
  some I knew from Tejas···
Strangers too,
  two men and two women···
  must have worked for Tejas
  after I left·
The Tejas people told me
  the company paid
  for funeral since
  she had no family·

Local Woman Found Murdered

Elaine Gage, a local Hallettsville High School graduate, was found murdered in Houston over the weekend. She was discovered inside an abandoned car across the street from the Dome complex early Sunday morning. She was discovered as police ran random checks on derelict vehicles abandoned on the lot. The circumstances of her death have not been released by Houston Police, but anonymous sources have revealed that the girl had been sexually assaulted before her death. Homicide detectives have assured the public they will be investigating her murder and as soon as more information is available, they will be releasing what they know to the press. Miss Gage graduated in 1991 and immediately got a job working for Tejas Petroleum in Houston, where she was living. She had been a member of the Hallettsville District Championship Lady Brahma volleyball team. She leaves no family and services will be held in Houston at the Westbury Cemetery, Wednesday, March 1, 1998 at 11 A.M.

Charity Kills

CHAPTER ELEVEN

The Show Must Go On

Monday morning Detective Storm was waiting in the dazzling reception area of the Show. Today the coming and going of numerous people made the place appear even busier than it had been yesterday. People scurried around everywhere; the chatter of workers on cell phones and radios filled the hallways; serving people carried trays of food; people pushed carts loaded with signs and ladders. All were finishing up the last minute details. Some people whizzed by on electric scooters that carried them from one end of the monster building to other. To Storm it all looked like total confusion, but he was sure as big as this endeavor was, it all made sense to someone.

Storm had come back to see Dakota Taylor and secure the video tapes from the stadium and the center from the night of the murder. He hoped the videos might show Leslie going or coming with someone, possibly a killer, or at least the last person to see her alive. At this point he needed a lead, any lead, somebody who had seen the girl, who had talked to her—someone who might have seen her killer.

Dakota arrived in the reception area, chatted a minute with the receptionist, and walked directly to Storm. With her hand extended, she said, "Good morning, Detective Storm, what can I do for you today?"

Storm took her hand giving one firm shake, thinking it was a shame this very attractive woman had ice water running in her veins. This morning she seemed even more aloof than she had on Sunday.

"Ms. Taylor, I would like to pick up the security camera videos from say, 8:00 PM the night before the girl was found to 4:00 AM Sunday morning."

"Detective, you will have to be more specific than that, you understand we have security cameras mounted everywhere."

Storm thought a minute. "OK, was this building open to the public Saturday night?"

"No, only employees of the Livestock Show and Rodeo or the NFL would have been able to get in here."

"Nobody else? How about Show officers and their guests?"

"Oh, yes, they would have been allowed in to visit the VIP Room."

"Then I would like those, as well as those from the stadium," Storm added, as if he had just thought of it.

"The stadium videos don't fall under our jurisdiction. You will have to request them from the appropriate person in the stadium offices."

"Would you know who that might be?" Storm's patience with her stonewalling was already running thin.

"Yes, I believe your police Sergeant Hebert can help you with that."

That raised the hackles on Storm's neck. Why would Hebert have access to the security cameras of the stadium and why hadn't he said anything about them yesterday? What the hell was the old fart up to?

Ms. Taylor then sent Storm to see Jeff Osborn, the head of security for the Center, to retrieve the videos for the times he'd requested. Osborn had a video of the main west entry and one of the escalators going to the second floor, but when asked about the VIP Room he stuttered, hemmed, hawed, and sheepishly said no, they didn't use surveillance in those rooms, but he gave no explanation as to why. He took Storm's card and said if he found anything else he thought would help he would get in touch with him.

As Storm left the office, he saw Jeff Osborn immediately reach for his phone and place a call. He thought, *I'll just hang around to hear what's so important.* Storm ducked around a support beam and listened to Osborn's side of the conversation.

"Osborn here.... Yes, he just left...."

"No, he has no idea. Don't worry, the scrubbing was good, it would take a pro to find where I changed it." That said, Storm heard Osborn hang up the phone after he had passed the word to whoever was on the end.

Storm got on the elevator, not satisfied with the way things had just gone, pretty sure the man had not been totally truthful with him, but hoping he would get luckier and the girl would show up on the stadium video disk somewhere. He headed off to see Hebert and found him in an office just off the north gate of the stadium, next to the workout area for the Houston professional football team. Storm couldn't help whistling to himself at how state of the art the workout area was. He had only seen rooms like this one on TV. It was outfitted with all the latest equipment. Given the problems the new team had had in their first season, it was ironic that the place was empty. It seemed to Storm somebody ought to be in there working with the offensive and defensive line since God knows neither could block or tackle. But I'm not here to ruminate about the failings of the team, he reminded himself. I need to talk to Hebert.

As he reached Hebert's office, he got another smartass Hebert jibe. "Did you find the killer yet, Desk Boy"?

"Nope, but closing in on him. You sure you don't know him?"

"What the hell do you mean?" From the sharp defensiveness in Hebert's tone, Storm knew he had hit a nerve. *God, I love the payback...*

"You watched the videos from that night yet, Hebert?"

"Why?" Hebert squirmed in his seat. Storm smiled, thinking, he must be wondering if he's being accused being accused of something. *Good. Let 'im squirm.*

"Why didn't you tell me you were in charge of security in here?"

"You didn't ask," Hebert smirked, trying to put Storm back in his place.

"Well, I am now, and I need all the videos from the ten hours before the girl was found to two hours after." Catching a breath, he continued to push Hebert. "What did you see on the videos?" Sometimes the direct way was the best way, Storm had learned in many sessions interrogating suspects and witnesses over the years. So he acted as if he already knew the answer, a tactic that often caused a reaction from the one being questioned, and that reaction often led down the path to the truth.

The way Hebert blew Storm off was almost as good as a direct answer: "It will take a couple of hours to get them for you. We are pretty busy around here with the start of the Show and I have to break someone away from other duties to make you a copy," countered Hebert.

Storm shot Hebert a look that said, "I know you are lying to me. You've seen them." But Storm knew, and he figured Hebert knew, he couldn't prove that. "I want the videos from every entrance used by anyone from staff to Show members that night. Have one of your 'boys' bring them downtown to me."

That nagging feeling in the back of Storm's head began to crawl down his neck. He was more and more sure that everyone out here was lying or covering up something and that everyone seemed to know more than he did at this point in time. He had to get back to Russell to see if he and Grady had continued digging around at the station and found anything more.

* * * *

Russell and Grady had met up early that morning to go over more tapes and take notes, recording anything they could find about other girls who had been found dead under suspicious circumstances, throats cut and dumped anywhere. They were being as surreptitious as possible so as not to attract attention from the overeager-looking-for-a-big-break types. They for sure didn't want Chu or her cameraman to find out what they were doing. If the *chihuahua* with great legs found out, their cover would be blown and anyone who might know something would most definitely go underground, ending all chances of untainted information. They wanted to help Storm solve this case. If they helped him they would be helping themselves; this could be the coups de grace for two veterans. Old dogs can find a bone occasionally and this bone could be a career maker.

* * * *

When Storm arrived at the TV station he made his way back to Russell's small office which, as always, was chockablock with papers, computers, and one large screen TV. Grady and Russell were huddled together over his desk watching a much smaller TV screen with a built-in disk player.

Russell looked up. "Hey, Colombo, what did you find out at the show this morning?"

Storm replied, "Got the security disk from the Center and waiting for more from the stadium. Guess who I had to see to get those?"

Grady looked at Russell, raised his eyebrow, and Russell just shrugged. "Who?"

"Hebert."

"Police Sergeant 'I am a coonass which means I am better than your ass' Hebert?" Russell snorted. He had trouble with Hebert years ago as a reporter and since then the man's inability to get along with news outlets had grown into legend.

"Yep."

"What the hell is he doing with security videos from the stadium?" asked Russell.

"He is in charge of security out there."

"Isn't he still on the city payroll?"

"Yep, but with all the events at the stadium and center, he is assigned there. He even has an office near the team workout center."

"Wonder if he gets two checks?" wondered Russell, just shaking his head.

"Who knows," shrugged Storm, "but that old fart knows more than he's tellin.'"

"Think he already looked at the disks?"

"Oh, yeah, I am sure of it, but he wouldn't admit it. He said he didn't have them and would have to get them to me. So I told him to send one of his 'boys' to my office with the copies. God, I loved digging him with the word 'boys,' too," Storm chuckled to himself, as Russell just grinned.

Looking at both of them, Storm asked, "How you two doing? Find anything new?"

"Yes, actually we did," Grady grinned. "Looks like there have been a few suspicious deaths of young women around the Dome grounds and it looks like it's been going on for the past seven years."

"Seven years?" whistled Storm. "All during the Show?"

"Yep. All during the barbecue or while the Show was in full swing."

"What else?"

"Six young women, plus your new one, all in their twenties, all brunettes, all from small towns, all found naked with their throats slashed."

"This is getting hinky. Why hasn't this been on someone's radar screen before? Were any of them solved?"

"Not that we can find. Not even a mention of a suspect or if the cases were ever solved."

Russell pulled out a list of names and pictures of the six girls. "All young, all pretty, and all dead," he commented. "All killed the same way, all to add to the Leslie Phillips case. We're not any closer to this one, are we? All we've done is add more unsolveds to the list."

"Looks that way. We got one hell of mystery going on here, fellas, don't we?" Storm said afraid to say what he really thought. These could all be the handiwork of a serial murderer, and someone—or lots of someones—were complicit in covering it up.

"Look, guys, keep digging but don't let it get out, keep it under wraps, okay?"

"Don't worry, Grady and I have lots more traps to run and dirt to dig, but we're playing this close to the vest. Chu and her bunch of ankle biters won't get their hooks into this 'til we break it and the bad guys get caught."

Grady laughed. "It's nice to be doing something again and doing it with you guys makes it even better," he said. "I'm not letting this one get out."

"Can I have a copy of that list?" asked Storm, as he prepared to leave.

"Sure. What you planning on doing with it?"

"Going back to see Alisha, see if she has anything more on this girl and see if she can pull any files on the other girls without anyone finding out what she is doing."

"Oh, yeah, the assistant M.E. Last time I saw her I asked her, 'How you like your new boss?' At which time I got a snide sneer and a kiss-my-ass smile. She knew that I knew M.E. Roberts is another blithering idiot political appointee. What more could she say?"

* * * *

Back at the Show offices, another meeting was taking place. Dakota Taylor and Sergeant Hebert were in Leon Powers' office and they had Vern Nagel on the speakerphone. Powers just stared across his desk at Dakota and Hebert and he didn't have a happy look on his face. Hebert knew that this was no time for him or Dakota to hide anything or polish the apple. Powers was serious and wanted to know what was going on. "What does he know?" referring to Detective Storm.

Dakota responded, "Nothing yet, or at least he doesn't seem to. He came in and asked for the video disk from security. All we had to give him was the main entrance and escalator going to the second floor. Jeff gave him copies and he left and went to see Sergeant Hebert for the stadium videos."

Powers turned to Hebert. "Well?" His lips puckered up in a way that said without words, "This is not the time to do anything but lay out the all the facts as they are known at this time. So get on with it."

"He came to see me, told me what he needed, and I told him I would have to get them. He said to have one of my people deliver them to him downtown." Hebert didn't say anything about the animosity between him and the Desk Boy, and he sure didn't want to mess this gravy train up. He had been given the opportunity to take over this plum from his predecessors, and the money he made here equaled his police salary for a year. The added income was his retirement fund and nobody was going to screw that up. Nobody. Most of the money was unreported and buried tin cans full of the cash filled his back yard. Not even Powers knew about the under the table money he got for turning a blind eye to certain goings-on and directing his men and the one lone woman under him to do the same.

"Have you seen them? Did you see anything that could prove to be embarrassing a liability to the Show?" Powers demanded, looking directly at Hebert to see if he twitched.

"Yes, sir. I watched them all once closely," replied Hebert. "I didn't see anyone take her out of the stadium."

"Did you see her go in then?"

"Yes." Hebert knew the next question and readied himself to answer it.

"Who with?"

"Joe Dresden," Hebert said in a hushed voice, as if someone might overhear him.

Every eye in the room rolled, and Vern just gave out a loud sigh on the other end of the phone. Hebert and everyone else in the room knew Joe Dresden. He was a ne'er-do-well who had married "up" and lived like he'd earned every bit of it. His wife, the former Ellen Hitchcock, now Ellen Dresden, was one of the richest women in Houston and from a family that built a solid business from the ground up. Ellen had taken over the helm of her father's business when he passed. Joe was her second husband and had worked for her as a sales associate when they met. He moved up to president of the company when she became the CEO as the successor to her father. The company was the biggest distributor in the Southwest for a locally owned air handling supplier. The company had contracts with everyone in Houston, mostly because of her father's business savvy and later due to Ellen's own shrewdness in getting the business classified as "minority owned" when she took over.

Ellen had been a member of the Livestock Show for a number of years and when she started dating Joe, he became a fixture in the VIP clubs and restaurants. Everyone knew about Joe and Ellen. Ellen was homelier than a mud fence, obnoxious, pushy, and generally not a nice person, but she put a lot of money into the Show, so everyone kissed her ass. After they married, Joe became the leader of the kissers. Joe had always been a philanderer and Ellen knew it, but as long as she didn't get hit in the face with any of his dalliances she turned a blind eye. People laughed and whispered behind their backs, but nobody overtly would utter a word. Her money was too important to piss her off, so they just let Joe be and let him act as if he was one of them.

"OK, so she went in with Joe Dresden. What exactly did you see, Sergeant?"

"About 11:00 PM on the night of the murder I saw Joe and the girl go up the elevator, headed, I assume, to the VIP club on the ninth floor. They were with a group of people, all directors and above, and a bunch of other women."

"Did you watch the entire tape?" interrupted Powers.

"Not a tape anymore," Dakota officiously threw in, "it's a disk now."

Looking as if he was trying not to show his frustration, Powers ignored her. "OK, did you watch this disk?"

"Yes, sir."

"Well, go on with the story then."

"Nothing more to tell. I saw Joe and a couple of the other men leave about an hour later but I never saw the girl leave."

"Nothing at all, not hide nor hair of the girl again anywhere on the disk?" Powers growled.

"No, sir."

"Right. So how did she end up in a garbage dumpster?"

"I don't know," answered Hebert, deciding brevity was best in this situation.

"Dakota, have you seen this disk?" asked Powers

"No, sir," Dakota said, shaking her head.

"OK, I want you to watch it with the sergeant and I want you both to double check it to see if there's anything— anything at all, that might embarrass the Show."

"Yes, sir," chimed in Hebert. "We're on it right now." He rose hurriedly, eager to be on his way.

"By the way, can you sanitize this disk?" This was not an unexpected question from Powers, but it still caught Hebert, and Dakota, too, he suspected, off guard.

"What do you mean, Mr. Powers?" The idea of suppressing evidence scared both Dakota and Hebert and the shock registered on their faces.

"If you find something we don't want out, I want it cleaned. You have to make a copy for this Storm fellow, anyway, don't you? Well, when you do, erase anything you think might embarrass us." Leon Powers didn't have to repeat himself to make himself understood.

"Do we leave out Joe taking her in?" asked Dakota.

"No, leave Joe in. He may have to be the sacrificial lamb if we need him," said Powers dismissively, and with a wave of his hand the meeting was over and everyone knew it was time to leave. Nagel hung up after saying he'd fill in the mayor.

* * * *

Not trusting that Vern Nagel was on top of things, Leon Powers reached for his phone. It was time for him to talk to the mayor directly and make sure His Honor understood the significance of control and silence.

Leon Powers was the CEO of a multibillion dollar concern with thousands of employees and huge revenues coming in daily. With a heady Ivy League education and a willingness to sacrifice anything or anyone to further his own prestige and career, he had risen to the top by always being in control of his own destiny. For years he had had to deal with politicians and he retained one of the best lobbying firms in the state of Texas. So dealing with the new mayor was not just a concern, it was a necessity.

He had accepted the role of president of the Livestock Show and Rodeo for his pleasure. It was a voluntary job but not without its perks. It added to his resume, put him in the public eye as a philanthropist, and meant he sat on an executive board with some of Houston's most powerful, rich, and elite families; exactly where he wanted to be. His term as president was three years, at which time he would move to the executive committee, where he would continue as a member until such time as he wanted to step down or he died. Leon was married, and although his wife had never showed any interest in the charity, his children did, and he made sure they were placed on high profile committees. He also saw to it that they were allowed to use the Rodeo as their private playground and, of course, granted all the privileges to which the children of the president are entitled.

Mayor Richard Lemay answered his private cell phone. Only a handful of people had the number.

"Richard, this is Lee." Leon Powers had never liked the name "Leon."

"Yes, Lee, what can I do for you?"

"I know you are aware of the unfortunate events of Sunday morning out here."

"Yes, I am." The mayor waited.

"You've got some cop out here digging around and we can't have him finding anything that could be scandalous for the largest contributor of incidental income to the city. Do I make myself clear?" The threat was not veiled. Powers knew the mayor would understand exactly what Powers was saying.

"I am aware and I have been assured by chief of police and Lieutenant Flynn, who is his immediate supervisor, that the detective they assigned to the case fits our standards perfectly, perfectly, for this job. Lieutenant Flynn has assured me that Detective Storm is a burn-out waiting for retirement."

"Richard, there are many influential people involved out here and I know you don't want anyone connected to the city embarrassing them or their favorite charity."

Powers got some satisfaction from imagining Lemay cringing. The threat was not veiled. Leon Powers and the people that ran the Livestock Show were among the richest and most powerful kingdom builders in town. He knew the mayor didn't need or want to piss them off; he needed their support if he was going to continue to run the fourth largest city in nation.

"Lee, I will dig into this as soon as we are off this call and this will go away, or if a killer is found, it won't be linked to the Show."

"I knew you would see it my way, Richard, and I know you can handle this. Thanks for your cooperation. You need to come out as my guest soon. How about the day of the President's visit? Good photo op for you, even if you are from that other political party!" With a small laugh, Leon disconnected the call.

* * * *

Goddamn it, shit, I don't need this now, thought Richard Lemay. The press was already all over him about the failure of his crime lab and his reneging on his pre-election promises to not raise property taxes. He pushed his intercom button. "Get Vern Nagel and the police chief in my office *now!*" he ordered his assistant. Almost as an afterthought he told her, "Add Lieutenant Flynn to the list, as well."

Charity Kills

CHAPTER TWELVE

One More Addition

When Storm got to the Sharps Building he checked in with the receptionist and went to meet Alisha. She was working on another body, this time a young kid who looked about ten years old. As the bile rose in Storm's throat he fought the urge to vomit. This was one of his most hated sights—kids dead.

"What happened here, Alisha?" Storm covered his mouth from the involuntary gag reaction.

"Floater, his father found him face down in next door neighbor's pool. Told the cops the boy had been missing about two hours and that neighbors were gone. Supposedly the gates were locked. But you know kids, when there is a will they will find a way."

"Damn, Alisha, that is three drownings this month, isn't it, and it's still too cold for a kid to want to go swimmin', isn't it?"

"Four, four kids, and it is just the start of March," said Alisha.

"Damn!" Storm shook his head, moving on from this objectionable subject. He had his own fish to fry. "Did you find anything new on our girl?"

"No, not much. I did do a DNA test on the semen found in the girl's vagina, but although there was bruising in her rectum, there was no semen there. She was penetrated both vaginally and rectally, but there was only lubricant in the rectum and everything indicates she was dead when that happened although still warm.

"If we find a suspect at least we got something to run their DNA against and we can run our sample against all the data bases I have access to." Added Alisha

"Could it have been two guys? One before she died and one after?"

"Could be, although without semen in the rectum, I can't be sure it was two. Either way, someone(s) had sex with her before and after she died from the front and from the back."

"So, it could it have been one guy?"

"The first must have been hurried, he must have been using a condom to leave the spermicide but it must have broke or he was sloppy, because he left traces of semen for us to find. If there was a second, they took their time or the first was no longer in a hurry, but as I said, he left nothing to match except the brand of lubricant."

"Any defensive wounds on her arms or legs?" He paused and then went on. "Find anything anywhere?"

"None. She didn't put up a fight and there were no skin cells or blood under her nails, she didn't mark him."

"She would have had to know him or them, and had to trust them to put herself in that situation then," said Storm.

"Looks that way or she got caught totally off guard by one or both. Whoever took her last is the one you want, I'm sure of it, whether it's one or two, and whoever he or they are, they covered their tracks pretty damn well." Alisha was still looking at her deceased child.

Storm thought out loud. "The way she was killed and the lack of evidence suggests he knew what he was doing ...Hey, Alisha, you got a copier?" he asked suddenly.

"Yes, over there, why?"

Storm hesitated. He had already drawn Russell and Grady into his anonymous detective team and now he was about to attempt to bring Alisha into it. He looked her directly in the eyes. If she wavered she was out, but if she held his gaze, he had another recruit. "Alisha, I think our girl is one of seven girls killed over the past seven years. I think whoever killed her might have killed them all, and if that is true, you know what we got."

Alisha gasped. She looked back in Storm's eyes and he saw she understood this was no time for teasing.

"Seven girls over seven years? How do you know? What has led you to this jump to conclusion? How come it hasn't come up before now?"

"I think there has been a cover-up. I think some very powerful people are behind the cover-up and I think police personnel and the mayor's office have contributed to it, too."

"Shit, Storm, what are you getting us into?" Her shock registered but she had listened this far and he could tell she would let him go on before she made up her mind.

"Alisha, this is what I know." Storm showed her the list of the seven girls in total including Leslie, whose bodies had been found near or on the grounds of the stadium.

"Each girl died of mysterious circumstances, each died by having their throats slashed." Alisha nodded.

He told her about his meeting with the people from the Livestock Show and how the mayor's rep has been there, as well. He told her about how Russell and a friend had researched all the girls deaths they could find from television archives and all of his suspicions. When he finished his recap, he again looked her directly in the eyes. It was her turn to talk, to join him or walk away.

"OK, if I'm in this, what do you want from me?" asked Alisha, still sounding uncertain as to what she could add.

"You now have the list of the six more girls' names. These would have all happened before you got hired. I want you to pull the files on them to see if you can find anything that connects them. This has to stay on the down low and you have to do this without the director or anyone knowing about it. If we get found out by anyone not only will we all be screwed, but I feel these murders will stay covered up. And Alisha, I promise, if we break this, you get credit," added Storm.

"Bite me, Storm. I don't give a shit about credit. If one guy or a gang did this, I want' em; fuck the credit."

Storm just smiled. He handed her a copy the list of names Russell and Grady had given him. He put his finger to his lips, making the sign that said, "Shush." That's all he knew he had to do—Alisha would do the rest. He then waved goodbye.

Storm had been thinking all day about one more recruit to enlist to the team. He thought he knew who he could trust and who he couldn't. Inside the department he came up with a big goose egg, that is with the exception of the man he was going to see next.

Returning to Reisner Street, he saw Sergeant Hernandez sitting at his desk shuffling papers for the lieutenant. Busy work occupied much of Hernandez's days and Storm knew Hernandez was bored to death. Hernandez was a street cop and a good one, and by now he would have been a detective if he hadn't been hurt. He needed Hernandez in the group to do some research on serial killers and look for files on his list of girls in police archives. He needed Hernandez to pull the unsolved case files on these girls and see if any connections could be made between them, much as he had asked Alisha to do. Hernandez could do the research on the computer and no one would be the wiser. To Storm's knowledge, Houston had never had a serial killer before, but he knew theory, profiles, and documentation would exist in the FBI files and that there had to be background on what led people like Ted Bundy, Jeffery Dahmer, and John Wayne Gacy to commit some of the most heinous crimes in last century.

Storm was convinced the team he was assembling had only a short time to digest as much as they could that might lead them to a killer. He needed Hernandez to round it out. He caught Hernandez's attention and motioned him to follow him, disappearing around the corner toward the coffee room. Hernandez got up and followed him.

Charity Kills

CHAPTER THIRTEEN

A Team Comes Together

Storm returned home again after dark, but this time, no angst or melancholy accompanied him. In the past years he would have simply bought himself a bottle of Jack, drunk himself into a coma and woken up the next morning with a bad hangover and absolutely no direction in his life. Tonight he had other things on his mind and sleep evaded him, but this was no call for a drink. His mind sought answers to tough questions even though some of those answers might scare him. He scrawled the questions on a yellow note pad:

1. *Why was this girl killed?*
2. *Why was she singled out? What did she have in common with the other girls we've found records on?*
3. *What kind of person kills attractive young women?*
4. *Why is the mayor's office involved at all, let alone having a spy at his meeting with the Show's people?*

5. *What does Hebert know? Why isn't he sharing it?*

He thought a minute and then added the most disturbing question of all:

6. *Do we have a serial murderer hunting in Houston????*

He had put his covert plan in motion and now there would be no going back. He had talked to Russell and planned a meeting with his co-conspirators for the next morning at Russell's condo. It was a place they could meet without fear of being seen or overheard. Nobody knew of his relationship with the group and it needed to stay that way.

* * * *

Russell had eagerly agreed to the meeting for the next morning, and although 9:00 AM was a little early for him, this mystery and solving the girls' murders had become more important. Russell's anticipation also was mounting and he was anxious to know who besides Grady and Storm would show up in the morning. Nobody from the station would know or care that Grady had gone to his place to help him with something, but what about the others? How were they involved and why? Guess I'll just have to wait until tomorrow morning, he realized.

Russell was up at 7:00 AM—an hour he hadn't seen in years. He had had trouble sleeping, but his lack of sleep had come from excitement. He had purpose for the first time in a coon's age. No long night out in a local watering hole, no waking up with who knows who in his bed and not caring, except for when she left. He and Storm were working on something together, something important, a mystery he wanted to solve.

* * * *

Storm arrived at Russell's at about 8:30 AM; it was an easy drive that time of day since it was against the flow of the ghastly lines of commuters all traveling in the opposite direction going to work. The guest parking at Russell's building was wide open and the doorman just waved to Storm as he entered the building. Seeing him reminded Storm that he needed to tell Russell to put together a story for the doorman to cover any suspicious activity the next few days. He didn't know how long or how many meetings they would have to have, but he knew they were all in it now and they needed to keep it under wraps for as long as possible.

The coffee was already on when Storm walked in. Right behind him was Grady with a box full of files and tapes. Russell was prepared for the tapes and disks; he had the latest in flat screens and players.

When Alisha arrived she also carried a box stuffed with files. She had just been introduced to Russell and Grady and they had gathered around the dining room table when the doorbell rang again.

This time Storm answered it and invited Sergeant Hernandez in. Storm had left Hernandez with a decision to make the night before, and it looked as if he had taken him up on it. He, too, carried a large brief case overflowing with the files, all he could find on the girls without garnering any suspicion when he left the precinct.

Each of the five poured their coffee, doctored it up, and sat down. The mood was excruciatingly serious at the table when Storm started off. "Each of you has a piece to this puzzle and I trust all of you. This is not your normal investigation. This is something we all have to keep so quiet you could hear a cockroach fart." He looked around the table, and everyone grinned in agreement. "Let me start with what we do know."

Storm began to lay out the facts as they knew them:

"Fact # 1: On Sunday morning around 4:30 AM a young woman was found dead in the trash dumpster outside the stadium by a cleaning person. By the way, that guy was freaked out and we can assume he had nothing to do with the crime.

"Fact # 2: Her throat had been cut and she bled out, but not in the dumpster; there was not enough blood there, so she had to be dumped there after she died.

"Fact # 3: Her clothes and purse were found later in yet another dumpster on the other side of building. Her clothes were bloody, so she had to have been killed while she was dressed, then stripped and abused.

"Fact # 4: She had had sex with someone prior to the killing; spermicide and semen were found in her vagina and on her panties, so she had put her panties back on after the first guy."

Alisha piped in, "The girl had been molested after her death, as well. It's important to note that the person who did that was most probably the killer; she had been anally abused postmortem, but no semen was found."

Storm went on to tell them everything he knew about the murder and the girl. Around the table the shock of what they were hearing began to turn into disgust and rage. Not a person at the table was unaffected by what they were hearing.

"Now I want to go over my suspicions and what I base them on. Sergeant Hernandez was the first to give me a clue that there had been multiple murders in the Dome area, when he mentioned that I got *another* dead girl found at the Dome. It started me wondering about what he meant, so I got Russell involved and he brought in Grady to help me check old data at the station to see if they could find any references to other murders near or around the stadium grounds. They found reports of six girls having been found dead near the stadium or on the grounds; that makes one a year for the past seven years. All young, all pretty, and all unsolved.

"I recruited Alisha and Sergeant Hernandez to go through their files to see what they could find with the caveat that they had to keep their searches under the radar of their respective offices." He looked at Alisha and Hernandez. "Since they are here, I have to assume they are with us and until we solve this, we all have to keep what we are doing secret. There could be a lot of heavyweight pressure come down on us if this leaks out, so we will only talk on safe phones and meet here at Russell's till we figure this out. Russell, you wanna start?"

Beginning with Russell, each of them proceeded to report on their individual discoveries to the moment. Russell and Grady told how they had found the names of the other six girls and showed the videos of news reports from the times of the murders.

Alisha had found files on all six of the girls from the M.E.'s office records and she went over the method of each girl's death. All had been killed by having their throats cut and all had been anally raped postmortem. None had defensive wounds, and each had been choked before death. She also went on to describe each girl's appearance and concluded by noting that they were similar in appearance and age.

Sergeant Hernandez pulled his files and followed along. He, too, had found all six murders. He had found the reports in the unsolved case files of the precinct, he told them. "I remember the last four girls' deaths from my time working the desk. I also remember thinking that none of these murders were vigorously investigated at the time; they all seemed to fall through the cracks, no leads ever found and no person of interest ever named."

But now he also had more information; more background on the victims and ultimately, more commonality. All of the girls worked in or around downtown Houston. All worked for big companies where they were only a paycheck number.

All came from small towns in Texas; they had headed to the big city to pursue their dreams in the fast lane, find a job, and maybe a husband. None of the girls had any family to speak of, so nobody to stand up for them or push for their deaths to be solved.

Grady interrupted. "Does it appear any of the girls knew each other?"

"Not from what I can find, nor were any of them from the same town. Two of them worked for Tejas Petroleum (but at different times), two in big law firms, one for the county, and the last two for big firms servicing the oil patch," replied Sergeant Hernandez.

"Were they all killed during the Rodeo?" asked Storm.

"Yes, all of them, although last year's victim was killed later than the others, late in March."

Russell jumped in to remind them that the dates of the Show had been moved to later dates last year. They had changed them to coincide with college spring break crowd, which also made it last longer. By changing the dates the Show could run twenty days instead of fourteen.

Next, they watched the disk of the films from the security cameras that Storm had gotten from the Show. The surveillance of the center's main entry and escalator proved to contain nothing helpful. Leslie never appeared to have gone into that building. But the stadium disk was a different matter. They saw the girl enter and go to the elevator with other women and men, but one man seemed to be paying much more attention to her than to the other women.

"Anyone know him?" asked Storm.

"I do," replied Russell.

"Who is he?"

"Joe Dresden. He is married to Ellen Dresden."

"Why do I know that name? Isn't she the former Ellen Hitchcock?" asked Grady.

"Yep, the very same," replied Russell.

"She took over her dad's company, didn't she, and was written up as the lady entrepreneur of the year back a few years?" asked Storm.

"Yep, and Joe married her soon after. He worked for the company and after they were married she made him president," smirked Russell.

"Is he involved with the Livestock Show?" asked Storm.

"Only because she is; she's a big contributor and likes the notoriety she gets from it. They buy champions every year and she was elected to the Show Board of Directors a few years back, so he gets all the benefits she gets. He has become a fixture out there, or should I say, in the VIP bars, since they got married. When you see them together, he is the social one and always loving and attentive, but when she is not around he's the same horn dog he was before they got married."

"You do know why you didn't get any videos from the clubs, don't you?" asked Russell, grinning at Storm.

"No, but I bet you know. I wondered about that, but got no inkling from the guy at the show. Why?" inquired Storm.

"It's kinda like Vegas—what goes on at the Show stays at the Show. All the big wheels have their, as they call them, their "rodeo wives" and their "real wives" and they don't want it documented anywhere, so no security cameras or cameras of any kind are allowed in any of the clubs for that matter."

"Does everyone out there know that?" Storm asked the question that seemed to flash across all the faces at the table.

"Well, an outsider wouldn't know it, but people who spend any amount of time out there all know it."

"So you're telling me Joe Dresden has *"girlfriends"* and Ellen doesn't know about it?" Storm asked Russell, while making quotation marks in the air with his fingers.

"Oh, I think all the wives know about their cheating husbands, but as long as you don't slap them in the face with it and everything is kept under the covers, so to speak, they choose to ignore it," Many of these wives are mucho protective of their station and if they did ever suspect infidelities; it is easier to turn a blind eye to them than to accuse your paycheck of being unfaithful. It's usually about money and position and a dalliance here and there is treated like 'who cares as long as they don't bring anything home with them.'"

"Any of the wives have Rodeo boyfriends?" asked Grady with a twinkle in his eye.

"I am sure some do, and if they do, that would be a much better kept secret." Russell just smiled his shit-eatin' grin.

"Do you think the victim is one of Joe's Rodeo girlfriends?"

"Looks like it from what we just saw, but who knows? It could have been the first time he had ever seen the girl. They pass some of these girls around like you traded baseball cards when you were a kid."

Hernandez was going through the files while this discussion was taking place and interrupted, "Hey y'all, this Joe Dresden is mentioned in the police reports as the last one to see two of the other girls alive. It says he was investigated and nothing came of it. His alibi was that he was with his wife at the times the girls were killed."

"Still interesting he was last seen with both them and now seen close to Leslie's death," said Storm.

"Russell, do you still have all your credentials for the Show?" asked Storm.

"Sure do! Daddy keeps me on the list so I still get all my perks," Russell snickered.

"I want to go to the Show tonight. I want to go to this club and mingle with the big boys, but I don't want anyone at the Show to know I am coming ...or Hebert, for that matter," he said, almost as an afterthought. This was going to be a surprise attack; hopefully he'd catch some people off guard. It was always easier for a suspect to make a mistake when he didn't know he was being looked at than if he had prior knowledge.

* * * *

The meeting broke up, each contributor heading back to their jobs to do all the digging they could without raising suspicion. They each would be looking for anything else that tied the girls together or that might lead to a suspect. They had all signed on now; they were all going to do whatever they could to find the killer of Leslie Phillips and the other six girls, all feeling pretty sure the killer was the same person. None of them took the situation lightly. They knew this was no game or adventure, but none of them thought they could personally be in any danger, not physically, anyway, and not at this time.

Charity Kills

126

CHAPTER FOURTEEN

Joe's Big Saturday Night

Darkness still came early in early March to Houston, and, as always, the weather could change in a heartbeat, but opening night of the Rodeo meant that everyone who wanted to see or be seen would be there and the weather be damned. Hot or cold, it was the night all sizes and shapes of women dressed in their best leather outfits, some of them needing more leather than one cow could provide. Others wore only enough garments for propriety (using the word loosely) and left plenty of flesh to share with the practiced observer. Add to the outfit of choice a new 20X beaver hat looking like the ones worn by the cowgirls in an old Tom Mix movie and a new pair of exotic skin boots, uncomfortable yet fashionable, and the women were ready for the "Rodeo Parade." Annie Oakley in Buffalo Bill's Wild West Show had nothing on these gals.

It was a Tuesday night, but people attending the Show took off work early to go home and change to be at the festivities in plenty of time. Even with advance tickets, committee badges, and parking passes, parking would be horrendous, forcing people to park in adjoining and satellite lots or anywhere else they could get by with. The Show arranged for offsite parking with shuttles to the stadium and a new onsite tram system to get folks to the center or the stadium. The tram consisted of a long line of open cars of eight to ten rows, each row seating four to six people across, pulled by specially designed tractors leased for the Livestock Show. A new committee had been formed just for this function, with the members ferrying people from the bus drop as well as making round trips to the adjacent, but still remote, parking lots. There was also the new Metro train system, which had been inaugurated earlier in the year and could carry folks from downtown or the Medical Center and all the Metro lots in between to the stadium. All in all the Show was doing its best to make accommodations to get as many people in as they could.

The committee system and sponsors were a financial boon and a money saver for the event. Committees existed for every possible need the Rodeo might have (and some they didn't), and many of the committees even had sponsors, like the Tram Committee, sponsored by Ford, which paid for the rental of the tractors and other vehicles in return for free advertising. All the twenty thousand members of the almost one hundred committees were volunteers who paid dues to be volunteers! One could say the Show management was double dipping—not only were no salaries paid, but the Show received money to let folks volunteer. There were committees for everything, from ticket sellers and takers to event information to animal auctions to workers in the private clubs and exhibition areas, to lost children. About the only paid employees other than the office staff were the uniformed security, the bartenders, and the servers in the clubs.

Storm wasn't too worried about parking or getting in since he was in the company of Russell. Russell received all the perks his father's status allowed, from free entry into all the events to special director parking. It all came with a special badge and card, which also allowed him entry into every VIP club in the facility.

When they arrived at the complex, Russell merely pulled up to a guard gate, showed his parking credential hanging from the window and was directed to a special parking area reserved for the "big boys" of the Show, their families and guests. The lot was located adjacent to the center and even at that proximity there were special golf carts made available to make sure that "Show royalty" didn't have to scuff their boots by walking too far.

Russell had told Storm to dress the part. "We're entering the land of the cigar store cowboy and I don't want you embarrassing me," he said with grin, which was a tongue in cheek way of saying, "Don't go looking like a cop." They both wore starched jeans, a starched button-down shirt, sport coat, highly polished boots, and a properly blocked Western hat. In case it had been too long since Storm had worn a cowboy hat, Russell reminded him the silk bow went in the back of the hat.

It had been years since Storm had been to the opening night; the last time was with Angie when she made Russell take her to see Reba McIntyre. It had been fun and Angie loved the hobnobbing with the faux famous or even the infamous. She never went anywhere she didn't know someone and that night had not been any different. Russell had gotten tickets to one of the sky boxes at the top of the "Old Dome." The seats were actually terrible and the stage seemed miles away, but the box had closed circuit television and the drinks and snacks were free. The Old Dome sky boxes all opened on a common hallway which made for a promenade where folks could walk all the way around visiting the boxes of friends along the way, stopping to have a drink and catch up on the latest gossip. Storm always found himself following Angie's lead, shaking hands with people he didn't know (in most cases didn't care to know) and working to keep a smile on his face. To Angie and Russell schmoozing was the reason to be there, but not Storm. He would run into the occasional old football player he knew from the past or a fan who remembered him and they might recapture the old heroics for a while, but the real fun was watching Angie have such a good time. She truly was the social butterfly; an infectious smile covered her face as she beamed from greeting to greeting. Inside Storm was amazed at how truly happy it made him and how beautiful she was when she enjoyed herself so much.

This night would be a wholly different story. He was there to watch people, see what he could pick out and hopefully find out if there was a killer in their midst. He wanted to do it with as little fuss and recognition as possible. He was with Russell, just two good ole boys out to have a good time and enjoy the scenery. Their first stop was going to be the VIP room in the center. It was a room where the elite went to have dinner and drinks before they ventured over to the stadium to watch the entertainment and socialize away from the crowd of common patrons.

The room had been upgraded when the Show moved into the new facility. It was located on the second floor of the center at the end of a long hall in a location where the regular patrons and committee people couldn't see the perks the directors and VP's enjoyed. The entry was subtly guarded by special committeemen who checked credentials, along with one or two of Hebert's cops. No one was sure exactly why the cops were there, but the assumption was that they were there to break up any altercations that might erupt between over-served "cowboys" or jealous "cowgirls." Storm guessed the gig was mostly just a plum job for some of Hebert's handpicked underlings; a place they could meet and greet, look out for the big wheels, eat for free, and get paid for about four more hours than they really worked.

Going with Russell always had its own share of drawbacks, though, because everyone knew him, either because of his dad and family or from television. There were always people yelling "hello" or waving at him. Storm asked him once if he really knew all those people. Russell just laughed and said, "Hell, no, but they think they know me because of television." Storm knew he was right, of course; he was good in his role and he always made the public feel like they knew him and that he liked them, which Storm was sure he really did. It was what made him popular.

Even though the committeeman at the door recognized Russell, he still was asked to see his admittance card, which Russell waved in the committeeman's face as he walked past with Storm in tow behind him. The place was full even at this early stage of the evening. Men and women filled the seats at the tables and others stood in groups around the bar. Most eyes went up to see who came in, and then most went right back to their conversations as soon as they reckoned if they should be impressed or not. Was it someone they needed to wave to, invite over and speak to? And most important, was it someone who could make a difference to them?

Many of those at the tables waved at Russell or said "hello" and asked about his father. Some would go on to say what a great man his dad was, which Storm knew always embarrassed Russell. Russell had told his friend more than once that he was considered the black sheep because he had never become one of them and worked for the Show. Still, many of the younger women smiled and Storm was sure some of them were women Russell knew in one way or another or they wanted to be.

Storm recognized many of faces in the room, either because of his friendship with Russell or because they were the movers and shakers in the Houston business world. The ones Storm found to be most interesting were the women; the unattached women he remembered from previous encounters when he and Russell were running the streets as single men drinking and partying, all before he married Angie. By now, most of them were at least in their forties and fifties, still dressed in what he thought were the same outfits they had worn twenty years ago, still stuffing their bodies into leather dresses or tight pants with boots; attempting to still look the part of "young, vibrant and wanted." But in many cases time had been unkind to both their faces and their bodies. Storm had always thought women who tried too hard to stay young hurt themselves and their looks. In a way he felt sorry for them. They had run their traps for way too long, but they couldn't stop until time and gravity had taken the last vestige of attractiveness from them. Most were now relegated to a Saturday night booty call for anyone who had no luck finding a younger companion.

As they headed to the bar, Russell asked Storm what he wanted, but Storm just shook his head and said, "Nothing now." He was occupied surveying the room, watching the people and wondering if Leslie's killer was among them. On their way to the stadium Russell had again explained to Storm why there were no cameras, including security cameras, allowed in the clubs. He told him that if you were caught taking a photograph in any of the clubs, the cops or the committeemen working the door would make you stop and sometimes even confiscate the camera. Nobody in the clubs wanted there to be any proof of hanky-panky of any kind. So Storm was fairly certain that if the killer was in the room, he felt safe.

That was when Storm saw Joe Dresden. He got Russell's attention and nodded toward Joe. "Let's go say "hello" and you introduce me, okay?"

"You have that evil smirk on your face you always get when you think you're going to surprise a bad guy and the bad guy has no clue he's a suspect yet," Russell remarked, grinning at his friend.

They began to move through the crowd like it was any other social move, Russell saying "hello" to everyone who spoke, hugging the women, shaking hands with the men, and always introducing Storm not as "Detective Storm" but as his old college buddy "David Storm."

When they got to Joe and Ellen Dresden it was the same procedure. Russell shook Joe's hand and gave Ellen a friendly hug. He and Ellen had known each other since they were kids, so it was natural for them to talk and exchange hugs and pleasantries about their parents and childhood friends. This momentary diversion of the couple gave Storm the opportunity to talk to Joe one on one. He asked what involvement Joe had with the organization and Joe began elaborate eagerly about all the philanthropic things he and Ellen did to support the Show, especially their purchases of champion livestock from the kids who showed their animals at the junior Ag competition and sale.

Storm asked Joe if he had attended the barbecue, not actually waiting for Joe to answer. Storm mentioned how he had missed it this year and how badly he hated to miss such a great party. He bantered on about how many teams there were now, but guessed that just added to the free booze and food if you could get yourself invited into a team's booth. He laughed quietly. "The barbecue is also a great place to meet cute women," he said with a wink, giving Joe the impression he was a partner in crime.

Joe, who Storm could tell had been eagerly waiting for his turn to talk, agreed. "Yes you are so right; so many women, so little time. There are more cuties around out there and actually around here," he added waving his hand around the room as if throwing a lasso, "and they all want to be part of this thing and to run with the big dogs."

"I see things have not changed out here. It's been a few years since I've been out, but I see the cute girls still get access to these rooms and make sure the right men know they are available," commented Storm.

"Yes, they do, and they seem to get younger every year," laughed Joe.

Laughing, too, Storm poked Joe in the arm and said, "I'm sure it has nothing to do with us getting older."

Joe chuckled, "Nope, but if they don't care and neither do I."

"Then you were here Saturday night?"

"Oh, yes, hooked up with a little beauty; dark hair, great body. Ellen, the woman talking to Russell, my wife, never stays late at the barbecue, so I had myself a big time. This cute little slut took me in the bathroom of the VIP club in the stadium and gave me a blow job; then I put her up on the sink and fucked her. Goddamn rubber broke, though, so I hope she doesn't come back knocked up in a few months," Joe said, grinning.

"Wow, sounds like you had a big time. Did you happen to catch her name?"

"No idea. Leslie something. Why? You want to meet her?" Joe looked around the room as if searching for Leslie's face in the crowd. "If she's here, I'll introduce you," Joe snickered.

Storm wanted to bitch slap Dresden so bad he could hardly contain himself. He wanted to beat him to within an inch of his life, but he had a better a way of ruining this moron's night. "You know, Joe, I never did really introduce myself to you. I am Police Detective David Storm, Houston Homicide Division. And I got big news for you, sleaze ball. The girl you were with Saturday night, her name was Leslie Phillips. Were you aware that we found Miss Phillips' dead body in a dumpster outside the stadium at 4:30 Sunday morning? The morning after you had sex with her in a bathroom?" Storm then took out a picture of Leslie lying on a slab at the morgue and showed it to Joe.

Joe's face turned ashen. All the blood drained out of it, his shoulders slumped, and his hands began a distressed shake.

"What's wrong, Joe? Were you the last one to see her alive?" asked Storm with a rage-filled look in his eyes that betrayed the calm in his voice.

Joe was in an obvious state of panic. I bet he doesn't know whether to shit or go blind, Storm told himself. This man has just insinuated he might have had something to do with this Leslie girl's murder and I've caught him admitting to seeing her Saturday night.

Storm reached over, laying his hand on Joe's shoulder "Don't worry, Joe, I am not here to take you in tonight, but I do want you available to talk to me, so don't leave town."

With the fear of God instilled in Joe, Storm grabbed Russell's arm at the elbow and let him know it was time to leave. Russell said his goodbyes to Ellen and as he turned to say goodbye to Joe, he saw the look of stark terror on his face. As they walked out he said, "You've brought the world to bear on poor Joe, haven't you? It couldn't happen to a nicer guy." They both laughed as they went to their next stop, the VIP room in the stadium.

* * * *

After he was sure they were gone, Joe grabbed Ellen's arm and told her in no uncertain terms he had become ill. "It's time to leave and leave now," he ordered her. Even as she attempted to argue with him, he half pulled and half pushed her out the door. She wasn't sure what had happened, but she saw the mask of fear on Joe's face and conceded to his wishes.

* * * *

The crowd had grown from the time Russell and Storm had arrived, and outside thousands of people now swarmed the grounds that surrounded the stadium. Lines were forming to enter as people pushed to gain entry. George Strait was performing, and if being opening night wasn't big enough, George always attracted a huge crowd. Storm had to admit George was one of his favorites, too, although he suspected tonight he wasn't going to see much of the show.

Russell didn't have to wait in lines; he merely waved his credentials and went around the lines to a gate that read "Gold Badges." He and Storm walked up to the security person, Russell showed his badge, and the two of them entered, interrupted momentarily by the metal detector going off. Storm pulled out his police badge and showed his hip holster to the cop working the gate. A quick look at the badge and an "I'm on the job" from Storm satisfied the cop and he let him pass.

They rode the escalator up the outside and entered the stadium through the first doors on the right. This stadium is some kind of structure, thought Storm, looking around. It's a lot bigger than the old Dome and with a lot more pop and flash.

Next they went to a special elevator where Russell again had to show his credentials, and up they went to the VIP area on the ninth level. This club was huge, and like the other VIP room, there were committeemen working the door along with what appeared to be two more of Hebert's cops. At this club Hebert himself was also found holding court, chatting with his officers working the door. One of the cops was an older, balding man obviously not in shape enough to run anybody down and the other was a tall, pretty blonde woman who had a severity to her look that probably scared most citizens shitless. Bet it comes in handy in this job, Storm reflected, as they entered the club.

Hebert looked a little shocked to see Storm approaching the doors to the club and immediately questioned Storm to find why he was there. "You on the job?" He didn't bother to introduce Storm to the other officers.

"Nope," said Storm, "just here with Russell to enjoy George Strait. Any problems with that, Sergeant?" Turning first to Russell and back to Hebert, Storm asked, "Do you know Russell Hildebrandt, Sergeant? His father used to be the president of the Livestock Show?"

Hebert shook Russell's hand. "You're that weather guy, aren't you?"

"Yep. Do you watch my station, Sergeant?"

Hebert smirked, "Nope. A person can't depend on you weather guys anyway—you're always wrong."

Russell just smiled and shot back, "Yeah, meteorological maps are hard enough for those of us with an education to understand, so I can understand your difficulty." *Russell is as good at this repartee as anyone, so let this coonass run off at the mouth.* Storm smiled with his private satisfaction.

The action in the room was much the same as the room they had just left: people having drinks, getting food from the buffet, mingling, ogling the women, ignoring those they didn't feel were of their class. There were tables and chairs set around the cavernous space and a forty-feet long stand-up bar. There were plushy paddled stadium seats facing the action on the floor for those who wanted to sit and watch the show. Televisions were mounted above the seats and huge flat screens all around the club area, making it easier to see what was really going on, where the rodeo action was taking place. You didn't even need to leave the bar the watch the action.

The same assortment of people filled this room as in the last, all dressed up for "flash and trash night," as those in the know had always called opening night. The place was full of girls like Leslie—young girls with older men, all betting on the chance they would find the gold at the end of their rodeo rainbow. Some were even hanging out with the cops. Those were girls who probably didn't have credentials or a waiting sugar daddy to admit them.

While Russell visited with old friends and acquaintances, Storm went back to talk to the cops working the entry. The older man was probably in his fifties and the woman was maybe around thirty. Storm pulled his badge and introduced himself. He produced the picture of Leslie taken from her driver's license.

"Did either of you work Saturday night here?" he asked them.

"Sure, we both worked," answered the older cop.

"Did either of you see this girl Saturday night?"

"I think I saw her," said the female cop.

"Good. She was seen entering the stadium with a man about 11:00 PM," he explained to them.

They both looked again and again the female officer said, "I saw her come in with a man I'm pretty sure was Joe Dresden, but I'm not positive."

"Did either of you see her leave?"

They both said "no," that they were sure the place was empty when they left and only the staff was closing down and cleaning up.

Storm noted their names. The male was Riley, and the female was Stone. Storm wasn't sure if they were lying about seeing Leslie leave or if they had just missed it because they were busy in the room full of big wheels. So, other than Stone having seen her enter the club, neither of them was of much further help.

"Here's my number at the precinct," he said, handing each of them a card. "Call if you remember anything else, OK?" Each took the card and put it in their pockets without further comment.

A fleeting thought ran through Storm's mind as he walked away from the two cops: It seemed strange that an old crusty police Sergeant like Hebert had a woman working for him, and even stranger, that she had been given one of his plum assignments. Hebert was not exactly known for his stance on equal rights—that was an understatement. But the thought disappeared from his mind as quickly as it had entered.

After a "dinner" from the buffet Storm and Russell left. Russell still had to do the late weather and Storm had many unanswered questions to ponder.

* * * *

What they hadn't seen while mingling and eating was Hebert on the phone, and they had not overheard his conversation with the cops working the door. He made it clear to his staff that Storm and this Hildebrant guy were to be watched and he was to be informed of anything they did while they were in room. "I wanna know who they talked to and what they did—everything, including trips to the john," he told them. Hebert then called Dakota Taylor on her mobile to tell her that Storm was there and asking if anyone had seen the dead girl the night of killing. He also needed to know more about this Russell Hildebrandt. Should he be worried about him hanging around with Storm?

* * * *

On the other end of phone Dakota just listened. "I'll look into Hildebrandt. Meantime, get back with me if you get any more information on their activities." Dakota knew Russell and his family, but what would he be doing here with that detective?

Dakota also knew Russell Hildebrandt was a weather man, not a news guy. Were he and the detective friends? Had Storm told him anything about the girl's death? The questions were not a huge concern, but they were thoughts to keep in mind.

Charity Kills

CHAPTER FIFTEEN

A Little Sleuth in All of Us

Navigating through the noise and confusion of the crowd, Storm and Russell didn't know a shadow had attached herself to them. Peggy the amateur sleuth had recognized Detective Storm as she was headed down the escalator in the center and he was going up. On her way home after a twelve-hour day Peggy had decided to follow the tall dark detective and see where he was going. She would stay behind, trailing him and the other man, keeping her eyes and ears open, picking up a small detail or two she might want to remember as she filed away mental notes she would later transfer to her blue spiral notebook. Like many of the employees of the Show, her credentials allowed her the run of the place, and being a lower ranked employee, she appeared invisible to the Show hierarchy and most of the general membership. To other staff members she was a common sight throughout the facilities—she could have been doing anything, delivering tickets or merely running an errand for one of the managers. Her invisibility made it easy to hide in plain sight.

Peggy had wanted to talk to Storm when she saw him in the Show offices the day before, but she couldn't take the chance of introducing herself without risking that management might find out what she was doing. This chance encounter gave her the opportunity to follow him and look into the same places he was looking and see if he might run across something she didn't know. Peggy discreetly followed along well behind the two men but within sight of their progress. If Peggy had been detected by someone related to the Show she would tell them she had come by to check with the manager of the club, inquiring if there had been anyone asking about purchasing unused tickets.

The two men's first stop had been the Center VIP club and she had seen the man with the detective flash some identification and the two of them precede as if they owned the place. She watched the detective stop and chat with the policemen working security at the door. He produced what looked like a picture from his pocket, obviously asking them if they knew the person in the picture. Each had shaken their heads "no" and the detective had replaced the picture back in the pocket of his sport coat.

It was then Peggy got her first really good view of the man the detective had come with. He was the weatherman on Channel 5! She knew he was the son of one of the retired presidents of the Show. His name was Russell, Russell Hildebrant, but why would the detective be with him?

Confused but undaunted, she continued to observe them, following every move without appearing as if she was watching. She had closely followed the two men with her eyes, watching them traverse the crowd, noticing how so many of people in the crowd spoke or shook hands with the weatherman as the pair made their way, meandering through the tables filled with ladies in garish dresses and men in boots that looked they hurt their feet.

It was then she saw the men separate. The weather man was chatting to Ellen Dresden, while the detective visited with Joe. She watched as the expression on Joe's face went from his normal ruddy self-confident leer to a mask of complete and total terror. Whatever the detective had said, it obviously had scared Joe, and his intimidation increased when he looked at the picture Storm pulled from his jacket and held in front of Joe's face. Joe's face had turned the color of a dead fish.

Immediately after the confrontation with Joe, the weatherman and the detective left and she needed to follow them but before she could go, she saw Joe grabbing Ellen's arm and amidst Ellen's plea to stay they fled in a flash as Joe dragged Ellen out of the club. In Ellen's hasty retreat she mouthed a hasty hello to Peggy, but was in too big a rush to say more.

Peggy knew Joe's reputation and she had seen it first hand on more than one occasion. She knew her friend Elaine had met Joe; Elaine had told her so. She had warned Elaine about Joe, but Elaine had just laughed and blew it off, saying she knew how to handle jerks like Joe. What was the face-off between Joe and the detective? Does the detective think Joe could be a killer? Could Joe be a killer? Peggy asked herself. It didn't seem likely but at this point, who knew?

Joe was a better lead than Peggy had at the moment, but it just didn't seem possible. From what she knew, Joe was a puss. He was addicted to Ellen's money and he liked his lifestyle, but he was a wimp. Peggy had seen more than one girl slap his face and watched him retreat like a scalded dog. No, Joe couldn't be the killer. But the question remained.

After the abrupt departure of Joe and Ellen, Peggy caught sight of the two she was following as they made their way through the crowd headed in the direction of the stadium and the Gold Badge entrance. Peggy was not supposed to go the stadium, but being invisible did have its perks. She followed the weatherman and detective upstairs to the ninth level on the next elevator, going up immediately after the one that had taken the pair of men up.

When she got to the entrance of the VIP club. she stopped dead in her tracks, her senses suddenly alert. Standing just inside the entry she saw police Sergeant Hebert and two cops loitering in front of the door. She also saw Hebert excuse himself from the door officers and go talk to the detective, but it was the tall blonde female policewoman who got her attention.

Peggy was originally from Victoria, Texas, a medium-sized Texas town about ninety miles from Houston, and she knew she had seen this woman before. She had seen pictures of this female cop in the Victoria newspapers about nine years ago. The blonde had been the roommate of a girl who had disappeared, and as far as Peggy knew, her disappearance had never been solved. No trace of the girl had ever been found. Although the sheriff's office had reasoned she had met with foul play, no body meant no crime, and the girls remained as missing, never being declared dead yet. Peggy remembered her family had not given up hope that they would ever know where she was or what had happened to her.

Now she remembered. The blonde female cop's name was Tess, Tess Stone. Around Victoria, it had been rumored that Tess and the missing girl had been living together in a lesbian relationship, but then again Peggy didn't know if there was any truth to it—she had just heard the rumor.

Peggy remained in the shadows long enough to see the detective speaking to Hebert and later to the officers working the door. She waited until she saw him and the weatherman fix themselves plates of food from the buffet and reasoned they were done investigating for the night. Stealthily she slipped away so she could return to her office and access pay records from the Show. She had to see how long the blonde cop had been on the payroll.

* * * *

All the time Peggy had been following the weatherman and the detective, she hadn't realized her invisibility had abandoned her. She had not been the only person that had seen the detective checking out possibly the last place Leslie had been seen, nor the only person who knew of his confrontation with Joe. The killer knew it was not a coincidence that a staff member was in a place she shouldn't be.

It appeared Peggy was following the two tall men. Did she just happen to be in the same place as these men, or was she tailing them? What could this girl possibly think she knew, or did she suspect something, and who had she talked to? As methodical as the killer was, nothing could be left to chance; this girl would not be the destruction of a perfect plan. Something would have to be done about her and soon.

Charity Kills

CHAPTER SIXTEEN

Method and Madness but No Motive

The Rodeo telegraph was in full swing and operating without delay. Policewoman Stone had been told of the banter between Storm and Joe Dresden; she had been told of the shock that had registered on Joe's face and how Joe had jerked his wife's arm, hurriedly leaving the club. She waited until Sergeant Hebert had finished with the detective and his friend and then updated him on the message she had just received from the officers working in the center.

* * * *

The next link in the chain was for Hebert to quickly follow up with Dakota Taylor and inform her. He didn't know what Storm had, but he did know what was on video and why he would be interested in Joe. Independently Hebert and Storm had come to the same assumption, and that was that

Joe was probably the last to see Leslie and he was a player, if not the killer, in this mystery. The conclusion had already been made that if a sacrificial lamb was needed, Joe would be the easiest to give up. It would come out that Joe had the morals of a tomcat; everyone knew that Joe's reputation as a ladies' man was not limited to the Show. Joe had a real problem keeping it in his pants and with Ellen's money, he could fish in many of the more expensive creeks around town.

* * * *

On the ride home Russell had filled Storm in on some more of the Show's little peccadilloes that were hidden from the public, like how money and influence made the difference in who rose in the power structure and who didn't. How membership in this closed society was passed down from father to son and grandson. How the unpublished ban on cameras was the way for the leadership of the Show to make sure they and their friends could enjoy all the "perks" in a friendly, nonjudgmental environment. Influence, benefits, notoriety, and secrecy all went hand in hand for these birds of rare air. Over the years there had been rumors in the inner circle about various members, but among these powerful men such innuendos and even sometimes negative truths were hushed and forgotten as quickly as they were discovered.

But...with media scrutiny having become what it was over the past few years, secrets had become harder to keep. There had been occasions that couldn't be covered up, like a director convicted of child molestation, a vice president arrested for growth and intent to sell marijuana, and an older member of the inner circle "outed" for being a homosexual. Married with grandchildren, that member had paid for young men to be flown around the country to spend weekends in extravagant hotels with him. His passing shortly after it all became public assured, like other transgressions, that all would be forgotten and never mentioned again. The Show distanced itself from such incidents as quickly as possible to avoid any fallout that might tarnish its reputation of squeaky clean family fun and philanthropy.

As a multimillion dollar cash cow for the city, the charity connected to the Show and Rodeo had always had the cooperation of the police and mayor's office. Only one mayor had ever tried to take on the Show, wanting to change the image of Houston to a more metropolitan big city image, but she was promptly put in her place. In her case, it was "Cowboys 1, Mayor 0." Since that time most mayors were more concerned with their wallets than the city's image anyway, the mayors elected after her all understood it was beneficial to everyone involved to get along and leave things be.

* * * *

After an abbreviated night's sleep, Storm woke up early, not really unusual, but this morning it was with a sense of vigor and vitality after the best night's rest he had had in years, or at least since Angie's murder. He still had had some disturbing dreams, but this time they were about Leslie Phillips and how to catch her killer. As he thought about all the girls, he was more and more convinced they had all been killed by the same person.

He dressed quickly and headed to Reisner Street. As he walked in, Sergeant Hernandez waved him to the coffee room and Storm followed. "The lieutenant is waiting for you and he has company," said Hernandez.

"Who?"

"Some guy from the mayor's office."

"Know his name?"

"Nope just that he was sitting in the lieutenant's office bright and early. How did it go last night?" Hernandez asked.

"Great. Scared the shit out of Joe Dresden," Storm said, smiling a little.

Hernandez smiled back; he knew it doesn't take much for a cop to scare a citizen, especially if the citizen doesn't know what the cop knows.

"Can you get me pictures of all the girls?" Storm asked.

"Sure, but I have to be careful. They will be copies," he answered, his eyes asking if that was OK.

"No problem. Cover your tracks, but do it."

"Storm, we are going to catch this *pendejo*," promised Hernandez.

"Damn straight, Pancho." What a great addition to the little team of investigators Hernandez was. He could see Hernandez was feeling like a cop again and that was good.

"Have you gotten any information on serial murders or any hints on what we should be looking for?"

"Yeah, some, but I will have more when we meet again." Hernandez's smile showed he was pleased with what he had found.

Storm saw the lieutenant waving him to his office, so he grabbed a cup of coffee and went in. Sure enough, there sat Vern Nagel, the guy he had met at the Show with Dakota Taylor on Sunday.

"Detective, I believe you have met Mr. Nagel from the mayor's office," said Lieutenant Flynn.

"Yes, sir, we met the other day."

"Well, he is here to get caught up on where we stand with the murder at the stadium."

"Lieutenant, I am working on it. We don't have a suspect or a motive yet, but I have viewed the security videos from that night and the victim was on it entering the VIP Club with a man. We don't have an ID on him yet," Storm lied.

"Is this man you don't know the killer?" piped in Nagel.

"I don't know yet. The video shows him going into the stadium with her, but he left with other men around midnight without the girl."

"The video doesn't show her leaving?" the lieutenant inquired.

"No, the only place she appears is going in, not leaving."

"Then she didn't leave with him?" the lieutenant responded.

"Seemingly not." As the questions became more repetitive and inane, Storm was becoming more irritated and his replies more terse. They were talking about things that shouldn't be discussed in front of an outsider. He had to be careful; he knew everything he said was going directly back to the Show.

"Do you know the victim's name?" asked Nagel.

"Yes, Sergeant Hebert's people found her purse and her driver's license in another dumpster on the other side of the stadium. Her name was Leslie Phillips," said Storm.

"What else did you find, Detective? We can be forthcoming with the mayor's office, David." It sounded strange, the lieutenant using his Christian name.

"Yes, Lieutenant, well, her clothes were found in the dumpster on the other side of the stadium from where her body was found, but no bloody crime scene could be found anywhere." Storm replied. Something gnawed at Storm about that, and he felt a renewed urgency to get out of the waste of time that he had become inadvertently a part of and back to discovering where she had actually been killed.

"How was she killed?" asked the lieutenant.

"Throat cut completely through her wind pipe. She couldn't have screamed if she'd tried. She bled out. This was not the work of an amateur." Storm left out the other things they knew. He sure didn't want to tell them he believed there had been seven murders and they were connected. That cat had to stay in the bag for the time being.

"We need to find the crime scene. With that much blood, it had to be a mess," the lieutenant commented and then asked, "Who's working on that?"

"Sergeant Hebert has men who work out at the Show full time, so I'm going to ask him to have his guys continue their search," Storm said. "And there is always the possibility that the cleaning crew may find something."

"Good idea. Get him on it," the lieutenant replied.

Storm knew that nothing would come of asking Hebert and his men to do the search. Hebert resented him and all cops that worked downtown. But he would ask, indicating that the request had come from his boss and the mayor's office, although he didn't think that would change anything.

"What's your next step, Detective?" Nagel again. What a nosy son of a bitch, Storm couldn't help thinking.

"Today I am going to the vic's apartment to see if anything there might give us a lead; messages on her answering machine, threatening letters, photos, or anything that might give us a clue. Then I am going to meet with the man we saw in the video and see what light he can shed on this."

"I thought you didn't know his name." Nagel sounded angry. "Who is he? Do you know his name or not?"

Storm could have kicked himself. He knew if he gave Nagel Joe Dresden's name the word would spread to Dakota Taylor within minutes of his leaving the police station. But, oh well, it was done now. Besides, they had seen the videos. He was sure of that, and Storm suspected they knew Joe was with her, so what did it matter? But Storm thought he would try to throw a curve ball with his answer, anyway. "Lieutenant, since this is an ongoing investigation I can't release that information to Mr. Nagel."

The lieutenant didn't back down. "Detective, Mr. Nagel is representing the mayor's office and they want this wrapped up as soon as possible, solved or unsolved. Get it closed with as little public attention as possible. Do you understand me?"

Storm knew that look. And he knew something else, something new. He now knew how the other murders had been dispensed with. He now understood the pressure that must have been put on the other detectives working those cases.

"OK, Lieutenant, but this has to be kept quiet. We don't want him running or covering his tracks. I need to question him before he knows that he is a suspect." Storm's voice softened as he spoke. "He might not have had anything to do with it," added Storm. "His name is Joe Dresden."

Storm saw Nagel's eyebrows arch in recognition, but the lieutenant didn't seem to have a clue who Dresden was. The lieutenant was new to Houston, so the name most likely didn't mean anything to him. Storm knew he had just given Dresden to the dogs; the Show would be separating itself from him as soon as they could. It might cost them some of Ellen's money, but they would find someone else to replace that with and keep themselves clean. They couldn't replace their holy reputation. Dresden would be the latest pariah. Storm knew giving Nagel Dresden's name was a dirty trick, and he wished he could have taken it back at this stage of the investigation. He had to admit he didn't like Joe, but feelings aside, Dresden was a sleaze, so maybe—maybe—giving Nagel and Flynn a possible sacrificial lamb wasn't all that bad.

"Detective, we're done here," said Lieutenant Flynn. "I need to have a few words with Vern. Close the door on your way out." Storm knew that was his cue to leave. Storm was sure they were discussing any further exposure the city might have.

Storm got Leslie's address from the file and as he headed out the precinct door Sergeant Hernandez handed him an envelope. Storm waited until he got to the car to open it. The photos of all seven victims fell out onto the seat beside him. All seven were the morgue shots; all seven death masks, but the similarity of the masks was what struck him. The killer definitely had a type.

The first girl was Elaine Gage. She was twenty-five, brunette, from Hallettsville, Texas, no family to speak of, and she had worked for Tejas Petroleum. She was found naked in an abandoned car on Fannin Street across from the Dome. She, too, had been raped and anally abused, and her throat had been cut in the same manner as Leslie.

The second girl was Debbie Turnbull. She was twenty-three, brunette, from Needville, Texas, and again, had no family. She was found naked and abused in the new construction area for the light rail system next to the Dome.

The third victim was Michelle Canter, twenty-four, also a brunette, from Yoakum, Texas; Linda Black, twenty-three, from Shiner, Texas was the fourth; Sissy Debuse, twenty-five, from Kingsville, Texas was the fifth; and last year's victim was Stephanie Gilgore, twenty-five, from Lufkin, Texas. All of the victims were found near the Dome, all looked enough alike to be sisters, all had little to no family to push for an investigation, all had been abused and had their throats severed and windpipes cut through, and all had been forgotten until now.

Not only did the killer have a type, he had a method. What Storm didn't have was a motive. He hoped that Hernandez had found something in FBI reports that could help them. He also needed to ask Hernandez if there was anything in the files of the other girls about their clothes. Something about that was still nagging at him, but he couldn't put his finger on it.

Before going to Leslie Phillips' apartment, he would first stop by Joe Dresden's office. He called to check to make sure Joe would be there for a while. Catching Joe at his office would give him the perception of "home field advantage" and hopefully give him a false sense of security. In Storm's experience, people made mistakes when they felt at ease.

CHAPTER SEVENTEEN

Ellen's Dilemma

Ellen Dresden's symbol of success was the facility she had built after assuming the controls of her father's company. She had bought an expansive piece of land virtually littered with small brick and metal buildings all in need of refurbishing and had torn all those eyesores down. In their place she had erected a grand, opulent, very modern three story building with a flair for Texas architecture. A sandstone and mortar façade covered the front of the facility, emulating a rendition of the first Christian missions that had dotted the Texas landside of the past. Ellen was definitely a Texan, and like all true Texans, was proud of her heritage. Anything resembling the Alamo was perfect in her mind.

The inside of the building sparkled; it was all marble and chrome, with a large circular reception desk and leather chairs inviting waiting guests to take a seat in the reception area. The non-administrative part of the distributorship was the latest in mechanized sorting tables and robotic arms used for overhead storage. The commodities the warehouse stocked were all electronically coded and put on their appropriate assigned shelf. When an order was taken an order entry clerk would input the list of items in a central computer. The computer would automatically create a "picking slip," which identified where the items were stored, the number ordered, the price, weight, and shipping instructions. The robotic arms would retrieve the items, assembling them at the end of each row of storage, where a floor person would load them onto a cart and verify the order with his or her copy of the order. Forklifts or push carts would then move the products to shipping and out they went. Efficiency was the word for this place. The floor was immaculate; the equipment pristine, and even the workers' uniforms were spotless.

* * * *

Storm gave his name to the receptionist and asked for Joe. When she asked the nature of his business he just replied, "Mr. Dresden will know."

About five minutes later Joe appeared, as if by magic. If he was a little shaken by Storm's visit, his outward demeanor was that of a businessman meeting a colleague or vendor. Joe extended his hand and Storm accepted with a quick one-time pump and then suggested they go somewhere they could talk in private.

Joe's office was exactly as Storm had imagined; a massive burled wood desk at least seven feet long sat in front of windows that overlooked the glistening warehouse. Pictures adorned most of the walls; including some of Joe and Ellen at the Show with the champion animals they had purchased. Golf trophies sat on a side table—Storm realized golf was probably the only sport Joe participated in. Joe was a pretty boy and would never have been a part of something that might cause physical pain. Joe was, just as Storm had thought, a weenie.

"Please have a seat, Detective," Dresden said, walking around to his oversized chair behind his desk. Storm wasn't intimidated—he'd had plenty of experiences with this old Napoleonic businessman's trick. Storm's chair was lower than normal, placing him in a position of looking up at Dresden. Since Joe was also short in stature, Storm was sure the furniture had been built to make him feel more in control of whoever was visiting him. For Storm this supposed disadvantage was easily remedied, as he was about to show Joe some more pictures and to do so would require him to stand up and lean over the desk, thus breaching Dresden's comfort zone. Two can play this game, he thought.

Storm laid the envelope of pictures he had brought on the desk, and looking at Joe, he leaned across the desk and pulled out the first photo, the picture of Leslie lying, obviously dead and with her throat cut, on the metal examination table in the morgue.

Storm said nothing, just waited a few seconds to let the significance of what Dresden was looking at sink in. This picture had a much more sobering effect than the one Storm had shown Joe the night before that had been copied from her driver's license photo. Noting the look on Dresden's face, he queried, "Do you know her, Joe?"

Dresden flushed. "You know the answer. I told you last night I knew her. So yes, I know who she is. But I didn't have anything to do with killing her."

"But you were with her?"

"Yes." Dresden's voice was shaky and weak.

"You told me last night you had sex with her. Do you like hitting girls, Joe, beating them up? Is that part of your sex play with them?"

"No, I never hurt that girl." He averted his eyes from the morgue photo on his desk.

"What did you do with her?" snapped Storm.

"I told you, we had sex. That's what she wanted, I wanted her, too, but that was it. Honest. I had nothing to do with her death." There was a strong quiver of fear in his answer.

"How do you know that? Did you ask her if she wanted to get screwed in a bathroom of the VIP club, Joe?"

"No, but she had been around before. She was at the barbecue Wednesday, Thursday, Friday, and Saturday night. I am not the only guy she was with; she was with other guys out there, too. It could have been some other guy."

"You see, Joe, I am only interested in Saturday night, the night you were with her. The night you pulled her into a bathroom and raped her."

"That is a lie. I never raped her. She was the one who suggested the bathroom. I only met her Thursday night. She was with Alex Flanders that night and they had already done the nasty."

Alex Flanders had been identified as one of the men seen entering and leaving with Joe on the video. Russell had commented when he saw the men in the group that they were the regular horn dogs and show dignitaries. This gaggle of nefarious reprobates was usually in each other's company.

He's pleading with me now. Let's see where this leads. "How do you know that?" Storm moved closer to Joe's face as he asked.

"Everybody talks about the Badge Bunnies out here. Everyone knows who they are. They're not sacred or anything."

"'Badge Bunnies'? What the hell are Badge Bunnies?" asked Storm.

"Girls like her, ones that come out to party and be a part of this whole experience. Girls looking for wealthy connected men that are at least directors of the Show."

"Then you and your buddies pass them around?"

"No, it's not like that. You just know if they are available. You know what they want and they know what they have to do to get in."

"So you take them up to the VIP club, get them drunk, take them in a bathroom or a stairway and do them?"

"Kinda." Dresden's voice had begun to shake. "How do you know I was with her Saturday?"

"You were caught on security video taking her up to the VIP club."

"How? Cameras aren't allowed in any clubs." Storm could see Joe thought he had him there.

But he's so wrong, Storm thought with satisfaction. "Oh, Joe, tell me you don't know." Storm just looked at Dresden and shook his head. "It's funny, people like you have already forgotten about 9/11. The world has become much more Orwellian since then. All buildings and facilities have to have security cameras at all entries and exits. Big Brother really is watching you. Did you think because you can stop pictures from being taken in the clubs, you and your buddies can stop public security? I guess Homeland Security hasn't heard about your elevation above the law."

Storm went on. "Who else 'knew' her, Joe?"

"I'm not sure. Alex probably knows some of the others." Joe looked as if he was still processing the idea that cameras now were being used for surveillance at the Show and that neither he nor probably most of his friends were aware of it.

"OK. Enough about Leslie for now, Joe." Storm pulled the rest of the pictures out and arranged them across Joe's desk. Joe's face went from flushed pink to putrid green.

"You know any of these girls?" The shock and fear in Joe's eyes gave him away. It was obvious he knew at least one of them. Not waiting for an answer, Storm asked, "Joe, you ever in the military?"

Dresden's gag reflex kicked in, and he swallowed hard before answering. "No. Why?"

"Well, each of these girls was killed in exactly the same way. Each had her throat cut and windpipe severed so she couldn't scream. Do you know how to do that?"

"God, no. For God's sake, put those away."

159

"Not 'til you have looked real close and tell me if you know any of these girls."

"I know two of them," Joe stuttered. His hands were shaking so bad he held them in a clinched double fist.

"Which two?" Storm pressured.

"This one and the one on the end." His well manicured index finger touched the bottom of each photo.

Joe had picked out Elaine Gage and Stephanie Gilgore. Stephanie was the girl killed last year.

"How did you know them?"

"Like I knew that other girl."

"Then you raped them, too?"

"Yes. No. I mean, I was with them. I never raped anyone." Dresden seemed to be shrinking behind his desk. Storm knew he realized he was not in control anymore and actually never had been.

"Did you kill them, too?" Storm didn't expect any other answer than a "no."

"*No!*" Dresden pleaded, yelling. He's totally falling apart, Storm told himself.

"Joe, I want a DNA sample from you."

"Why? I already admitted I knew them."

"To verify that the semen found in Leslie's vagina is yours and to check against any DNA findings from the other girls."

"I didn't know any of the others, just those three."

"OK, Joe, then giving me your DNA will eliminate you from suspicion in other murders."

"Am I a suspect in the deaths of these girls?" Joe asked, indicating the three he had identified.

"No, Joe but you are a person of interest, though, so I wouldn't leave town if I were you. And one other thing, Joe, you keep your mouth shut about this. You talk to no one, not even your wife. If I find out this has gotten out with rumor mill at that damn Rodeo I am coming for you first, you understand? I can assure you won't enjoy county lockup.

Pretty boys like you don't do well there." Storm had to scare Joe bad enough to keep him from talking to the Show.

"OK, now, Joe. Here's what you need to do: You will report to the medical examiner's office no later than noon tomorrow and they will take a DNA sample to compare the semen left on Leslie to verify you were the one who had sex with her. If you are not there by noon I will come back and I will place you under arrest and take you out of this building in handcuffs in front of your wife and all your employees."

Storm knew egomaniacs like Dresden would do just about anything to avoid the perp walk. He packed his pictures back in the manila envelope, and left Joe's office to return to his car. He wasn't sure about Joe yet and no one could be written off as a suspect—well, no one who had anything to do with the Show.

* * * *

Ellen had seen Storm come into the building and recognized him from the incident with Joe the night before. Her office was positioned she could see the visitors who came in to Joe's office. She had watched the entire episode and had seen the look on her husband's face and his hands shaking as he looked at the papers the man had arranged on his desk. Whoever this guy was, showing Joe whatever he was showing, it had totally unnerved him. Who was this guy and what was he doing with Joe? She had to find out.

She reached across her desk, which was a match to Joe's except just a tiny bit bigger just as her office was just a little bigger than his, and took out her personal phone book to look up Russell Hildebrandt's phone number. This man had been at the Show with Russell the night before. What was their connection and what did it have to do with Joe?

When Russell didn't answer his home phone, she called the TV station and after a few minutes Russell came on the line.

* * * *

"This is Russell Hildebrandt."

"Russell, this is Ellen Dresden. I need to talk to you."

"Well, imagine this. I see you last night and here you are on the phone so soon with me. What can I help you with, Ellen?" said Russell, his mind now racing in overdrive. What could she want? Had Storm already been to Dresden's office? What did Ellen know? Storm had told him and the others to keep quiet and that was exactly what he was going to do.

"Who was that man with you last night?" Ellen was always direct and a little mannish, but then, she was her father's daughter.

"You mean my friend Storm?"

"I guess. Is that his name? How do you know him?"

"We have known each other since college, why?"

"Well after he talked to Joe last night Joe pushed me out the door and wouldn't speak to me all the way home. And just now he was here in Joe's office and it is obvious Joe is even more upset this time. Who is he and why is he bothering Joe? What is going on, Russell?"

"He is a homicide detective with HPD, Ellen. He is my best friend; he is the one whose wife was killed about five years ago—not sure if you would remember that or not."

"That doesn't answer why he was here and why he just scared the shit of Joe."

"Ellen, I'm sure I don't know," Russell lied through his teeth. The less he said the better off he would be.

"Does it have anything to do with that girl found dead Sunday morning? Or does it have something to do with his dead wife?"

"Again, Ellen, I seriously have no idea. Storm doesn't talk to me about things like that." The lies continued to roll out of his mouth like they were warm molasses.

"That girl from Sunday was a tramp, you know. You know the type. They hang around the Show hoping to meet

162

someone with money. You've been there and you've been with them."

Damn, his next thought caused Russell to consider something that would have never entered his mind earlier. Did Ellen have anything to do with this? If Joe was later considered a suspect was Ellen getting ready to build an alibi for Joe? *I'm not sure I should even ask the next question but in for a penny, in for a pound, this is no time to back away.* This realization led to his next question.

"Ellen, really I have no idea, but I'm sure if Storm was there to talk to Joe, he's checking all leads to see if Joe had ever seen the girl or knew anyone who might have known her. I am sure it has nothing to do with the murder of his late wife." As if an afterthought Russell asked Ellen, "Did you know the girl who was killed Saturday night, Ellen?"

"No," she spat out. "I don't bother myself with whores like her out there."

With that, Ellen abruptly hung up the phone.

What the hell was that about? Damn, he had to get hold of Storm. Could his old friend Ellen have gone from being a childhood playmate to being a killer or an unwitting accomplice? That idea disturbed him to no end.

* * * *

Meanwhile Ellen was fuming. She knew about Joe's dalliances, but she also knew Joe was a pretty boy wimp who jumped when she screamed. She knew he had married her for her money and his womanizing had long ago worn thin on her. It was time to confront Joe. She had confronted one of his little flings, what was her name? Stephanie, yes, Stephanie, and the girl had backed off. Nobody was leaving her for some little gold-digging slut. If Joe left her he got nothing, and he knew it.

Charity Kills

CHAPTER EIGHTEEN

Joe's Naughty Little Secrets

Dresden was standing at the bar in his office pouring himself a glass of bourbon when he heard his office door open and immediately close. From behind he heard a voice. "Must have been quite a conversation for you to need a drink already. It isn't even lunch time."

It was Ellen and he was sure she had seen the man from last night come into his office this morning. He tried to stop his hands from shaking by gripping the glass he held tighter as he turned around to confront her.

"No, honey, just a bit of the hair of the dog," he replied, trying his best smile as he shrugged, hoping to disarm her.

"Bullshit, Joe, I know who he is and we are not going to talk about this in your office. Meet me at my car in five minutes. Do you understand?" Ellen glared as she held up five fingers. This was not a request and Joe knew it.

Five minutes later Joe opened the door to Ellen's white Escalade and got in. Her change of clothes for the Show hung in back. Hat boxes filled the cargo area, along with at least six pairs of boots and small bags of lingerie.

Ellen looked over as Joe got in and quietly asked, "What does that detective want with you?"

I need to think. I have to be quick to give a plausible answer. But Joe Dresden's mind went completely blank.

"Before you answer, I want you to consider your answer very carefully, and don't you fucking think you can lie to me," growled Ellen.

"I'm not going to lie." Joe paused momentarily. "He came here to talk to me because I knew the girl that was found dead on Sunday out by the stadium. He just wanted to know what I knew about her. If I might know anyone who might have seen her last or wanted to kill her." Joe was trying to conceal the truth, but he could see in Ellen's eyes he wasn't succeeding.

"That's not the whole truth, is it?" demanded Ellen, her piercing eyes boring into his face.

"Yes, it is," Joe was quick to answer, though he knew right away his answer was *too* quick, actually.

"I told you not to lie to me. There is a hell of lot more or your hands wouldn't be shaking like that and you wouldn't look like a dead trout."

Joe's entire body was tense and shaking. He was trying to control himself, but it wasn't working. He knew he would have to tell her everything or there was no telling what her reaction would be.

"OK, OK. He came here to ask me if I did it. If I killed her," Joe croaked, his head slumping over in his lap, the sweat running down his brow over his nose.

"Why would he think that, Joe?" Joe knew all too well that Ellen was not stupid. She was not going to let him off so easy. She knows it's time to call me on it, he realized. I think she's about to let me know she's known about the other women. I'm in deep shit.

"He has video of me taking her into the VIP club in the stadium the night she was killed. He claims I was the last one seen with her," Joe croaked again.

"Were you, Joe, were you the last one to see her alive?" Ellen asked through clenched teeth.

"No!" Joe's voice was almost inaudible. "I left her in the club. I went with the guys to Fuad's and that was the last I saw her till he showed me her picture."

"What was she doing with you at the club, Joe?" Ellen's voice had calmed and she seemed more in control of herself.

"She was around all last week, hanging out with all the guys. She was at the barbecue every night and she asked me to take her to the VIP club." Joe thought, that's partially true, anyway.

"Did you do anything with her? Did you have sex with her and goddamn you, I mean even a blow job, you're not Bill Clinton, understand?" barked Ellen.

Joe just sunk his face toward his chest again and said, "Yes."

"So she was another of your fucking tramps. The little whores who follow you men around the Show hoping to snag a rich husband and sleep with anyone they think has money." This was more of a statement than a question from Ellen.

Joe nodded his head "yes" as his eyes concentrated on the floorboard of the SUV.

Ellen was again calm. "The one last year was just the same. I had to pay her off to get her to stay away from you. She disappeared after that and was not seen in the clubs again."

The shock registered on Joe's face and he turned to Ellen, "What do you mean you 'paid her off'?"

"I gave her ten thousand dollars to go away and not come back."

"When did you give it to her?" Joe asked, incredulous.

"The second week of the Show. I got her name from the security guard working the door. I called her, met her for lunch, and gave her the ultimatum: take the money and stay away from you and any other married men out there, or else."

"Ellen, that detective had her picture, too. She was killed last year," Joe said. When he looked at Ellen's face it was cold as stone and dispassionate. She doesn't care, he realized.

"Ellen, I told him I knew her."

"Did you kill her, Joe?"

"Hell, no." He knew the shock was painting his face—that was probably a good thing—and it made his answer sound more authentic.

"Then, so what? You knew her, but if you didn't kill her. Why worry?"

"Ellen, he had pictures of seven girls, all young, all found dead somewhere on the grounds of the Dome. He asked me if knew any of them. I told him I knew two besides the last girl. The girl from Sunday, the girl last year (the one you paid off), and the very first girl killed." Joe could feel his fear running deeper now. It was almost palpable.

"Did you have anything to do with any of the murders?" Ellen whispered.

"Goddamn it, Ellen, I could never kill anyone. I just knew them, the same way I knew the girl from Sunday. Actually, I knew all of them, but I didn't tell him that. If he finds out, I really will be his best suspect," Joe's voice quivered even more.

"You were doing the horizontal bop with all of them and now all of them are dead?" Ellen asked, sounding as if she was about to laugh.

"Yes, but I didn't do it. I didn't even know some of them had been killed. Ellen, if it gets out I was with them and you paid one of them off, it could get really ugly." Joe was in a state of panic and he knew it showed in his voice.

"No one will know that I paid off some slut who was fucking my husband and no one is gonna find out you knew them all. There are a lot of men who probably knew them all. They were sluts, anyway."

* * * *

Ellen thought it was funny to watch him squirm like this. *He's such a pussy. He could never go to jail.* He would be the favorite on the cell block with his cute little tight ass. Joe also didn't need to know that she had paid off more than one of them.

"From now on you don't talk to anyone about this, not your asshole buddies at the Show nor anyone here at work. You keep your mouth shut and never talk to that detective again. You don't talk to anyone without me or our attorney with you. I never want to see or hear about you with another woman out there, do you understand me? If I find out you have been and you lie to me, I am going to the detective and tell him you knew all seven of those girls and had been with them all, and that's a promise. Now go back to your office. Stay put 'til it's time to go to the Show. Tonight you go with me, you stay with me and you keep your mouth shut."

"But Ellen, he told me to report to the medical examiner's office for a DNA test or he will come back and take me to jail, right here in front of everyone."

"I told you—you don't do anything without an attorney, you don't go for any test unless he shows up with a warrant. Do you understand?" Her icy glare told him she meant business.

* * * *

Ellen didn't leave Joe any choice and he was too frightened to argue. Anyway, Joe knew she was serious as a heart attack and there was no way he was going to cross her. Until all this went down and they pinned these murders on someone else he had to hold himself together. He got out of the SUV and went back to his office and the bottle of Jack. Drinking wasn't gonna help, but it wasn't gonna hurt, either.

Charity Kills

CHAPTER NINETEEN

Playing Hunches

Back in the Livestock Show offices, intrigue hung like a storm cloud over everything. In one part of the building Dakota Taylor was meeting with Leon Powers and Sergeant Hebert to update them with the information she had just received from Vern Nagel. They were in agreement that all of them were more than ready to let Joe Dresden take the fall if it came to that. Now the question was how to distance themselves and the Show from Dresden and what damage control they would have to do to cover it with Ellen.

"I want to be sure that the current investigation is into the murder of only the girl from the other night and that this Detective Storm doesn't or isn't going to relate this to any other situations that might shed a negative light on the Show," Powers said. "Those goddamned security cameras put the girl here in the facility. Although the whole world has become more security conscious since 9/11, it aggrieves the inner sanctum to know there's a connection to us and I want it stopped," Powers ordered the two.

Hebert and Taylor assured Powers that to the best of their knowledge the detective didn't know about anything else. "I'm tellin' ya, Storm is a washed up has-been," Hebert added, as Dakota nodded her head in agreement.

"OK. Now that we have that clarified—and you better be right—it's business as usual for now. Keep up an outward appearance that nothing unusual is going on, at least until we hear Dresden's been arrested or something breaks."

Powers got up and showed Hebert and Dakota the door. He's obviously done with us for now, Hebert reassured himself. At least I hope so.

* * * *

In another part of the offices Peggy was going through her binder on the girls' murders. Peggy had pictures of all the girls except for this last one. She also had every write-up she had been able to find in the newspapers at the times of the murders. She felt she knew the background of these girls better than the cops did, and last night when she followed the detective, she had come upon something she felt was major, something only someone with her combined knowledge would have recognized. Late last night she had accessed show records and confirmed her suspicions. She had to talk to that police detective. He might think she was looney tunes, but she had to tell someone and right now she thought he was the only one she could trust.

* * * *

Not far away, Storm had gone to Leslie's apartment in a modest neighborhood off the Southwest Freeway and the Loop, just south of the Galleria. Not a bad neighborhood, but not the best anymore, either. In the '70s it had been the area to live in if you were single and into the club and bar scene of Houston. Over the past few years it had become more rundown and was being encroached upon by the barrio. Dollar Stores, Mexican bars, and bodegas lined the streets now, and most of the apartment complexes had fences, concertina wire, and gates surrounding them. But it was still convenient to downtown and much cheaper than the new complexes on the near west side of town.

Her apartment was clean and tidy, without many worldly possessions—just a TV, couch, chair, and breakfast table in the main living area. A queen-sized bed and dresser occupied the bedroom, and her closet was filled mostly with skirts, blouses, and jackets befitting a working girl's budget. There were few photos of family or friends. Although he did find pictures taken at the Show, there was no one he recognized in them.

Appropriately, in many of the pictures she was dressed in her best cowgirl outfits, standing with men and women all dressed similarly. They were taken outside of both the stadium and the center as well as inside the center where the exhibits were set up. Nothing too surprising or noteworthy, many of the men in the photos were much older than she, but there were no photos of her and Dresden. Storm gathered them up and decided to take them with him and to see if Russell knew any of those men pictured with her.

Storm's next stop was the Tejas Petroleum building downtown. The Tejas building (actually one of two twin buildings called in combination "Tejas Plaza") was one of the first major buildings built in downtown Houston as the home of large Tejas Petroleum Corporation. The first real high rise was the old Humble Building built in 1936; after its construction there had been a long drought before the spate of new super structures that had started with the Tejas Buildings. Built in the late 1960s, the two Tejas Petroleum Plaza buildings were white marble and black glass and the lobbies were nice, if somewhat cold and austere.

Tejas Petroleum had its own full-time security and after arriving at the desk of One Tejas Plaza, Storm asked to see Dwight Parker, head of internal security for Tejas Petroleum. The receptionist called him and within minutes after being told there was an HPD Detective there to see him, he was in the lobby shaking hands with Storm. Introducing himself he asked, "What can I do for you Detective?"

"Mr. Parker, I'm here doing some follow-up on a murder that occurred last weekend. A young woman named Leslie Phillips was found dead on the grounds of new stadium. We understand she was an employee of Tejas Petroleum." Storm continued. "Have you been notified of her death?"

"Yes, we got notification Monday after she didn't show up for work and our attempts to contact her failed. A Sergeant Hernandez from HPD called and notified us of her death and asked for any records we might have of her next of kin. In our records we showed she only had one set of grandparents surviving her. Seems her parents were killed many years ago." said Parker.

"I'm the lead investigator on the case, Mr. Parker, and I'm chasing down any information that might help us find a clue to her killer. Would you happen to know what department Miss Phillips worked in? I would like to talk to anyone who would have known her or might be able to tell me more about her."

"I think she worked in our purchasing division, but I'll introduce you to the human relations director and he can tell you exactly where she worked and who her supervisor was."

With that, Parker led Storm to the elevators. Parker was an older man and had probably worked for Tejas for many years. He obviously ran a tight ship. He carried himself like ex-military, his back ramrod straight, but he had gentleness in his voice.

They found the human relations department and Storm was introduced to Peter Bonham, the director of personnel for Tejas Petroleum in Houston. After Parker and Storm were seated in Bonham's office, Parker explained who Storm was and what he was doing there.

"I was sorry to hear about Miss Phillips," Bonham said. "From all accounts she was a good employee. I'm sorry to say I didn't know her personally, but I have her file on my desk because I need to review it for details like insurance and reports to the IRS." He told Storm he had already concluded that she had worked for Tejas Petroleum for the last four years and that her work record was spotless. Her immediate supervisor was Maxine Davenport, office manager in the purchasing division, which was located on another floor. He apologized, telling Storm he couldn't escort him to that department as he had another meeting, but asked if Mr. Parker would take Detective Storm to Ms. Davenport's office.

"Mr. Bonham, I appreciate your seeing me on short notice and I won't take much more of your time then needed, but I do have one more question. There was another girl who worked here about seven years ago who was also murdered. Would you have any records on her that would tell us if anyone who still works here who might have known her?"

Storm was playing a hunch. While sitting there listening to Bonham relate what Leslie's employment file showed, Storm had remembered that the first girl killed had also worked at Tejas Petroleum; might as well check it out. Bonham reached over to his computer keyboard, rebooted it, and asked, "Do you know how long ago it might have been?"

"About six or seven years ago. Her name was Elaine Gage," said Storm.

While Bonham scrolled through the human resources records, Parker leaned over and whispered to Storm, "Why are you asking about this other girl?"

"She was found near the same area this girl was found and killed in the same manner. Let's call it a cop's curiosity, intuition, whatever."

"Then you think there might be a link?" asked Parker.

"I am not sure yet, it's way too early to know, but there are too many similarities to ignore the possibility," said Storm.

"Do you think it has anything to do with Tejas Petroleum?" Parker asked. Storm saw the concern on his face, and for good reason: the idea that someone might be killing Tejas Petroleum employees would, of course, be a worry to him.

"Not that I know of now, but I promise to keep you posted," said Storm

"Well, I hope to hell it doesn't. I got enough shit on my plate right now with this terrorist crap I have to deal with," sighed Parker. Storm nodded, silently acknowledging that in this post-9/11 world, everyone had to be careful to notice even things that seemed insignificant.

It only took Bonham a couple of minutes to find the file on Elaine Gage. She had worked in the accounting department for three years. Again, perfect reviews in her personnel file. Her supervisor had been Shirley Young and she was still the manager of that area. Bonham offered that Parker could take Storm to see her, as well. Parker agreed. "I'll call ahead and alert the two women of our impending visit and ask them to cooperate as much as they can," he told Storm.

Storm again offered his thanks to Bonham and he and Parker were off to purchasing to see Maxine Davenport. When they arrived on the floor that housed the purchasing division, Storm noticed it was much different than the offices they had just left. It was full of cubicles about four feet high, each with a matching desk, a couple chairs, and a bookcase—sterile but functional. There was a small conference room on the floor where they were greeted by Mrs. Davenport, a portly woman of about forty-five who told Storm she had worked for Tejas Petroleum for twenty-five years. She had started her career with Tejas Petroleum as a clerk in the purchasing division and she was quite proud of the fact she had worked herself up to manager. She quickly gave Storm the ten-cent tour on the workings of her area, obviously proud of her operation.

"How well did you know Miss. Phillips, Mrs. Davenport?" asked Storm.

His question set off a surprising series of events Storm wished he could constrain, but knew he had no control over. Mrs. Davenport was apparently one of those people who wore their emotions on their sleeve. When Storm brought up Leslie's name, Mrs. Davenport began to sob.

"I apologize for barging in and upsetting you, Mrs. Davenport," he said, as Parker offered her a box of tissues from the side table. "I need to know as much about Leslie's life as I can."

Mrs. Davenport nodded her head in understanding. "I knew Leslie from her first day of working here. I even trained her." She blinked to hold back the tears, as she fought to gain control of her emotions.

"Was she good at her job?" Asked Storm.

"She was wonderful. Her paperwork was perfect. Her buyers loved her and her vendors even brought her presents, small things like pens and those goofy bobble head dolls," said Mrs. Davenport. "Leslie was never late for work and she was always back before the lunch hour was over. That's why I became so concerned when Leslie didn't show up for work Monday morning."

"How did you get the news of her death, Mrs. Davenport?" Asked Storm.

"First we called the phone numbers we had for her, and when there was no answer we called security to look into it," she answered, beginning to sob again. "I'm so sorry...I can't seem to stop crying....It was just a few minutes later that one of Mr. Parker's people called to say they had been contacted by the police department and told that she had been killed sometime late Saturday night or early Sunday morning."

"Mrs. Davenport, do you know if she had any family?" asked Storm.

Stopping to blow her nose, she began typing on her keyboard and looked at her monitor. Then she copied something down on a scratch pad and tore off the top sheet. She handed it to Storm. "Just her grandparents. That is the name and address she listed as her emergency contacts. She grew up living with them in Hallettsville after her parents were killed in auto accident. She was an only child, no brothers or sisters."

"Are they both still living?" Asked Storm.

"Yes, as far as I know. Leslie had a picture of the three of them on her desk and I know she went home to Hallettsville to spend Christmas every year. They were all she had since the loss of her parents, not even aunts or uncles I ever heard of," Mrs. Davenport said, suppressing another sob.

"Have they been contacted by someone here in the office?"

"Yes, Detective, and they are making funeral arrangements for their granddaughter. They are not wealthy people Detective, so Tejas Petroleum is going to help with that as well as with getting her body home to Hallettsville. The funeral will be as soon as the body is released from your morgue," Said Maxine.

"I will look into the release of her body for you, Mrs. Davenport," Storm promised, although he knew it would be an easy promise to keep since the M.E. had finished the autopsy and Leslie could now be taken home for burial.

"Detective Storm, these people who work for me, especially the younger ones," waving her hand in the direction of the cubicles, "are like my family. They know my door is always open and we chat and I try to keep up with their lives." Once again, the water works started.

Storm tried not to smile, though in spite of himself he found it amusing that Mrs. Davenport referred to her door being open since her office was a cubicle, as well, only with taller walls and no door, the sign of her stature in what he suspected was a strictly defined pay-grade hierarchy.

"Since you were so close to Leslie, did she ever mention a boyfriend or significant other?" asked Storm.

"Detective, Leslie was a beautiful girl; she had guys all over the building knocking her door down. She could have dated any single man in the place, but she didn't. I told her when she first came to work here, 'Don't play where you get paid,' and she took it to heart and never did," said Maxine.

Storm wondered if that was true, or if Leslie had chosen what information she shared with Maxine. "Do you know if she dated anyone?"

"Yes, I am sure she did. She was a wonderful girl and any man would have been lucky to have gone out with her. I know she got involved with the Rodeo and Livestock Show thing two years ago and I heard she dated some of cowboys out there, but nothing serious. I think if she had had a serious boyfriend she would have told me," Maxine sniffled.

"But she didn't tell you specifically about any of the cowboys, mention names or anything?" Asked Storm.

"No, she took vacation time that time of year, or would have started it, next week. She said she wanted to be free to be out there all of the time, as she loved meeting new people and attending all the social events, and when her vacation was over, she came back and really didn't talk much about it, just exclaimed she'd had fun," Maxine said.

"Well, I think that's all I need for the moment, Mrs. Davenport, but this is my card. If you think of anything else that might help, please call. Thank you for your time and assistance. By the way, you're right, she was a beautiful girl. I'm sure her loss will affect everyone who knew her," said Storm.

Parker's and Storm's next stop was to see Shirley Young, who had been Elaine Gage's boss at the time Elaine was killed. If Storm thought the purchasing division was austere, the accounting department was downright Spartan, with computer terminals everywhere, lots of silence, and no personal touches at all. Shirley Young was probably fifty, with severe butchy looks and a mechanical quality about her. She didn't offer to show them around or explain what they did and she acted annoyed that she had to take time out of her day to talk to them, especially about something that had happened six or seven years ago.

There would be no tears on this visit; it was all business and Storm knew to get on with it if he wanted to get any information she might have. Without preliminaries, he asked, "Do you remember an employee named Elaine Gage?"

"Yes, she worked for me about seven years ago. I think she was found dead somewhere out by the Dome," Ms. Young said matter-of-factly.

"What can you tell me about her?" Asked Storm.

"She was good with paperwork and kept up with her job, although she never volunteered to do more than was asked of her."

"Did you ever wonder about her murder?" Storm asked.

"No, it was of no concern to me; it was only a matter of filling her job as soon as possible."

"Did the police contact you when she was killed?"

"No." Ms. Young was starting to sound not just rushed but annoyed.

"Do you know if she was dating anyone?" Storm inquired.

"No, I do not make it a practice to get involved in my employees' lives." Her tone was curt as she stood up and glanced at the large watch on her wrist.

"Did she have any friends that worked here?"

"As I remember it, she had one friend, a girl named Peggy Wise. She worked in this department, also. I always saw them eating lunch together in the cafeteria," Ms. Young said, sounding a little calmer.

"Does this Peggy Wise still work here?"

"No, I think she went to work for the Livestock Show out at the center a few years ago."

"Is there anything else you can tell me about Elaine?" Storm pressed.

"No, Detective, as I said, I don't get involved in the lives of my employees. Now I'm very busy and I need to cut this off. If there is anything else I can do for you, please call me and make an appointment. If I think of anything else, I'll call you," Ms. Young's tone made it clear the interview was over. With that Storm handed her a card, thanked her for her time, and he and Parker left. When they reached the lobby they exchanged cards, shook hands, and Storm went on with his day.

Storm now had a new track to follow. Who was this Peggy Wise and what could she tell him? Storm made a mental note to see her on his next trip to the Show.

Charity Kills

CHAPTER TWENTY

The Mind of a Serial Killer

Assembling his team of unlikely investigators for another session of comparing facts, brainstorming and planning their next move was not as easy one might think. Russell and Grady had to finish the early nightly news and would not be free to leave the station until a few minutes after 6:30 PM. Pancho and Alisha found it necessary to leave work casually, as if they had put in a full day and were merely clocking out to go to their homes. With all these considerations in mind, Storm called Russell and arranged to meet him and the rest of the team back at the condo no later than 7:00 PM.

Storm found Russell, Grady, Hernandez, and Alisha all waiting for him when he arrived carrying boxes of pizza, which was the only reward he could offer them. The dining room table was covered in files and video disks. Hernandez had brought his laptop and since Russell had wireless service in his building it was easy to find Internet access. All participants stood ready to go to work.

"Hey, big dog, where you been and what you got there, dinner?" Russell inquired as he answered the door.

"Long day. What's going on here?" Storm handed the pizza boxes to Russell and waved his hand, indicating the mass confusion that already was strewn across the table.

"We're ready to go and we started without you. Hope you don't mind, Baretta."

After a round of "hellos," the five dove into what they had found so far. They had seven dead girls, and according to Alisha, all had been killed in the same manner. To add to the curiosity, all the girls had similar looks, all were brunettes, all were around 25, all were from small towns, and all had very little family to miss them. They had discovered the killer definitely had a type. But what else could the team conjecture?

"If we now believe, and I think we do, that we know the killer's type, there are some other important questions. Like, how does he find them?"

Answering his own question, Storm said, "He finds them somehow at the Show. How does he know so much about them, to know they are from small towns and are basically alone in life?" Again he answered his own question: "The killer has had to spend time with them get to know them."

"There are no defensive wounds on the girls, or we think we know that in the cases of the other girls, but in Leslie's case we are sure because we saw the body. Why not? If I was about to be attacked by a stranger it's probable every one of these girls would surely have fought back. So the only conclusion we can draw is they knew their killer. But again, how?" The group around the table sat silent each pondering the questions Storm had just laid out.

Grady finally spoke up. "We also have seven murders with very little publicity on any of them. The newspapers dropped them, television dropped them. There was nothing more reported after the initial reports of them being found."

"We got Joe Dresden on video," said Hernandez.

"You think he is the one?" asked Alisha, looking to Storm for an answer

"No, I don't," said Storm.

"Who then, if not Joe?" asked Russell.

"Not sure yet, but that's what we are going to find out," added Storm, knowing he sounded a little more positive than he felt.

"By the way, I told Joe he had to come see you and get a DNA swab to test against the semen you got from Leslie," Storm told Alisha.

"Do you really think he will come in voluntarily?" asked Alisha.

"Probably not. I'm sure I scared the shit out of him, but if he doesn't show up don't worry about it, I will get a warrant and make him do it." With that said he moved on.

"What else we got?" Storm asked his fellow conspirators. "Pancho, what did you get from the FBI?" He explained to the others that he had asked Hernandez to do some research into the modus operandi of serial killers like Bundy and Gacy to see if the research would give them any insights into their killer.

Sergeant Hernandez took out a notebook containing all the facts and theories he had been able to find on serial murders and killers. "First, we need to look at these murders as if they are connected and ask whether they are the result of a *mass murderer* or a *serial murderer*. In both scenarios the victims die as result of the murderer gaining control of his or her victims' lives. The mass murderer kills multiple victims at the same time, usually in a big display for public attention, fear, and media blitz.

"The serial murderer, on the other hand, kills methodically over time—weeks, months, even years—and usually not for public attention. Wanting attention, the mass murderer usually operates within a designated area like the city or sometimes an area as small as the neighborhood they grew up in. The outcome for a mass murderer can come in a variety of forms: they are caught by police and arrested, they spend days in court, and their photo is featured on the front page of every newspaper in the country and on every television news report. Sometimes they are killed by someone else who takes the execution of the mass murderer into his own hands, but with the same results, lots of coverage on newspapers and TV. Less often, they commit suicide, and even more rarely they turn themselves in. But the outcome is always the same—they become notorious, and that was all they were looking for in the first place. They believe they have spread their message even in death.

"In complete contrast, the serial killer usually wants to stay under the radar and to elude detection so they can go on killing. They are organized. They kill over time, one victim at a time. They may even stop for periods of time or change their modus operandi. Although there is a difference of opinion as to the numbers, in theory, there may be as few as thirty-five to fifty serial murderers, or as many as five hundred, operating in United States at any one time."

"Shit! You got to be kidding! Five hundred of them?" asked Storm, aghast.

"Yep. And I think we all feel it is obvious we have a serial murderer, since our victims have appeared to be one a year for the past seven years," added Russell.

"Go on, Pancho," Storm said, pushing Hernandez to continue on with his tutorial.

"Both types scare the hell out of the community, but the rampage of a mass killer usually ends with a "final statement" that often ends their life at the same time. The serial killer goes on and on believing that the many murders they have committed won't be or haven't been discovered yet and certainly not all of them can be linked to the single killer. They strongly believe that they are smarter than anyone in the police departments. You would think that the community would recognize that a person is acting unusually strange, but the serial killer knows how to manipulate people's perceptions and will even go through a cooling off period that may last for months or years before he kills again. These killers suffer from antisocial personality disorder and not psychosis. They appear normal, many times charming; a guy named Cleckley—he studied the personalities of some psychopaths and wrote a book about them—called that the 'mask of sanity.'

"Serial killers are motivated by power and sexual compulsion. They may have been abused in childhood or are compensating for their self-perceived inadequacies because they grew up poor or came from low socioeconomic background. Killing gives them power to take revenge for perceived slights and bad things that happened to them when they had no control. Killing gives them back power and they bask in the afterglow for a period of time until they need another power fix and kill again. The time between killings varies depending on how disassociated the killer becomes. Most find they need to kill more often as time goes on because the 'glow' wears off more quickly. Some only kill when they are set off by some perceived outside slight. For most, the knowledge they have terrified a community and baffled authorities adds to their sense of power.

"There are two types of serial killers," Hernandez continued. "The *organized* types are deliberate and highly intelligent, many with IQs of over 110. They plan their crimes, usually abducting their victims, killing them in one place and getting rid of the body in another. Does this sound familiar? They are likeable and charming and they often lure their victims with ploys like appealing to the victim's sympathies. Ted Bundy would put his arm in a cast and ask women to help him carry things to his car, where he would beat them senseless and haul them away.

Some serial killers choose victims who will go with them voluntarily, like prostitutes looking for a trick. They maintain a high degree of control over the crime scene and usually have a working knowledge of forensic science, enabling them to cover their tracks. They follow their crimes in the media; part of the afterglow thing I talked about earlier. They feel pride in what they have done. They are the guy or girl next door; the person the neighbors are always surprised about because 'he or she was such a nice quiet person.' They may even have spouses and children.

Many times they try to inject themselves into the investigation. They want to appear helpful and even become a hero if they can. They sometimes even leave clues leading the investigation to someone else in the community viewed as not as nice as them. They hunt their victims like prey."

Hernandez stopped momentarily looking around the table "Again sounds familiar, doesn't it?"

"Conversely, the *unorganized* serial killer kills impulsively and the kill is messy. They usually have a low IQ, around 80. They don't clean up the crime scene. They strike randomly without warning and have no plan. Often in retrospect, they are described as having been creepy or very strange by the people who knew them."

He paused. "I think we have an organized serial killer," Hernandez said, and as he looked around the room everyone shook their heads in concurrence.

Hernandez went on. "It looks like we all agree we have an organized serial killer, but the next part of the description is trickier, as there are more types or profiles under this heading. The first type is the *visionary*, who may claim he was forced to kill by voices or direction from afar. Rarely are serial killers insane, nor do they hear voices telling them to kill. They often make that claim after they are caught, but it's usually to stay off death row. For instance, the Son of Sam killer claimed his neighbor's dog told him to kill all his victims and that the dog was possessed by a demon.

"The next type is the *missionary*. They kill because they believe they are doing society a service. They choose types of victims that they feel don't belong in society, like prostitutes, particular ethnic or religious groups, or the rich, you name it.

188

Aileen Wournos stalked and killed men who used prostitutes. She was the one Charlize Theron portrayed in the movie *Monster*. They believe they are helping the community.

"The next type is the *hedonist*. This is the killer with the sexual appetite. They enjoy killing and they think their victims deserve to die. They enjoy the hunt as much as the kill. Some kill fast, others slowly, to enjoy the torture and humiliation they inflict on their victims. They also enjoy abusing the body after the kill. The Son of Sam liked killing young couples found necking in parked cars, making one watch the death of the other. Jeffery Dahmer enjoyed necrophilia and cannibalism.

"Next is the *gain motivated* type. These are the hit men, people who kill for money. I don't think ours is that, so moving on we come to the big one—the *power and control* killer. They kill to gain power and control over their victims. They probably had been abused as a child and been left to feel powerless or they might be shunned by society for their lifestyle or some abnormality, mental or physical. They abuse their victims sexually, either before or after they kill them. They are not motivated by lust as much as revenge and they want to humiliate their victims by sexually degrading them."

"So," said Storm. "Where does this leave us?"

"Well, number one, I think we all have to agree this killer is the organized type, right?' said Hernandez.

"Damn straight. I think we all agree on that," said Grady.

"I also think our killer is a hedonist and/or the power and control type," said Alisha.

"We know our killer is careful and organized," said Russell.

"And our killer likes to degrade the victims, i.e. the anal rape," said Alisha.

"Obviously, our killer must look normal and fits in," said Hernandez.

"The killer has definitely found a hunting ground," added Grady.

"Yes, and the killer either knows these girls or appears trustworthy," contributed Storm. "Maybe the killer is someone in authority, like a big wheel at the show."

"Or a cop, a bartender, or anyone that is fixture out there," agreed Russell. The idea had not crossed his or anyone else's minds before Hernandez's report—their focus had primarily been on the sleaze dog officials who always had a girl around.

"Possibly," said Storm. "This puts a whole a new spin on the cases. That's why this group is so great. What else do we have?"

"Let's walk through what we know about the killer, like they do on the cop shows on TV, and see where it takes us," suggested Grady.

"All right. Given Alisha's breakdown of the 'how' the murders were committed, we probably have someone who has medical training or Special Forces training in how to cut the throat, hitting a major artery and severing the windpipe quickly and efficiently," Storm theorized.

"Yes, and they didn't get that knowledge from the Internet. Also, they used something seriously sharp, like a scalpel or a boning knife," chimed in Alisha.

"Although these girls weren't very big, the killer still had to be strong enough to subdue them without a lot of struggling since they didn't have any defensive wounds," said Storm.

"That indicates they trusted the killer," suggested Hernandez, "which means they had to know them pretty well."

"Although we still haven't found where Leslie was killed, and the other crime scenes were clean. The killer is meticulous, careful, and cleaned up after themselves," put in Storm.

"In order to have had access to Leslie, at least, they had to have been in or around the stadium Saturday night," added Hernandez.

"The only people who had access to the VIP rooms that night were big wheels and their guests," threw in Russell.

"That's not entirely true, Russell," said Storm.

"Who else?" said Russell

"The employees—waiters, bartenders, janitors, hell, even the cops working the door," said Storm. He looked at Russell. "Can the employees get people into that room?"

"Sure. They're not supposed to, but I've seen the cops and committeemen working the door let in single girls if they are cute," said Russell.

"It's a place to meet and greet and party and the more cute single women the better. I saw that for myself the other night," said Storm.

"Unfortunately, none of this gets us any closer to a killer," commented Grady.

"No, it doesn't, but it could help eliminate pretty boy philandering husbands like Joe Dresden," said Storm. "Guys like Joe don't have to kill a girl; they can just ditch them when they're through. His girls are toys to be used and discarded."

"That narrows the field," said Hernandez, lifting his eyebrows as if amused with the thought of how eliminating one man might actually do that.

"Now that we've agreed we know we have a serial killer and even have a quasi description of the type, my big question is why?" said Alisha.

Everyone seemed to be in agreement that there had to be an underlying common element to the killer's need to kill these particular women, though what it was still a mystery, and why only one girl a year?

"What else do we have?" asked Storm.

"We have a cover-up," said Russell.

Each of the other team members sat still for a minute, as if trying to think of what to add. The elephant in the room was out. Everyone had been thinking it, but no one wanted to be the first to say it.

"Who is covering these murders up and why?"

"Well, the Show for one," said Grady.

"Who else?" asked Storm

The police?" asked Hernandez.

"Why?" asked Storm.

"It's in their best interest to hide it if they can't solve it. The Show is big and they can't or won't have the public thinking their venue could be dangerous," said Hernandez.

Storm looked at Alisha, "You think the cops are covering this up, too?"

"It looks that way to me, maybe not intentionally but all the same, yes," said Alisha.

"In my research into the girls' files I saw two other things that bother me," Hernandez volunteered. "I guess this is as good a time to throw them out on the table. Detective, there is something else. Did you or any of cops at the scene ever find the girls' shoes?"

"Not that I know of, why?" asked Storm. He thought of his earlier hunch. Leslie's shoes had not been found with her clothing.

"When I was telling you about serial murders and the hinky kinks there is one thing I left out, one in particular, and that was, most of them keep trophies of their kills. I didn't notice it at first when I went through the files, but I did when I kept looking at the similarities from each report. In the list of personal items found in connections with each girl there were always bloody clothes found, their purses were always found with money still in them. So robbery wasn't a motive. But in each case there was never a mention of shoes of any kind. I think the killer is keeping their shoes, or boots in this case, as the trophy. With everything else that connects the way these girls were killed, it adds to the support that this is the same person." Hernandez took a breath as he looked around the room, seeing the acceptance of what he had said register on the faces of the others.

"And I think our killer picked these girls for all the reasons we already concluded but I think the killer knew them all well enough to really 'know' these girls, and I mean pretty well, and none of them had much family. Each and every one of them only had like one or two family members left in the world. The killer is picking the prey very carefully, the killer stalked them." With that said, Hernandez sat back and let his theory sink in.

The room got even quieter as they each digested what they had heard. It was Alisha who was the first to speak. "OK, so we think Sergeant Hebert knows more than he is telling, but who else is involved in sweeping these murders under the table?"

"The mayor's office," said Storm, and he told them about his visit with Lieutenant Flynn that morning and Vern Nagel's proprietary interest in his progress.

"Do they know you know about the other girls or do they know we might?" asked Hernandez.

"No, I don't think so. I haven't said a word to anyone, except Joe Dresden, about them yet," Storm.

"Have any of the rest of you caught anyone sniffing around?" asked Storm.

"Chu asked what Grady and I were doing today at the station earlier than I would normally be there," offered Russell.

"What did you tell her?" Storm.

"Told her we were going over his old vids for his retirement."

"Did she buy it?"

"Think so, she didn't ask anymore."

"Did she talk to you, Grady?" Storm turned to the cameraman.

"Nope. Although, she did ask when I was retiring. Guess she wants to dance on my grave or buy me a cake." That broke the tension and everyone had a good laugh. "OK, so where do we go next?" he asked.

"Did you have any luck at the girl's apartment?" Hernandez asked, turning to Storm.

"Zip. But I did bring along some photos that look like they might have been taken last year at the Show. Wanted to see if Russell recognized anybody." With that he handed the photos to Russell, while the others looked over his shoulder.

As he looked at the pictures he asked Storm, "How did it go with Dresden today?"

"He said he knew two of the other girls and admitted he had been with them. He is one scared piece of crap."

"He should be, he is candidate numero uno, isn't he?" said Hernandez.

"He is right now, but I'm not sure he's good for it," said Storm.

"Why?" asked Grady.

"Alisha said the girls were murdered by someone who knew what they were doing. Their throats were cut in such a way they couldn't scream and they didn't fight back. Joe Dresden is a pussy. He never was in the military or even played any contact sports. I doubt he's ever played anything but pocket pool or 'hide the trout' in high school. He is a pretty boy dilettante who married for money and the freedom to play golf every day."

"But that doesn't totally rule him out," said Hernandez.

"No, but he says he only knew two of the other girls."

"You can't believe everything you hear from a guy like him, so I don't think that rules him out for sure," argued Hernandez.

"No, but it does if we can prove he didn't know all seven of the girls. He sure didn't look like he recognized the others, with the exception of the gag reaction to the morgue photos."

It was then Russell broke in. "There is something else you need to know, Storm. When you went out to Joe's office Ellen saw you and the exchange you had with Joe. She called me and began giving me the third degree, like 'who are you, what were you doing in Joe's office' and so on. At first I didn't think it was a big deal but damn, she hasn't called me in years and now here she was on the phone asking me about you."

"Did she say anything that would make you believe she knows anything or knew Leslie?" asked Storm.

"Yes, actually she did, she called the girl a slut, she told me I was just as bad as Joe and I knew what kind of sluts that hung around out there and what they were looking for," replied Russell.

Russell quickly tried to add humor as looked around the table and asked with feigned innocence, "Do any of you think I would keep company with soiled doves?"

A collective groan was heard from everyone and smiles again appeared on all their faces.

Storm caught Alisha eyes and asked, "Do you think a five-foot-five about one hundred-fifty pound woman could have done this?"

Alisha thought a minute. "No, where would she have gotten the training and knowledge to kill someone like this? Plus, these girls were all pretty tall, probably at least as tall as most females. It would have been almost impossible for her to subdue them, hold them down, and kill them without one of these girls scratching her and there has never been any skin found reported under any of the girls' nails."

Hernandez spoke up. "Storm, we never saw her on any of the disks, and didn't Dresden tell you he went in with Leslie and a bunch of other people? If his wife was there he wouldn't have been in the bathroom getting laid."

"Are you going back to see Joe again?" asked Russell.

"Probably, but right now he isn't high on my list to go see again, why?" replied Storm.

"Well, I think you may have to ask Ellen where she was the night Leslie was killed. We didn't see her on the security disk, but does she have an alibi?" asked Russell.

Each collaborator considered the possibility but moved on.

"OK, if not Dresden and not his wife, then who?" asked Alisha.

"If we are right and all these girls were killed because they were around the Show, then we have to assume that the killer has had access to the Show for at least the last seven years," Storm commented.

"Are we sure they were all involved out at the show in one way or another?" asked Russell.

Storm looked around the room. All shook their head in the affirmative. "It's my guess we do," he said, "but I'm going back to the Show offices tomorrow to check for any records on the six other girls. I'm also going to ask for any video tapes that might still exist on the nights the other girls were killed and see where it leads."

"Shit!" yelled Russell. "You know that will tip our hand."

"Only tip off those who are trying to hide the facts and we've got to know for sure if the killings are related. I know I'm putting myself out on a limb, but I have to take the chance to get concrete proof of what we feel in our gut is true."

The room got eerily quiet.

"What do we do then?" asked Russell.

"Keep yourselves out of it for now. Stay quiet and don't let anyone know we have met or talked. If anyone takes a fall for this, it will be me. All of you have a great deal more to lose than me, especially Pancho," said Storm.

Storm knew, and he knew the others were in agreement, that this was a big step and all hell could break loose, but it was the right step to take. If there was a conspiracy, then the proverbial shit would hit the fan by tomorrow and there would be nothing they could do to stop it except to get a yellow slicker and duck.

For now Storm was on his own. God, tonight it would be hard to sleep, but then he thought, get over yourself, Storm, old buddy, people have been writing you off for years, so what's the big freakin' deal now?

CHAPTER TWENTY-ONE

"Peggy Won't Be in Today"

The next day was one of those special and somewhat rare days in Houston when not only is there not a cloud in the sky and no smog, but the temperature is cool, there's no humidity and just a light breeze blowing. It was one of those early March days when everybody wants to be outside enjoying nature. One of those days the people up north could only rent for a day at this time of year, Storm thought, the kind of day you feel alive.

The drive to the Show offices was easy. Storm had stopped at his favorite taqueria on Kirby and Alabama for a Mexican coffee and two breakfast burritos—his taste for those filling, high-cholesterol gas factories was one of the few secrets he had kept hidden from Angie. She had hated his eating habits, so he had had these treats on the sly. His mantra was, "if it tastes good and doesn't kill me it's safe," but he saved actually eating them for when she wouldn't catch him.

With a satisfied smirk on his face he finished the burrito as he pulled through the main entry gates to the complex. The place was bustling; committeemen were running around on golf carts or helping contestants stall their show animals, and vendors were replenishing their booths with food. With the wonderful weather, this was going to be a glorious day for all concerned.

Storm stopped at the reception desk, asked for Ms. Taylor, and then took a seat to wait. A different female gatekeeper seated behind the elevated reception desk reached for her telephone and made a call.

Dakota Taylor soon came through the doors that separated the inner sanctum from the reception area. She flashed her corporate smile and held out her hand. "Detective Storm, you're here early. How did you hear about it so soon?"

Storm couldn't hide his puzzlement; he had no idea what she was talking about. "Hear about what, Ms. Taylor?"

"Why, one of our employees is missing." Dakota now, too, looked confused, as if she was wondering, why is the detective here if he hasn't heard?

Storm was so dumbstruck he didn't know what to say. Questions ran through his mind. Who was missing? Why hadn't he been called?

"You don't know, do you?" asked Dakota.

"Who is missing, Ms. Taylor, and how long have they been missing?" asked Storm.

Dakota gave a look that was hard to interpret but which Storm took to be a "Damn, I just let the cat out of the bag" look.

"Oh, it's probably all a misunderstanding, I'm sure she is just running late. Maybe she had an accident and hasn't had a chance to call."

"Who is it?" asked Storm.

"Oh, never mind, Detective, I shouldn't have bothered you with it. It was just seeing you here unexpectedly; I thought you had come to help."

"Ms. Taylor, I am always ready to help. Has anyone called the police and put in a missing persons report?"

"I thought they had when I saw you, but I am not sure now."

"Who is it?"

"Peggy Wise, our assistant manager of ticket sales, but I am sure she is just running late."

Damn. This was the woman Storm had wanted to talk to. *If she is missing what the hell is going on out here?*

"Ms. Taylor, do you want me to report it? Do you have her address? I can always call it in and we can send a car by her home to check."

"No, no, Detective. Like I said, I am sure she is just running late, but I will notify you if there is any change."

Damn, this bitch is cold, thought Storm. She soon went right back to her stone-faced-fake-smile-corporate self. "Now what was it you wanted to see me about, Detective?"

"This might be better done somewhere private, not out here in the lobby."

"Of course, Detective." They went to the same small conference room off the lobby he had been in before.

"Do you keep records of all the members and people involved in the Livestock Show?"

"I am not sure what you are asking, Detective," Dakota replied cautiously.

"Ms. Taylor, I have reason to think that the murder of Leslie Phillips is related to other murders in the Dome area over the past six years and I need to see if there are any links between them and the girl from Sunday in your records."

Only Dakota's eyes betrayed her, darting away from his, trying to look somewhere anywhere but at him. He knew she had them and he knew she was going to lie.

"What could you possibly mean, Detective Storm?"

"Over the past few years, six girls have been found dead in or around the area of the Dome, all killed in the same manner as the girl from Saturday night. I have their names and I was hoping you had a record of whether they had been members of the Show. If they were, then we may need to check out members of the Show as well as employees, vendors, security staff, anyone who might have had a connection to them."

It was then that Storm pulled the morgue photos of the girls from out of the manila envelope he was carrying, and as he did, a sheet of copy paper with the girls' names also fell out onto the table.

"Detective, I can't give you that kind of information."

"Why not?" asked Storm.

"Our records are privileged," she answered. Her throat made an involuntary clutching sound as if she was trying to keep from gagging.

"Ms. Taylor, I am not asking you to give me your list of members or donors, even though you are a charitable organization. I only want you to tell me if any of these girls were members or if there were any documented relationships with the Show. Of course, I can always request a subpoena if I have to."

* * * *

Dakota cringed, looked away, and groaned. She wished she could be anywhere but sitting at this table. Her natural reaction was to flee, but she knew she had to fight. Flight was out of the question. The pictures made her sick to her stomach and she fought to control the urge to vomit, but the sight of the dead girls was overwhelming. She covered her mouth and turned away.

Dakota knew she was caught. The Show had promised to help with the investigation and she didn't want to appear to be stonewalling. She knew the Show could get the subpoena quashed, so her best bet was to stall. Storm may have been a washed up drunk, but he had found out about the other girls.

Peggy Wise had slipped her mind completely now. She had a bigger dilemma and bigger fish to fry.

Smiling sweetly and seemingly backing down, Dakota said, "Of course, Detective, if you will give me a list of their names I can run a search of our database to see if these girls are on any of our member or vendor lists. I'll get back to you with the information as soon as I have it."

Storm handed her the piece of copy paper with girls' names on it and added, "Miss Taylor, if you will give me your missing employee's address, I will send a car by to check on her."

"No, no, that's okay, Detective. Let me get on this for you and I will call later today with what I find."

* * * *

All Storm could do was wait and see. He hated waiting, so he was going to see about the missing employee, this Peggy Wise. When Storm got to the parking lot he called Hernandez from his mobile phone, thinking to himself that the shit was about to hit the fan now.

"You out there?" Hernandez meant "the Show." "What happened?"

"I just met with Dakota Taylor and I asked for the names and any records they may have on the six dead girls. She knows about them, it was all over her face, but she is good; she didn't blink an eye, but she did flinch, and she lied to me. She told me it would take some time to find out if any of the girls' names were in their database."

"What do you think she knows?"

"I think she knows there's a cover-up and who's behind it. I suspect she knows a lot more than then she is telling me."

"Then the Show is in on it?"

"Yep. Hey, Pancho, I need for you to get me an address on a Peggy Wise. She works here at Show."

"Who is Peggy Wise?" asked Pancho.

"She is the girl who worked with the first victim we found, the one who worked at Tejas Petroleum six years ago and was found with her throat cut like Leslie. Her supervisor told me this Peggy girl and Elaine, yeah, that was her name, were friends and now this Peggy works for the Show. I thought while I was out here I would see if she knew anything about Elaine's death. Did she know if Elaine was dating anyone out here. Ask her if she knew any of the others."

"Why, then, do you need her address?"

"When I got here this morning, Ms. Taylor was not surprised to see me and thought I had come because they have a missing employee. It turns out they hadn't called it in yet and were just passing it off as she must just be late. But if you can get her address I want to go check on her. If she's missing, it may be connected. I'd like to run by her house and see if she's at home and you check to see if she was involved in some car wreck or something and just late for work."

It took a few minutes for Hernandez to find Peggy's address, but it was close by. Her small house was just south of the Dome off Stella Link in a neighborhood that was like the Heights—finding new life because of its location. People moving to Houston to be near or a part of the burgeoning Medical Center wanted to live close by and this area was perfect.

Storm approached the door and found it open. He went inside, announcing himself. "Houston Police. You here, Miss Wise?"

No answer. He stepped in cautiously, gun drawn. The place had been ransacked. The furniture was turned upside down with books and papers all over the floor. In the bedroom he found the lifeless body of Peggy Wise. Damn, what the hell?

It was plain to see the girl had had her throat slashed just like Leslie and she had been posed for discovery. Was this part of his case? Did this woman have something to do with the other murders? As he ruminated on this latest turn, he called for backup and for the M.E.'s office.

While he waited for the response teams he called Hernandez. "Hey, listen. . ." He told Hernandez what he had found.

He then called Alisha. "This is Detective David Storm. I was out on a missing persons call and discovered a homicide at the home of Ms. Peggy Wise. The victim is a young woman, maybe about twenty-eight. She has been murdered, her throat cut in a way that has some distinctive characteristics." He chose his words carefully and spoke formally, not knowing who else could be listening. "You'll be officially notified soon. CSI is on the way and as soon as they've processed the scene you'll be receiving the remains." He paused. "I'd appreciate knowing your conclusions, Doctor."

Though Storm was intentionally vague, he figured Alisha would catch the hints he dropped. Within minutes patrol cars working the area arrived; even Hebert showed up. Storm watched over the crime scene until the on-call processor from the M.E.'s office arrived. Nobody was touching this body or disturbing the scene until everything was photographed and logged into evidence—he'd hang around to make sure of it. Hebert's officers began to canvass the neighborhood. All the neighbors were shocked and surprised to hear something like this had happened in their neighborhood, but no one had seen anything suspicious. They knew Peggy's hours were long this time of year, so they didn't expect to see or talk to her until the Show was over.

Storm watched as the onsite exam was completed. This victim had fought back. She didn't go down easy, but the pool of blood surrounding her body was big enough to be the entire capacity of her body. Her bloody right hand was dropped in the pool and her index finger pointed outward. It appeared as if she was trying to write something but what? There was too much blood to make any sense of it. She was lying face down, her clothes were ripped, and her naked bottom was posed as if stuck up in the air. He had to wait for verification, but he was sure she had been violated. For the moment, all he could do was wait for Alisha to do her magic and tell him what she found. He wondered if the wreckage in the house was from the fight or if the perpetrator was looking for something.

Irony seemed to be the only reaction to the scene Storm could come up with. I need to call Dakota Taylor and tell her that Peggy Wise won't be in today, he told himself. Guess questioning this girl is out of the realm of possibility.

CHAPTER TWENTY-TWO

A Mentor's Confidence

Dakota Taylor sat quietly in her office trying to regain her composure. Seeing the morgue photos of the all of the murder victims had left her totally unnerved. She was sure she would never get those ghastly faces out of her mind. Even her cold corporate heart wondered how someone could do what had been done to those girls, not once, but seven times. She knew she had to pull herself together and call Vern Nagel, so he could get the mayor and the police chief more involved, and do it immediately. Someone had to put a leash on the detective. She made the call.

* * * *

The mayor heard him coming. Vern Nagel didn't even wait to be announced. He bolted through the mayor's office door gasping for breath from the short run down the hall.

He brought himself up short of his boss's desk looking more than a little alarmed. "Mr. Mayor, that detective that works for Flynn, he knows about the other girls."

"Jesus Christ, Vern, you can't just run in here babbling about something inane and interrupt me." Mayor Lemay was pissed. The veins in his neck popped out as his blood pressure began skyrocketing and he assured himself, I have a right to be.

"Sir," Nagel ran on, screeching, "That detective Lieutenant Flynn assigned to the murder of the girl at the Dome knows about the other girls, the ones found over the last few years."

"How the hell do you know that?" The mayor put the papers down he had been reading and looked at Nagel as if he had lost his mind.

"Dakota Taylor from the Livestock Show just called. She said the detective was there this morning with their names and morgue photos of each of them. She said the pictures made her sick. He asked Dakota to run their names against the Show's database to see if any of them were connected to the Show in any way."

"Goddamn it, Nagel, Lee Powers has already called and chewed my ass out about this. He basically threatened me and it wasn't a warning. He was clear that he expected me to take care of this. Get the police chief, Lieutenant Flynn and that dumbass director of the M.E. department in here now! If that detective has morgue photos of all of the victims, he probably had help from someone in the M.E.'s office." The mayor knew he was getting more upset by the minute and he didn't care. Was he surrounded by idiots and buffoons? Couldn't anyone around here control some drunk and pathetic old washed-up cop ?

It only took a few minutes for each of the men Richard Lemay had summoned to arrive. Also in the group was a gray haired cop the mayor didn't recognize. What in world could be in Flynn's head that he would bring this old guy along? Who the hell was he and what could he add? The largest concern, could old guy be trusted?

"Flynn, this is a private meeting. Who is this gentleman and what is he doing here?" asked the mayor, looking directly at Lieutenant Robert Smith.

"Mr. Mayor, this is Lieutenant Bob Smith. I asked him to join us because he knows Detective Storm better than I do and I think we may need his insights here, Lieutenant Smith from the training division was the detective's first instructor and has followed his career ever since."

"Lieutenant Smith, I don't have time for niceties. I didn't ask you here and I am not sure what you can add, but since you are here, please be aware anything said in this room is for our ears only. If anything said here comes to light, it is you I will come after. Is that understood?"

Lieutenant Smith shook his head affirmatively and seated himself back from the table behind the higher ranking officers; he was no stranger to the pecking order. He wasn't sure why he was here, either, other than it had something to do with Storm and he wasn't sure he was happy to be involved.

"Flynn, your man just showed up at the Livestock Show offices with names of all the girls found killed near or around the Dome over the past seven years. Not only did he know their names, but he had photographs obviously taken from the M.E.'s files, as they were morgue shots. Is there any other place they could have come from?" The mayor looked right at Dr. Alex Roberts, the presiding M.E. and Alisha's boss.

Before the M.E. could answer, the chief broke in and said, "Sir, there would also be a copy in our unsolved case files."

"Where are those files and who has access to them?" The mayor stormed.

"Since they are homicides they would be in our archive records," answered Lieutenant Flynn.

"OK. How he got them is a mystery we can solve later. Right now, the Show office tells me, he is trying to make a connection between those other unsolved homicides and this one, he was assigned to investigate this murder. And, gentlemen, he has to be stopped *now*! I have already had my ass eaten out by Lee Powers and I will tell you, you don't want him or the people he represents at the goddamned Show up our asses. Do I make myself clear? Lieutenant Smith, tell us about this Storm character," directed the mayor.

* * * *

Smith had been sitting back trying to stifle a grin during the mayor's tirade. It looked like Storm was back and had stirred up a hornet's nest. Obviously, something had called him back into the game and Smith knew the powers that be weren't ready for the old Storm.

"What I can tell you, Mr. Mayor, is that growing up in Houston, he was a local football hero and went on to play at Texas Tech. After college he came back to Houston and enrolled in the police academy. I was an instructor there at the time and he did well. He had all the physical attributes and he was smart; not just book smart but street smart. Then five years ago his wife was murdered and her killer was never found. That's when he fell off the edge. He began drinking, he either didn't show up for work or if he did, he would come in drunk or drinking. He screwed up some major cases and we had to give him a choice; take administrative leave and sober up or get fired. He took the leave and as far as I know has not had a drink since."

Smith looked at Flynn. "He's been on your watch since he returned, hasn't he?"

"Yes. I've kept him in a support mode, canvassing and so forth for the lead investigator and filing the reports."

"Why did you give him this case?" asked the mayor.

"When I got the call from Sergeant Hebert on Sunday morning, I was led to believe this was not a priority case and not to assign it to a lead investigator. The inference was that the case would be open and shut with little or no follow-up and would probably just go away, so Storm seemed to be the perfect choice. Since his return to the force, he hasn't shown any desire to work a case that's hard nor has he appeared to be committed to solving anything. He stopped a moment as if thinking and then continued. "Although he does dig into the files of his wife's murder every once in awhile."

* * * *

"Do we take him off this case?" the mayor asked, a question he deliberately made more wide-ranging than directed at any one participant.

"No, sir. In my opinion, that would send the wrong message to the other detectives in my division and might even make this case more visible," said Flynn.

"Sir," pushed in Nagel, "Dakota has told me he also runs around with that weather guy from Channel 5."

"So what?" the Mayor fumed, not appreciating Nagel's constant interruptions.

"We need to take a look at—" Nagel began, but didn't finish because Lieutenant Smith jumped in.

"Sir, Russell Hildebrandt and Storm have been friends since college. Russell was Storm's best man at his wedding and he has been there for Storm since his wife was killed. I agree with Mr. Nagel. He may not be a news man anymore, but he still would find it interesting that his best friend, a homicide detective, was pulled off a murder case, especially one where Storm may have found more questions than answers."

"OK, OK. Leave him on it, but put a muzzle on him and a very short leash," the mayor barked. "And I want to know how he found out about the other girls. I want that source to be dried up. You all understand?" Richard Lemay scowled at every man in the room.

"Yes, sir. I will have Storm in my office first thing tomorrow morning," Flynn quickly said.

"Good. And I want Vern and Lieutenant Smith there, as well. Make sure he understands he is not to stick his nose into these old cases, he just works on the one from Sunday. You got it?"

Every head in the room nodded "yes."

CHAPTER TWENTY-THREE

The Bomb Drops

Leon Powers' cell phone began to beep with the text message that it was time to meet and the 911 notice on the screen left no doubt that it was an emergency. Somewhere the shit had hit the fan, but where?

* * * *

By 11:00 AM Peggy Wise's body had been dropped at the M.E.'s office and Alisha had been pulled off the autopsy and investigation. She had started the examination, but was sidelined by her boss with the excuse that she hadn't finished the drowning victim and that he needed a definitive answer to the cause of the boy's death. He also warned her that if she was helping Detective Storm in any way with any information or files on any unsolved cases she could be severely reprimanded. "Terminated" was what he implied, but Alisha didn't scare that easily; if she was in for a penny she was in for a pound, and she wasn't backing out. Her political appointee pansy boss had never seen Saturday night in the "Ward" where she grew up, and verbal threats like his rolled off her back like water off a frog's ass. It didn't matter what it took. She and the others were going to help Storm solve the killings.

Before she obeyed her orders she had just enough time to examine Peggy's body and find the evidence she needed. No orders from her shithead boss, or for that matter the Mayor's office, were going to deter her. Politics were one thing, but solving a murder was another, and the latter was what she was all about. Now it was time to share her findings with "Storm's Troopers," as she had begun calling the detective's team, and she texted a request for a meeting to each of them. She hid the records of her tests and the resulting findings and waited for 6:00 PM to come so she could meet with the other four.

By the time the team assembled Alisha had a lot more than speculation about the killer and whether the deaths were connected and she could hardly wait to drop the bomb. "Guys, we've all assumed we were looking for a killer who was male, right?" With all heads nodding positively, she continued, "Well, guess what? It's not a man!"

The others were caught off guard and it showed. "The skin under this latest victim's fingernails tested positive for female DNA," she continued.

"No shit!" resounded around the room.

"Yes," said Alisha. "Peggy Wise's killer was a woman."

"So, does that help us link her murder to the others?" asked Storm.

"I think so. I'm not one hundred percent sure, but I'm close. Her throat was slit in the same manner and her anus was abused, so the M.O. is the same."

"Could it have been a copycat?" asked Grady.

"It could be, but I don't think so. She was sodomized just like the other girls and that fact is only known to the people in this room. My final report on Leslie has not been filed yet. I thought it would be better if only we five knew the whole truth," answered Alisha.

Storm took up the story from there. "The house was a mess. I figured it could have been the result of the fight, but the more I think about it, the more I think it looked as if the perp was looking for something," said Storm.

"I must say that although I think the killer was probably the same person, I don't think this particular killing was part of the pattern. I think this killing was one of necessity," said Alisha.

"What do you mean by that?" asked Hernandez

"It's the crime scene and the aftermath. Although the method was the same, the scene isn't. The victim was only naked from the waist down. There was no cleanup of the crime scene. The body wasn't moved or dumped. This was hurried, not planned. This was a killing of necessity." Alisha beamed like a kid on Christmas morning.

"You found her, Storm. Did you see anything weird or out of the ordinary at her house?" asked Alisha.

"No, nothing that jumps out at me except like I said, it looked like the perp was searching for something, and, of course, unlike the others, there was blood everywhere."

"Tell me again what you saw. Think about it. Go slow. Visualize everything," Alisha instructed him.

"I saw her lying on the floor of her bedroom, naked from the waist down, and there was blood everywhere." Storm slowly re-enacted his discovery of Peggy's body.

"Anything else?"

"Yes. It looked like someone had written something with her blood, maybe with a finger, but the letters were smeared. Maybe it was the perp leaving his calling card, his initials maybe. I am not sure Ms. Wise would have been able to write anything but I remember thinking one letter looked like a

213

C or a G and the last letter could have been a B or a P, but I won't swear to it. Crime scene photos give a perspective that the naked eyes misses but again I don't know."

"Her hand was covered in blood, so she could have been writing anything," said Alisha. "Did you look through her house?"

"A little, but of course I was trying to preserve the crime scene till the forensics guys and the M.E. could get there. I wanted that scene sealed," said Storm. "Like I said, the house was a mess; chairs turned over, papers all over the floor, and at first blush I assumed it was from the fight."

"If the killer was searching the house they might not have found whatever it was, though obviously it was worth killing for if they were in fact looking for something," Russell commented.

"I'm going back to her house," said Storm. "Pancho, I want you to get back into those files if you still have copies and call anyone who might have known any of the other five girls that I haven't contacted yet to see if you can turn up any new leads or connections. Did they have boyfriends? Did they volunteer at the Show? Is there anything to connecting them to other people at the Show or to one another? The rest of you keep your heads down and your ears to the ground."

"Did she have her shoes on?" asked Hernandez.

"Truthfully I don't remember, but when we get the pictures from the crime scene we can see," replied Storm.

"There were no shoes to inventory with what she was wearing when we got the body," Alisha commented.

"No, but I will look around when I go back to her house," said Storm.

Hernandez nodded, as did the others. They were all in agreement, and no more needed to be said.

"If the killer is a woman, doesn't that throw Ellen Dresden back to the top of the listed?" asked Hernandez.

"It would have if I hadn't reread Sunday's paper," said Grady. "Ellen was, according to the Houston paper, out of town at a Rodeo charitable women's fashion show in Austin on Saturday with at least twenty other rodeo matrons. The fashion show didn't end until after midnight Saturday night, so if she killed Leslie she made the trip back in less time than anybody can drive that distance."

Storm just shook his head. It was a break to know Peggy's killer was a woman, but now their best suspect had an airtight alibi.

They all left convinced they had an eighth victim. They had bought into Alisha's theory this was most likely a killing of necessity. This was not a random or copycat murder—there had to be a connection to the other seven homicides.

Charity Kills

CHAPTER TWENTY-FOUR

The Big Reveal

Early the next morning Alisha reviewed the records again. Traces of female DNA were definitely under Peggy's fingernails. She had fought back, so the killer would have fresh scratches somewhere on her body. She also found a record of a short length of blue thread on the body, so she photographed it, scanned it, and typed its color and characteristics into the computer to see if a match would come back. The preliminary match identified it as consistent with the thread used in sewing together pieces of shirt weight fabric, and she recognized its color right away as the color and type used in manufacturing uniforms. Would this small and possibly insignificant detail mean anything or raise any red flags with her team?

Storm's phone had been playing "Stormy Weather" all night but he had turned it off. Early the next morning his home phone began another incessant chorus of rings. Why am I not surprised he's calling already? Storm thought, as he saw "Lt. Flynn" flash on the caller ID. Flynn started right in with the accusations." I hear you've been asking about six other murders, not just the Phillips homicide. You're trying to establish a relationship between those other ones and the show."

Storm was sitting at his kitchen table studying the crime scene photos from Peggy Wise's murder. Peggy was lying face down in a pool of blood with her hands outstretched. Her skirt was up around her waist and her feet were bare. The killer hadn't had time to move Ms. Wise's body or hide the crime scene. Alisha appeared to be right that this was not planned out as well as the others, but Storm felt in his gut it was same perp; call it "cop's intuition" or whatever you want, he told himself, but he knew.

It appeared she was trying to write something, but what? Her hand was drenched in blood and the letters, if they were letters at all, were smeared and messed beyond his ability to read them. Was she trying to tell someone who her killer was, or was she asking for help? Could the killer have been taunting the police with some bogus clue? He had to get back into Peggy's place and take a more careful second look around.

"Come to my office as soon as you get in," Flynn ordered. When he arrived, he glanced at Sergeant Hernandez with a question in his eye. Hernandez nodded affirmatively—signaling the files were all back in their place and had not been missed, but he did have copies. They had put that plan together the day before when Storm had made the announcement to his team that he would be putting the word out at the Show that he knew about the other girls. All records were to be replaced—Hernandez would only keep copies, so if someone went looking to see if files were missing they would find everything in order.

Storm knocked on the lieutenant's door and was waved immediately in. Through the glass windows of the office he had seen that Flynn was not alone, and now he saw a familiar welcome face among those waiting for him, a surprise one but a welcome one. But he wondered why Lieutenant Smith was there.

"Who do you think you are?" Vern Nagel attacked first, launching into a voice that was so loud everyone in the precinct turned to see what was going on. "What do you mean going into the Show asking about six old cases about a bunch of girls you are not authorized to be looking into?"

Flynn slammed the door behind Storm as quickly as he could. He was trying to keep this as quiet as possible and Nagel's yelling was not helping that situation. Rumors circulated quickly around police departments and the lieutenant didn't have any idea of what was truth and what was rumor at this point.

"Hold on, Mr. Nagel, this is my office and my meeting and you will keep your voice down. I understand the mayor is upset and you're feeling some pressure but I would ask that you hold your tongue until we clarify some things and we'll get through this. Storm, did you go to the Show yesterday and ask for records on six people unrelated to the specific case you're supposed to be working on?" asked Flynn.

"Yes, Lieutenant, I did," Storm said quietly. He had found that speaking softly in confrontational situations usually made the other person even angrier and often exposed their vulnerability and real purpose. It was a trick he had learned when he had argued infrequently with his mom and even less frequently with Angie. The softer his voice got, the louder and madder they got. Having Nagel react this way pleased Storm to no end.

"Those are old cases that have nothing to do with the murder of that poor girl last Saturday," yelled Nagel.

"Mr. Nagel, please. Keep your mouth shut," Flynn said, scowling at Nagel. He then turned to Storm and said, "Storm, why do you want that information?"

"Lieutenant, I believe these murders are all related," said Storm.

"Why would you think that, do you have any evidence of that?" yelled Nagel.

"Nagel, I have asked you to be quiet and I will not ask you again." Turning back to Storm he said, "Now why do you think these old cases are related?"

"This weekend's victim's throat was cut in a professional way so she couldn't scream. There were no defensive wounds, so she didn't fight, which means she knew or trusted her killer. She was in her early twenties, brunette, cute, single, no family to speak of, and last seen in the company of Show big wheels in the VIP room of the stadium. We have video of her going into the stadium, but none coming out. The man she went in with admitted having sex with her in the stadium rest room, but claims that was the last time he saw her," said Storm.

"Then you have your killer," announced Nagel.

"No, Mr. Nagel, I don't believe we do," Storm said.

"Again, I ask what does this have to do with the six old cases?" The lieutenant was not asking anymore—his tone made it clear he was demanding an answer.

"I believe the other six women were killed by the same person who killed Leslie Phillips." Storm knew he had put himself on the line now. "The circumstances of each girl's death is the same, the cause of death was the same, they were all similar in appearance, and they were all found dead either near or on the grounds of the Dome." Storm wasn't going to divulge anything more about what he knew, at least not in front of Nagel.

"Who is this man of interest?" asked the lieutenant.

"As I said earlier, he is Joe Dresden. He was seen on the video going into the stadium with the girl the night she was killed, and right now I wouldn't call him a suspect," replied Storm.

"So, you don't have a suspect?" Nagle's voice was rising again.

"Nagel, I am warning you for the last time, I will ask you to leave if you can't control yourself. You are not furthering anything with your tone and your interruptions," the lieutenant, obviously pissed. He directed his questions back to Storm.

"Why don't you think this man is your killer?" asked the lieutenant.

"When I confronted him about what he knew about this girl it scared the shit out of him, especially after I showed him the picture of her lying in the morgue. Also, in the video when he leaves the stadium, he doesn't look the worse for wear. He's in the same clothes, but they're not wrinkled or bloody. He admits to being with the girl, but claims when he left her she was fine and having drinks with other people in the club. We can reasonably believe she had consensual sex before the killing; there was spermicide found in her vagina and no evidence of rape. The damage and bruising to her anus was postmortem."

"How could you possibly know that?" Flynn demanded.

"That is the opinion of the medical examiner," said Storm.

"So, you interviewed this Dresden character and you scared him?" Flynn asked.

"Yes, sir. But he's no killer. He's a playboy and philanderer, but he's also a wimp with no background in the military or police that would fit the M.O. of our killer."

* * * *

Nagel had suddenly gone quiet, listening to every word Storm was saying. He had to report back to the mayor and Dakota as soon as he left the meeting and he wanted to make sure he got it all, although he knew he still needed to get this guy away from the idea that these murders were related. He knew the decision had been made that if it got that far and someone had to be the scapegoat, Joe Dresden made a good candidate. But this asshole, who was supposed to be a ne'er-do-well drunk, was headed in another entirely different direction and unless he could be convinced Joe was responsible, the police were going to starting looking for someone else. If they did, Nagel knew he would be looking for a new job, especially if what Storm uncovered turned out to cast any shadows on the Show.

"What came out of the interview? Did he have an alibi?" asked the lieutenant.

"Yes, sir, he left the VIP club with his friends to go to a place called Fuad's for more drinks closer to home and the video shows him leaving without the girl. Not only that, but there was no change in his clothing from when he entered. That would be pretty hard to accomplish given the way she was killed and the blood loss that had to have occurred," Storm responded quietly.

"Did you confirm he was at this 'Fuad's'?" What is it, a restaurant, a bar, or what?"

"Yes, it's a regular watering hole near the Galleria for big wheels from the Show. The wait staff remembered all of them, including Joe, coming in about midnight. Joe left his car there and was driven home by one of his buddies, Rob Turnsdale. He didn't go back for it until the next day and since the M.E. puts the time of death at between midnight and 2:00 AM, I'd say his alibi is airtight," Storm said.

"Back to the other girls. How did you know about them and why do you think they are linked to this?" the lieutenant asked.

"First, from the get-go I overheard other folks refer to this case as if it was "another one" of many over the past few years," Storm replied.

"Who was talking about it?" The lieutenant demanded, and the answer to this question interested Nagel, too. Whoever had been talking needed to be silenced.

"Some of the cops who work the stadium. I overheard them talking about other girls killed the same way."

* * * *

Storm was lying through his teeth, but he wasn't going to reveal his true source of information, not in front of Nagel. *And God knows, I'm not going to implicate Hernandez. Not now.*

"How did you get their names?" asked the lieutenant.

"I had the M.E. look through their files for the past ten years to see if there were any DOAs where the victims were young girls murdered in the same manner and in the area of the Dome. As it turns out, there have been six other girls that fit the bill almost to a tee."

"Why do you want information from the Show about them?"

"I think these girls were hunted by the killer at the Show." Now came the part where he knew the bottom would drop out for everyone in the room. "I think we have a serial murderer and I think they operate at the Show and choose their victims there."

There was no going back now. Storm had opened Pandora's Box, and everyone in the room caught their breath. Not the least affected was Nagel, who looked downright apoplectic. Storm knew he had just shortened his time to prove his theory, or he would lose what little confidence anyone on the force had left in him. Within hours, more likely minutes, the Show, the mayor's office and the police chief would be circling their wagons to deflect any responsibility or knowledge of any conspiracy to cover up the fact that there was and had been a serial murderer operating in their city or at their charity and for this long.

"Jesus Christ, Storm, that is one hell of a conclusion. Are you nuts? If this leaks out and you can't prove it, you are done. You will be gone and nobody will be able to save you," warned the lieutenant.

* * * *

Lieutenant Flynn knew he needed to get with the chief and lay this out for him as soon as possible. He also had to keep Storm close. He had to be kept in Storm's loop so he knew what Storm knew, but his bigger concern was who else knew. Who did Storm trust, and who would he have confided in? That last thought stopped him dead in his tracks. Damn, who else knew what Storm had deduced? Who else besides his source at the M.E.'s office was helping him? Shit, shit, shit!

* * * *

Nagel almost ran out of Reisner Street. He had to get to the mayor and Dakota Taylor. He needed to be the one to give them the news of this latest bomb. Maybe he could temper it somehow and make himself look good in the process. He didn't know how but he had six blocks to come up with an idea...

* * * *

As Storm left the lieutenant's office, Lieutenant Smith came up behind him and put his arm around Storm's shoulders. Smith had remained silent throughout the entire meeting, and Storm still wondered why his old mentor had been in on the meeting, to which he had added nothing to the discussion.

As they left together, Lieutenant Smith asked, "You believe everything you said in there, kid?"

"Yes, Bob, I do."

"That's all the answer I need. Then solve it, boy, solve it." As he walked away, he turned once more and continued, "Glad to see you back, boy." He smiled at his old protégé before leaving, and Storm knew his old teacher had his back.

Storm had to get back out on the streets before the shock of his revelation to Flynn and the others wore off. He had to get back to Peggy Wise's place and see if he could find what he hoped the perp had not found, and figure out how she was involved in this. None of the "persons of interest" they had identified before were all that interesting now.

He went over the details once again as he picked up his keys and badge. Joe Dresden had admitted to being with the girl the night she died, but he had an alibi. Alisha had found female DNA in the skin under Peggy's nails, which added more credence to Joe's being innocent. Ellen Dresden had called Russell to see what he knew about Storm and why he had come to see Joe, and since they now knew or were pretty sure the killer was a woman, it could have been her. But she had been out of town and that, too, could be verified. Still, damn it, thought Storm, I'm not any closer to the killer and time is running out. He only had about twenty-four hours before things got out of hand and too many people would know what he knew. Flynn would be calling the M.E. to find out what Storm had learned and who had given him the information. He had to hope Alisha had covered her tracks. He had to keep Hernandez under the radar and although he didn't know how, he wanted to keep Russell and Grady out of it, as well.

There had to be a link, something overlooked at Peggy's house that could help him. He had to know what she had known, because he was certain it had gotten her dead. He had to warn Alisha to get out or be unavailable to her boss for the rest of the afternoon.

As he walked out of Reisner Street, he nodded to Hernandez and put his little finger and thumb to his ear and mouth, letting him know he would be calling him.

CHAPTER TWENTY-FIVE

Backseat Treasure

Storm rushed to get back to Peggy Wise's house, repeating his prayer that he would solve the murders. Considering what he knew, he had to get Leslie some kind of justice. He kept thinking of how his old boss, Lieutenant Smith, had taught him to organize and work his way through a problem to find the ultimate answer.

The police tape was still up on Peggy's door and lab guys would have already combed through the house looking for evidence left by the killer, but Storm felt there had to be something else; there was something Peggy knew that got her killed. The house and the murder scene were the same as when he had seen them last, except that the body had been removed and the blood cleaned up once the photographs had been taken to preserve the scene.

There was no trace left of any kind of writing or message Peggy may have left in her dying moments pointing to the killer, no dying scrawl that appeared to be the word COP written in her own blood, but there had to be something. He leafed through books and sifted through papers scattered about the floor and tables. He saw fingerprint dust on every surface—doors, windows, tables, and chairs; even the commode had been printed. He also knew this killer was smart and there would be no fingerprints that would lead to whoever it was.

He had to keep digging until he did find something, though it didn't seem like much, a picture of Peggy and a girl he recognized from another picture. It was the first murder victim, Elaine Gage, standing next to Peggy outside the Tejas Petroleum building, and the two women were smiling, with their arms around each other. He knew it! Peggy had been friends with at least one of the girls killed.

The house had been picked clean and he found no other leads. As he was about to throw in the towel, it occurred to him that Peggy's car might have been overlooked. He found her purse lying on the bed with the contents dumped beside it including what appeared to be the keys to her car, which he hoped was in the garage. It was ironic how many times the victims' automobiles were overlooked, especially when most people use their backseat as a mobile closet/safe and some even carry tool boxes in their trunks. Many times those items never make it into the house.

Opening the doors, he saw it was apparent that the car had not been searched, and in it, he discovered a surprising find on the back seat. It was a blue three-ring notebook like ones kids use in school. Except this was no ordinary book of class notes. It took him only a few minutes to realize what he had discovered.

I've gotta call another meeting—now. It had to be done quick. He immediately called Russell, Alisha and Hernandez. "I know the time isn't the best, but trust me, this is important," he told each of them. Grady was with Russell, so he would make sure he got there.

Russell got home before Storm arrived, so the door was open and Grady and Russell were standing just inside when Storm arrived.

"What ya got, Baretta?" asked Russell.

"I think we got the killer; actually, I think Peggy Wise, the girl who was murdered yesterday, got the killer, and I think Alisha was right, it's a woman. But let's wait for Hernandez and Alisha to get here so we can go over this together."

The anticipation in the room was thick enough to be carved with a knife, but they waited. Alisha was the last to show up only ten minutes after Storm.

Seated around Russell's dining room table, Storm laid out the blue notebook and began his description of what he had found.

"I think we've all been pretty much in agreement that we probably have a serial killer on our hands and that after Peggy Wise's murder yesterday we all felt the killer was the same person who had killed the other girls; even though the venue was different, the method was the same and the anal rape fit the same pattern."

Everyone nodded.

"This Peggy Wise was one hell of an amateur detective herself. First, I found this picture of her and the very first victim, Elaine Gage." Storm laid the picture of Peggy and Elaine on the table for all to see. "This time I searched the entire house, even the garbage, but found nothing else." Then, snap," and Storm snapped his fingers, "I thought of her car, and sure enough, lying in the back seat was this blue three-ring notebook. Inside this notebook are pictures of all the victims, clippings from the newspapers on all their deaths, personal notes listing what she knew of each girl, and the details of each death. This girl was keeping a diary of sorts on a serial murderer."

"She was the killer?" asked Grady, confused. "If she was, why was she killed the same way?"

"No, but she was one damn fine sleuth. Look at the last pages of the book." Storm opened it to the last page. Peggy had written the name "Tess Stone." Beside it her notes read: "From Victoria, Deputy Sheriff, and Houston cop, worked for Show since 1997." He then flipped back a few pages so they could all see Peggy Wise's notes:

What I Know About The 7 Murders
And What They Have In Common
3/13/04

1. *All around same age*
2. *All brunette, slender, cute*
3. *All from small towns*
4. *Not married*
5. *Little or no family*
6. *Some I saw out here in VIP clubs,*
   married man hunting grounds
7. *All volunteers*
8. *All found naked and raped in area of Dome*
9. *All were killed near same time of year, only*
   one killed later in Show season.
10. *Doesn't appear they fought the killer, not*
    beaten or cut up, just their throats cut.
11. *Some clothing found, but no shoes.*
12. *All died on weekend night*
13. *All killings are the same, but disposed*
    of in different ways

Ideas I Have

- *Same killer, my cop friends think I am crazy.*
- *Didn't fight so had to know killer, or have*
  been knocked out with drugs, or passed out.

- *Killer lives out here during Show, knows his or her way around here or involved here·*
- *How did they meet the killer? Committeeman, staff or worker or big dog?*
- *A detective is here now· Am following him see what he knows· Maybe someone finally cares·····*

Tess Stone
I found the killer

✓ *Show records list police officer working the door at VIP room in Stadium·*
✓ *Worked here for seven years; always worked security at door·*
✓ *The same blonde woman I saw at Elaine's funeral*
✓ *She is also the woman who lived with a girl in Victoria when the girl disappeared 9 years ago· Her name was Gail Ponder· She disappeared from a trip to beach, never seen again· Tess was Deputy County Sheriff at the time· Rumor always had it that she knew something, but no one ever proved if she did or not*
✓ *Left Victoria after that· Now I know where she went·*

Got to get a hold of detective tomorrow and tell him·

Everyone leaned over and read until Alisha spoke. "The blue thread found under Peggy's nail matches the thread used in a HPD uniform shirt. I was waiting for the definitive reading on the match and it came back this morning. So, we know now it was a female and a cop, or at least someone wearing a cop's shirt that killed Peggy."

Russell reached for the picture of Peggy's body encircled in the pool of her own blood, "Now I see it, look." He traced the letters in the crime scene photo. "She was trying to spell *COP*, she was trying to tell you it was a cop who killed her." It was instant recognition from everyone—they could all see the letters now.

"Hernandez, can you get into personnel records of Houston cops working patrol now?" asked Storm.

"Yes, I can." Pancho looked at Russell and pulled his laptop from the case and laid it on the table, booting it up so he could access the wireless network operating in Russell's building.

"Russell, while Pancho is looking up this Tess Stone in HPD's database can someone use your computer to go on the Internet? If you Google someone's name you can find anything ever written or published about them, right?" Storm questioned.

"Yeah, not everything, but most things. Why?" asked Russell.

"In the diary she mentions the disappearance of a girl in Victoria nine years ago. Do you think we can find anything about that?"

"Probably, or if not, we can go to the Victoria paper site and look for old articles about a girl disappearing," suggested Grady.

While Grady and Hernandez used the computers, Russell asked his friend, "So how did the meeting go with Houston's finest example of the Peter Principle?"

"Yeah, what did Flynn want to know?" asked Alisha.

He told them about how his report had caused the color to drain out of both Lieutenant Flynn's and Nagel's faces. "They're circling the wagons—and by 'they' I mean all of them, the police chief, the city, and the Show. They're getting ready to fend off the wolves crying for blood when this story breaks."

"Got her!" yelled Hernandez. "Tess Stone has been a Houston cop since 1997. She's assigned to Hebert on the south side of town." The fact she worked for Hebert came as a surprise to everyone, because, as Hernandez pointed out, "Hebert's not known for his ability to work with the opposite sex." The whole department knew Hebert was the supervisor least likely to have a female patrol officer, yet here she was, reporting to him.

Within a few minutes Grady had her, too. "There is a story in the *Victoria Advocate* about a girl who went missing in 1997 from the home she shared with her girlfriend, a Miss Shannon Teresa "Tess" Stone. It says the girl went missing the Fourth of July weekend and had not been seen since. There was some suspicion the girlfriend might know of her whereabouts or had something to do with her disappearance, but nothing had ever been uncovered. It also says the girlfriend was a Victoria County deputy sheriff. It goes on to say that the victim was last seen going on a boating and beach trip to Port Aransas, but she never arrived to meet her friends. Later, in another article, it says that search had been suspended but all hope for solving the case was not given up."

It was then, as everyone crowded around the computer, that the picture of Tess Stone and her roommate came up on the screen.

The roommate was a cute dark-haired girl. "Oh my god, she looks like Leslie Phillips," Alisha whispered.

Storm felt his knees buckle and he almost fell over. Tess Stone was the cop working the door of the VIP room the night Storm and Russell went to the Rodeo. Staring at the picture on the screen, all Storm could say was, "Oh, shit."

He pointed to the screen. "Russell, this is one of the cops I talked to the other night when we brought all hell down on Joe Dresden. She was working the door of the VIP room. She said she had seen Leslie before—saw her come in with Joe— but didn't see her leave. People, we know Peggy was killed by a woman, we know she had a thread from a cop's shirt under her nails, and now we have a female cop, who was suspected in her lesbian girlfriend's disappearance, working the door of the VIP room at the Show on the night of at least one of the murders, for sure. I don't think it takes much of a leap of faith to begin to see the "how" to the pattern of all the murders, including Peggy's," Storm said.

"She is a person of authority, she is a cop, so trusted, and since she worked the door they would have recognized her and been comfortable with her. Her training fits the modus operandi and now we've found a link to the disappearance of a girl who fits the common physical characteristics of the murdered girls," added Hernandez.

"OK, y'all, as bad as I hate to say this, I need to go see Hebert and see what he knows about Tess Stone. Hernandez, you are going with me. Russell, we need to go in under the radar so you've got to help us get in. Over half of Hebert's people work overtime at the Show, so it's pretty solid she will be there. Hernandez, go change your clothes. Try to look less like a cop and more like a cowboy going to the Show and meet me back here by 5:00. Grady, you and Alisha have to sit this one out; no way I am taking any chances on getting you involved in something that could go south in a hurry, " said Storm.

Both Alisha and Grady nodded. They argued the decision, but finally agreed they would wait in the courtyard outside the center near the food tents.

Russell parked in his normal parking spot close to the center and stadium; after all, he did have perks. The three of them, Russell, Hernandez, and Storm, walked to the entrance to the chutes, flashing credentials and badges as they walked by the cops and security guards who were working the massive garage door that opened the way to the bowels of the stadium. Grady and Alisha took a park bench across from the massive doors, sat down, and began to watch as if they might be able to see anything. When Storm and his posse got near Hebert's office, next to the football team's workout room, Storm told Russell to wait outside; he and Hernandez would go see Hebert alone.

"Well, Office Boy, what are you doing here again? I hear you got a killer," said Hebert.

"Sergeant, I want to ask you some questions. Don't get froggy with me and don't you dare lie. This is serious and I don't want any shit," said Storm.

Storm took out a piece of paper with Tess's name written on it and looking straight at Hebert, asked him if he had an officer named Shannon Teresa Stone working at the stadium. Hebert began to fidget in his chair, clearly uncomfortable, unable to look back at Storm, instead staring at the floor as if deaf and dumb. The alarm in his eyes and face gave him away.

"Bullshit, Hebert, I know she works for you on the south side. Is she here?" The tone of Storm's voice and the way he leaned across the desk displayed his intent. He was not above pulling the old son of a bitch across the desk.

Hernandez stood by the door, assuring nobody would be interrupting them now.

"Yes, why?" was all Hebert could say.

"I believe she is our killer," said Storm, calming just a little, but still leaning over the desk.

"Bullshit, you are just trying to find a goat. I heard about your serial murder theory and I think you are full of shit!" yelled Hebert. The cop looked like someone had kicked him in the balls. Storm could almost read his thoughts: This drunk has to be wrong. I personally took Tess under my wing when she came to work for HPD.

"You can think what you want. I don't give a shit. Is she here?" asked Storm, lowering his volume as he let his quiet voice kick in.

"Yes. She works the door of the VIP room on the ninth level. You can't tell me you believe she killed anyone. She's a fellow cop." Hebert was becoming more irate by the second.

"We are about to find out. We have DNA from the last killing, the young lady who worked for the Show, and we found a notebook from her home that implicated Shannon Teresa Stone in her murder and those of the other seven girls in Houston, not to mention a girl in Victoria. All I want is a DNA test done to get her cleared of any suspicion. The M.E. is waiting for a sample that will clear her of any wrong-doing. Now that's not too much to ask for, is it? You do want her cleared, don't you?" Storm paused to let that sink in.

There was no reaction from Hebert, his face still blank of expression. Storm moved on.

"The ninth level is empty now, isn't it?" Storm asked.

"Yes, except for the people working there and for security," responded Hebert in a voice barely audible.

"Will she be there?" asked Storm.

"Yes, she should be. They're due on at 5:00 PM."

"Sergeant Hernandez and I are going up there. We will ask her for a DNA sample and we'll be out of your hair. If you call her and warn her before I can get there I am coming back down and I will personally jump down your throat. Then I will arrest you for tampering with a homicide investigation. You got that?" Storm couldn't believe how calm he was. He willed himself to slow down; he knew being too excited could lead to mistakes and now was not the time for errors in judgment.

With that, Storm and Hernandez left Hebert's office and headed back down the hall to get Russell and go to the ninth level. When they got off the elevator they told Russell to hang back and wait. As they approached the entry to the club, Storm motioned to Hernandez. "Move to my left and back me up," he mouthed. Hernandez nodded affirmatively.

Officer Stone was standing at the front door when she saw Storm coming. She turned and told him the club was not open yet and he would have to wait. She added, "Do you have credentials to get into this club?"

Storm calmly pulled his badge and explained to her he was there on official business. "There's been a break in the Leslie Phillips case and I need to ask you some more questions about the night you saw her in the club and get some details straight about her murder. Officer Stone, of course you are up to speed on the two murders that have occurred in the last week, aren't you?"

"Yes, terrible, isn't it? The girl you showed me the other night and now the girl from the Show offices."

"Yes, it is. The last victim, Peggy Wise was her name by the way, left some very damning evidence."

"Oh, really?" replied Tess Stone.

She's starting to look nervous. I wonder if Pancho notices the way her eyes are darting back and forth. Hope so. Looks like she's looking for a way to escape. "Yes. But first, how did you get those scratches on your neck?" Storm asked, pointing to the area where he had already noticed some marks and waiting to hear how she would explain them.

"Fought with a drunk in here last night. Why?" Officer Stone said, putting up her hand over the scratches.

"Just an observance, Officer Stone," added Storm.

"I am sure you didn't come here to ask about my well-being, Detective, so what can I do for you?"

Storm looked over at Hernandez. He wanted to say, "Do you see the urge to flee building throughout her body as much as I do?" But he didn't have to. Hernandez's face betrayed no emotion but Storm noted that his hand was near his weapon and his stance telegraphed "ready."

"I need a DNA sample from you, Officer Stone, because, you see, Peggy scratched her killer and traces of skin from what the M.E.'s DNA tests indicate was from a female, traces we believe came from her killer, were found under her fingernails. Add to that, we have a blue thread that matches the fabric used in HPD uniforms." Storm pulled a DNA swab from his jacket.

Trained police officer Tess Stone began to back away.

"Officer Stone, don't do this, don't make me come after you." Stone spoke softly, encouragingly. "It is your choice but you can clear this up right now and right here. Let us have the M.E. come up to administer the test and eliminate yourself as a suspect."

Tess made another step back, further away from them and closer to the door.

"Officer Stone, please stop! It's just a test. We need to eliminate you as a possible suspect." Storm's tone was quiet, again trying to calm Tess so the situation would not become any more volatile.

As Tess continued to back away, her hand fell to her side as if to unsnap her gun holster. Storm didn't move—he barely breathed. He noticed Hernandez's body language— he was on high alert, gun within a second's reach. He knew now she was desperate, and God knows what she would do if pushed.

"Officer, stop. Please. Let us help you. This is not the way for this to end. Did you love Peggy? Was it a love gone wrong? You can talk to me," Storm assured her. Even as he tried to stay one step ahead of her, he had no real proof yet there was any involvement between Ms. Wise and Tess. Maybe talking about Peggy will calm her so she'll say something concrete we can use as cause to take her in, he hoped.

In mere seconds Tess's actions seemed to become animal-like, feral. Like a cornered wild hog, her instincts seemed to take hold as she looked around for a means of escape, but with Hernandez now behind her and Storm in front, there was nowhere to go.

Then her demeanor changed once more. A serene expression eclipsed her face, as if in her mind the only and perfect way out had just dawned on her. She unsnapped her gun holster, put the palm of her hand on her 9 millimeter, and smiling like the Madonna, she began to pull the weapon.

Before Storm could react, a shot rang out of nowhere. He spun around, expecting to see Hernandez with his gun drawn and discharged; instead, he saw Hebert holding his service revolver at arm's length, smoke still escaping the barrel.

* * * *

Hebert stood there horrified. He had been a cop for thirty years and had never had to shoot a living creature, let alone a human being. Now Tess, his protégé, had pushed for this end, the act that was known as *"suicide by cop,"* a last ditch effort to escape a bad situation, and he had been the one to shoot one of his own.

During Storm's confrontation with Tess, Hebert had snuck up a back elevator to get to the VIP room, hoping against hope Storm was wrong. When Tess had come to Houston and applied for a job with HPD, Hebert had been the one to vouch for her. It had been obvious early to him Tess floated her boat in a direction that was not generally accepted for police work, but Hebert also knew many of the department's female officers' sexual orientation wasn't the norm. His own niece was a lesbian and he had seen the torment her lifestyle had caused her, but that didn't mean Tess's relationships away from work needed to be a problem as long as she kept her nose clean. Tess had proven to be a good addition, street smart, get-your-hands-dirty type of cop and she didn't flaunt her personal lifestyle. He had added her to his cadre of officers working the Show as a reward for doing a good job and he knew she could use the easy money.

In spite of how protective he felt toward one of his own, he had also seen Tess's reaction to her confrontation with Storm. He saw her looking quickly and frantically around to locate any possible exit. He heard what Storm was saying to her and he knew now Storm had evidence that would implicate Tess. When she reached for her gun, his experience and his reflexes took over and even he could not let the office boy die like this.

Rushing to Tess's body and cradling her head in his lap, Storm asked, "'Tess, did you kill all those girls?"

Still smiling, Tess said, "Yes, but I loved only one." And she was gone.

CHAPTER TWENTY-SIX

Peggy's Notebook

Storm was sure that DNA would prove Tess to be Peggy Wise's killer, and Tess's dying declaration would be written up, but they still had to find evidence to bolster the motive for killing the others Remembering what Pancho had told them, that most serial killers keep mementos of their crimes, he was hopeful; there would be something in Tess's personal things to tie her to the other murders.

* * * *

It was then Russell called Grady and Alisha to tell them the outcome and ask Grady to meet him downstairs with a camera.Russell was a news man again. He felt vital, and he and Grady were going to break the biggest story of the year. Alisha was to join Storm and Hernandez at the scene of the shooting.

* * * *

For the first time in a long time, Storm wished he could have a drink. All hell was about to break lose, the facts of this case couldn't be hidden from the public anymore, and there were careers about to be lost. He picked up Peggy Wise's notebook and thumbed through the record of her research.

Second girl:

Another found,
  looks like Elaine,
  tall, slender, brunette,
  young and cute·

Saw her at Show,
  seen her going in and
  out of VIP club·
Committee Volunteer·
Not seen her with Joe,
  but had with other
  married big dogs·

Cops say she was killed same
  way as Elaine,
  throat cut, raped
  and found naked·

Did not go to her funeral
  it was out of town·

Killed on weekend night

small town girl

no family

same time of year as Elaine

Cops found her clothes
  but no shoes or boots···?

Turnbull

Debra Ann Turnbull
Beloved sister of Jenna Hopkins of Needville passed away February 25, 1999, in Houston Texas. Funeral services will be held at 3:00 P.M. March 1, 1999, at Green Lawn Cemetery in Needville, Texas.

Young Woman Dies Violent Death

Houston Texas - Early this morning the body of a young woman was found against the fence on the north side of the Dome parking lot. There are some utility and storage buildings on that side of the parking lot, her body was discovered between buildings when a cleaning crew looked under what described as an abandoned tarp. When they pulled the tarp away, they found her naked body. Her throat had been severed and police spokesmen said the girl had been violated before her death. HPD is investigating, but have not yet released her identity, awaiting notification of nearest of kin. Police said no suspect had been determined.

Girl number three:

*Slender, brunette, young
and cute·*

*Small town girl only had
a brother·*

Canter

Michele Louise Canter, 24
Michele Canter of Joachim
passed away March 12, 2000, in
Houston Texas. Funeral services
will be March 15, 2000, at Mr.
Avery Cemetery, Joachim,
Texas. She is survived by her
brother Peter Canter
of Spokane, Washington.

*Cops say she was found
naked, throat cut and raped·*

*Didn't know this one but
she is listed as committee
member of the Show·*

Local Cheerleader Found Dead

*This is a pattern,
kills same time
every year*

Why?

*How does he find
these girls?*

Houston - Michele Canter, of the Class
of 1994 at Joachim High School, was
laid to rest March 15, 2000, in Mt. Avery
Cemetery. After graduation, Ms. Canter
moved to Houston, working for Harris
County as dispatch clerk for the streets
department. The roadside cleaning
crews she used to be responsible for dis-
patching found her body early Sunday
morning. Her death has been determined
to be a murder and the Houston Police
are now investigating. They added Ms.
Canter had been sexually abused and her
throat had been cut. Her naked body was
found near an abandoned eatery in the
Dome area of Houston. So far, no suspects have been identified. Her brother
Peter Canter lives in Spokane, WA. He
returned to Joachim for her internment
and asked all donations be made to the
Joachim Shelter for Women.

Woman Found Dead

A young woman's body was found early
Sunday morning by roadside cleaning
crew. The cause of her death is unknown
at this time, but is being investigated.
Release of the victim's identity is awaiting notification of her next of kin. The
body was found while cleaning crews
picked up trash just off Old Spanish
Trail and Kirby next to a derelict restaurant. #

3/18/2001 This is the fourth girl killed in four years· She was killed the same way as all the others· From small town, no family and looks just like Elaine and the others· Sgt· Hebert came around asking if any of us knew her, told I had seen her around knew she was volunteer and had seen her going into the VIP club in the center· Show has also made it clear we were to help with investigation but not to talk to the press or anyone else·

Girls in office are scared so at night we are walked to our cars or walk in a group· Nobody acts like this is same person, but I think it is, but who? They have to be out here, they have to be finding these girls out here·

Cops only know she was cute and they had a picture of her they showed us to see if we knew her· Told them I had seen her but didn't know her· When I asked if they thought it was same person who killed the others they acted like I was nuts·

Killer Sought

Houston Police are seeking the killer of a young woman. A young woman's body was found early Saturday morning behind dumpsters used for disposal of waste at the Dome. No facts have been released as the cause of death and the young woman's identity is being held awaiting notification of next of kin. #

Area Girl Found Murdered

Houston, Texas - The body of Linda Black was found Saturday morning in Houston. Ms. Black had apparently been raped and murdered by an unknown assailant. Houston police are investigating the killing of this Alice girl, but have yet to release any details of their investigation. Ms. Black was a very popular student and will be missed by the entire community. Her funeral was held at Restland Cemetery on March 21, 2001. Ms. Black will rest in her family plot with her parents and two sisters.

Black

Linda Elisabeth Black, 23
Linda Elisabeth Black of Alice, Texas, passed away March 16, 2001. Funeral services will be held March 21, 2001, at Restland Cemetery at 10 A.M. in Alice alongside her mother and father.

DeBuse

Danielle "Sissy" DeBuse, 25
K. DeBuse passed away March
the 9, 2002. Funeral services will
be held March 14, 2002, at 11
A.M. at Mem. Park Cemetery
in Kingsville, Texas. Ms. DeBuse
has no remaining family and
will rest next to her parents
Phil and Lois Debuse.

Houston Unsafe....

The crime rate in Houston is on the increase as the number of murders, home invasions and car thefts have skyrocketed in the nation's fourth largest city. One of the latest killings involved a young girl from Kingsville last week. Ms. Kitty DeBuse a 1995 graduate of Kingsville High School was found murdered and sexually assaulted near the Dome complex on Houston's south side. Police suspect Ms. DeBuse was killed sometime the night before and that she was found naked with a deep cut across her neck and throat. Due to injuries, the police doubt the girl had a chance to yell for help or fight her attacker. Ms. DeBuse if one of many killing that have gone unsolved in the Houston area. Violent crime statistics show murder in Houston has increased 10% over the past two years. Ms. DeBuse worked for Twinco Valve and Fitting in Houston.

Fifth girl in five years,
all similar killings

I don't have any clues,

I had seen this girl too,
but she was like the rest

didn't know her, only
really just seen her.

Cops say the same
but no one asked
about this,

nothing much about
on the news
or in the papers

only one article from her
hometown paper.

Almost like…
no one cares…

Huntsville Girl Murdered

A popular Huntsville girl was found raped and brutally murdered March 21, 2003. Stephanie Gilmore, a graduate of the Huntsville High School the class of 1998, body was found near the Dome complex in Houston. Police say a man walking his dog near the north entry of the complex found the young woman's body. The details of her death have not been released pending further investigation. Ms. Gilmore worked for a law firm in Houston and her body will be brought back to Huntsville for interment in her family plot. Ms. Gilmore had no remaining family in the Huntsville area.

Girl 6

Volunteer,

I knew this one,
  talked to her
  a few times·

Brunette, slim, cute,
  young all the same·

Raped
  throat cut
  clothes found

  no shoes or boots...

Cops not saying
  anything
  about this girl
  except how she died···

this girl late in season
  of show

not found till last week·

Gilmore

Stephanie Anne Gilmore, 25
Stephanie Gilmore will be laid to rest March 26, 2003. The funeral services will take place at 3 P.M. at Mt. Carmel Cemetery in Huntsville, Texas. Ms. Gilmore died March 21, 2003, and has no surviving family.

7th girl

Nothing in paper yet Detective came to see Ms. Taylor, again

I had to tell the girls and had to repeat no one talks about it or to press.

I am going to follow detective see if he can lead me anywhere, then I will talk to him.

I have got to tell detective I think this is same killer as Elaine and others

Phillips

Leslie Markus Phillips, 25
Leslie Phillips will be put to rest March 15, 2004 at Aransas Memorial Cemetery at 2 P.M. Ms. Phillips is survived by her grandparents Jake and Dorothy Phillips of Hallettsville Texas.

Charity Kills

CHAPTER TWENTY-SEVEN

The Trophy Room

This night was going to be a long one after the events earlier at the stadium. Storm and Hernandez were on their way to Tess's home to see what evidence they could uncover. Traffic at this time of night seemed lighter than usual, or maybe they just didn't notice how heavy it was, as their minds were elsewhere. The mental image of Tess lying dead and her Madonna smile replayed through their minds as they drove out of town on the Southwest Freeway toward Crabb Tree Road.

The farther they got into the country the darker it got, and the quieter. Neither had said much since they left the scene of the shooting at the stadium.

Storm sneaked a look at Hernandez and could tell that he, like Storm himself, was chewing over how things had gone so terribly wrong. The house was located in an old farming area just south of the freeway where developers had begun to build new homes sprouting up around it like mushrooms. They found the road that led to it, a long gravel and dirt combination that led to a two-bedroom clapboard house with a garage/tool shed behind it. Giant live oak trees hung over the drive as if it were a covered bridge, blocking out all light from the stars and moon. The yard was mowed and everything seemed in its place. The house was small; freshly painted in white with blue trim.

The inside was even neater. Tess's furniture was modest; a couch, chair, TV and a simple kitchen table and chairs; all looked spotless. The white porcelain in the kitchen and bathroom gleamed. The floors were scrubbed and no dust appeared to be anywhere. Her bedroom was the same; the bed made, pillows fluffed, and the chest of drawers lined with items she probably used on a daily basis all perfectly laid out in order. The clothes in her closet were arranged by type and color, her uniforms on one side, her jeans and casual shirts on hangers on the other. Her shoes were stored in boxes labeled by the type and color with the exception of her boots, both work and cowgirl. Those were all lined up on the floor and perfectly polished.

Nothing they found surprised either of them. From the information Hernandez had retrieved from the FBI profiles, everything fit the model of an organized serial murderer. They would have been shocked if they found things in disarray; after all, this lady was deliberate about the things she had done, or what they thought she had done.

After scouring the living area of Tess's home they still hadn't found anything to link her to the other killings, that was, until they entered the second bedroom. The door was locked, but a stiff shoulder cracked the jam. When the door smashed in, they found the other world Tess lived in and all the pieces of the puzzle appeared before them.

Across the room was a clear Plexiglas case that ran the length of the wall and was two levels high. The case sat on shiny chrome legs. It held two sets of clear cubes about two feet by two feet. Each row had four cubes and each cube held a pair of boots, with the exception of the last, which held a pair of running shoes. In front of each pair of boots was an engraved nameplate with the name of the girl they had belonged to. The only exception was the one with the running shoes; they must have been what Peggy was wearing the night she died.

There was a work table and chair with a role of clear plastic sheeting, a material used by workmen to protect floors and furniture from dust and paint spills.

She must have used the sheeting, probably Visqueen, Storm realized, to hide her crime scene.

A dozen combat knives, all in sheaths, arranged on a rack hung on the wall. These knives would be tested for blood and Storm was sure eight of them would be found to have traces of blood from each of the victims. They might even find blood evidence of the girl in Victoria who had disappeared nine years ago.

On the work table was a photo album and a diary. These were the pieces of evidence Storm and Hernandez wanted to look at, even though they both dreaded what revelations they might find.

An individual page had been dedicated to each girl in the photo album. There was a picture of each girl lying in her own blood, her face lifeless. The other picture on each page was of each victim posed with her bare bottom raised and with a large plastic phallic object protruding from her anus.

Although the album assured them that they had the right killer, it didn't answer the biggest question of all, why? Storm hoped to find those answers in Tess's diary that lay on the desk. The diary was meticulously kept and dated on top of each page, so he felt he could look for dates near the times of the killings and he would find the answers.

My Diary
Shannon Teresa Stone

Dear Diary   3/16/96
Today I met a beautiful new girl· She flirted with me and acted interested· She is tall, brunette and gorgeous· Her name is Gail, Gail Ponders· She is a year or two younger than me and told me she had had a relationship in college with another girl· I hope she wants another; Victoria is a terrible place to meet a girl who likes girls, the town is too small and prudish and I am getting lonely·

———————————

Dear Diary   3/17/96
Work was the same today· Nobody takes me seriously, everybody thinks I just got this job because I am a woman and they needed to fill a quota· I am a good cop and I know how to do the job· The other deputies tease me about being a lesbian but I blow them off· They are not sure about me and I don't say, but I guess they'll know if I start dating Gail· I called her today and she was so sweet on the phone, she made my heart melt when I asked her to lunch and she said yes· XOXOXOXOXOXO

———————————

Dear Diary   3/19/96
I went to lunch today with Gail· She is wonderful; she laughs and teases and even reached over and took my hand during lunch· She is bright and funny· I asked her out for Saturday night and she said yes· My heart is skipping from the joy at having found such a wonderful girl· The day can be terrible at work, but when I think of her my smile takes over my face·

———————————

Dear Diary   *3/23/96*
Today I had to arrest a man for beating on his young
girlfriend· He had left her with a black eye and bruises on
her arms and legs· After I arrested him, she wouldn't file
a complaint against him· The sheriff let him free· Why are
girls so stupid, why would she be with a man like that?

But I had dinner with Gail· She looked so cute in shorts
and the little top she wore· We had pizza and a couple
of beers and went dancing, we giggled and played till after
midnight· I get light headed when I am around her· I drove
her home and she kissed me good night· It was my wish,
to kiss her like that· She kissed me as if she loved me and
I hope she does·

———————————

Storm skipped ahead in the diary, closer to the dates of
the disappearance of Gail.

———————————

Dear Diary   *5/3/96*
Gail has moved in with me and we are together all the
time now· Her parents hate me; they think I have ruined
their daughter· People on the street look at us like we're
monsters· They all say bad things about us behind our
backs· It seems to bother Gail more than me, she hates
being looked at and ridiculed· She will be fine though our
love grows everyday and I know she will be my lover for
life· No one can come between Gail and me·

———————————

Dear Dairy   *6/16/96*
Today was a bad day· Gail stayed at her parents' home
last night and left me alone for the first time since we
moved in together· Her parents hate me and I know
her friends are trying to break us up· I am not sure
but I think her parents had her old boyfriend over for

253

dinner last night trying to show Gail the problem with being in love with a woman· She didn't come home till this morning, she said she just spent the night with her parents, but I think she is listening to them· She is mine now and nothing is going to change that, even if I have to confront her parents·

Gail is mine·

Dear Dairy   6/26/96

Gail has planned a trip to the beach in Port Aransas· She says she is going with friends; the same friends who want to break us up· She has been seeing them a lot lately and she has been seeing her old boyfriend again· I won't let her go· She belongs to me now and she belongs to me body and soul· I will stop her· I will make her understand she can't leave me· No one can take her from me·

Diary   7/4/96

Today is Independence Day and I am independent again· Gail is gone now and no one will ever find her· I gave her a chance to change her mind; she knew she belonged to me· I told her I loved her as her eyes went blank, my kiss caressing her lips and the blood covered my hands· She was mine· She belonged to me and now she will always be mine· She looked so cute with her hair pulled back in a pony tail sticking through the back of her white longhorns hat, wearing her shorts and my cowboy boots· She pleaded, but it was too late; she would never belong to anyone else· Holding her after death was as natural and exciting as when we made love· I am ashamed of how I felt, feeling her warm blood on my arms and hands caused my orgasm·

Diary   *7/4/97*

It has been a year since our loss of Gail· The local police and Sheriff's office have questioned me, but my regret of her disappearance is as bad as anyone else's· Her parents think I had something to do with it or know where she is but it will never come out· If I had done it, do they think I would have left anything to lead them to me? Everything is gone; her clothes, her body· The knife is hidden and only my boots remain with me· Something strange has come over me, I find myself fantasizing about the day she died· About how it felt to hold her as her life ran out· The way her eyes pleaded, the intense orgasm I had·

Diary   *9/1/97*

I have applied for a job with the Houston Police· With my time as a Deputy Sheriff in Victoria I am sure I will get on· It is time to leave Victoria; after all this time people still look at me strangely and I can hear them muttering under their breath about "the Dyke" and Gail's disappearance· Moving to a large city is the best for me· In a large city I can meet more women, maybe another Gail and get lost in the crowd·

Diary   *11/3/97*

Houston is wonderful and has opened up so much for me· I work on the south side of Houston for a Sergeant named Hebert· He is a crusty old fart, but seems to have taken a liking to me· I work days so my nights are free and he offered me a job working at the Stadium as security for one of VIP clubs that are open during special events· He tells me it is mainly making sure no one gets in without credentials and making sure the VIP drunks don't get in trouble·

Houston also gave me a chance to take classes in martial arts and an FBI course in distinguishing killing techniques· I still have the dreams and fantasies about Gail and the exaltation I got from it· I know I can do it again· Police are mostly stupid and would never think of a fellow officer, especially a woman officer· I know I can plan it, execute it, and never get caught· I would have to do it where I can be a part of the investigation, so I know what they know· I am looking forward to this work at the stadium; it might be the perfect place to find another Gail·

As Storm leafed through the diary quickly he saw the names of all the other girls and their deaths described ghoulishly. He wanted to find her entries on Leslie and Peggy. He hastily turned the pages until he got to the dates from the days just passed. There he read Tess's entries about Leslie. How Tess had seen Leslie on Wednesday of the barbecue and considered her another young beautiful tramp, one of those that hung out in the VIP clubs with older married men. Tess had then picked her as her next lover. Tess had done her research like she had all the other girls. She knew Leslie's parents were dead, she knew she was from a small town and she knew the likelihood that anyone would push the investigation of her death was slim. "Lover" was the term Tess used when she talked about the girls in her diary.

The diary detailed how Tess would talk to the girls, becoming comfortable with them and them with her. She described how she would set the scene for the murder and use the Visqueen to contain the blood so no mess would be found. She wrote how she took her own clothes home to burn them and left the bloody victim's clothes behind to be discovered close to where the body was found but not on the body; she wrote how she saved the boots as trophies and took photographs of the girls with a phallic device used on their anus. She did this, she explained, as a final humiliation of the girls and to make the cops think a man was doing it. It had to be obvious to the investigators that a man had raped these girls and then abused them anally. This kind of abuse would never be related to a female killer.

She talked about the cutting stroke that severed their windpipe and how the warm gush of air and blood felt so good on her skin. She described leaving the bodies where they could be found on the grounds of the Dome. After her first killing she had learned that the Show and police covered up events like this to save themselves the scrutiny of the public. She wrote about how very little was ever said or written about these girls and how the cases all seemed to go into the unsolved file quickly. That part had been a little disappointing. Actually, she wished she was creating more fear, but she satisfied herself with knowing it helped keep her secret of murder.

She described how she chose her victims. They all had to look like Gail and that was the first criteria. When she got to know them better the next hurdle was find out if all were from small towns and hopefully had little or no family that would push for an investigation into their deaths. She knew they all had been having affairs with older men during the show, making love to them in secret and secluded areas of the stadium. Each girl drank, normally leaving a little inebriated, making it easier for her to have an excuse to walk them outside. How they trusted her and felt safe with her! But the girls never made it outside the stadium or off the grounds and with each girl's death Tess would have another of what she called her "religious orgasms."

For days after each killing Tess would polish and stroke the boots, bringing herself to another sexual delight. Leslie had been just like the others. Tess reveled in the fact she felt that no one was going to get any closer to catching her, to discovering her secret life.

Then Storm came to the entries about Peggy. Peggy was a different story. Tess had seen Peggy following him when he hadn't that night in the VIP club, and she saw Peggy watching when he had talked to her. Tess was concerned Peggy had recognized her and was afraid that Peggy would tell Storm about the rumors from Victoria. She lost sleep that night and the decision was made—she had to get rid of Peggy and do it in a hurry, too much of a hurry to execute a good planning. Peggy didn't really fit Tess's type, but this was a necessity. In Tess's mind there was no option but for Peggy to die.

Like any good police person, Tess got Peggy's address and went to her house to check it out. There were no alarms, and she had broken in through the back door and left it open. She then drove back to the entrance into Peggy's neighborhood and waited. When Peggy came home, she followed and waited until she figured Peggy was getting ready for bed. She quietly entered through the back and caught Peggy unaware. Peggy fought back; she had scratched Tess, but finally Tess had pinned her down and was able to use her knife on Peggy's throat. After it was over, she staged the scene like she had with the other girls. She hoped it would lead anyone investigating the crime away from her and to the undiscovered killer of the other girls. She didn't have time to clean up or move the body because it was about then that an HPD patrol car came down the street. Damn the neighborhood watches! Tess snuck back to her car and left, taking Peggy's shoes with her to add to her trophy case.

EPILOGUE

So ends the case of Leslie Phillips and the seven tragically killed girls before her, including the beautiful young woman from Victoria, Storm reflected, as he filed the obligatory reports for Lieutenant Flynn. Storm hoped it would put Gail's parent's minds to rest to know her killer had been found. Although the prospective of finding her body was remote, there was the solace in knowing the final resolution of her killer.

Storm had mixed emotions about his work on the case. It was good to have solved the murders, but it was sad to know that these girls had died for the depraved fantasies of a lunatic serial murderer and their deaths had been ignored for so long. And for what? To keep the powerful of Houston and sleazeballs like Dresden and Leon Powers from getting their chaps dusty? All this to hush up bad publicity about the Show that might cause sponsors and their deep pockets to fly the coop?

He wondered how many heads would roll at the Show and in the mayor's office, or if things would be handled differently in the future. His conclusion was probably that there wouldn't be any major changes. Some things never change. But one thing was for sure, he was back to his old form and with a new partner, Hernandez, and he knew he didn't want a drink.

As he stuck the forms into Flynn's "in" box, he sighed. *Some careers are going to be made with this case, others will be lost, but in the scheme of things, nothing really changes.*

ABOUT THE AUTHOR

A thirty-year resident of Houston, Texas, Jon Bridgewater graduated from the University of Nebraska–Omaha with a BS in Communications and English. His career was in sales, where he worked his way up to Vice President of Sales and Marketing for a US-based manufacturer of electronic equipment, prior to becoming an entrepreneur and pursuing his writing aspirations.

An ex-college football player and Omicron Delta Kappa Honor graduate, Jon has always loved entertaining people and storytelling, enough so that for a brief time in the early seventies, he tried his hand at acting and stunt work in television series and made-for-TV movies until the lack of work forced him back into sales.

His desire to entertain and tell stories never abandoned him and with a push from close friends, he decided to follow their advice and develop one of his stories into his debut release, *Charity Kills*. Not content with only one title, he has already completed his second book, *After the Storm*, and is currently working on the third as yet unnamed book to complete the trilogy.

Jon enjoys outside hobbies and activities such as fishing, skiing, riding his Harley Davidson Dyna Wide Glide and watching college football. You can often find him volunteering at events for special children or at various other charitable causes.

To contact Jon, email: jon@jonbridgewater.com
or visit www.JonBridgewater.com

COMING FALL 2012

After the Storm
A David Storm Mystery

by Jon Bridgewater

In 2006, Hurricane Katrina blew more than just refugees into the city of Houston. Now, hardened criminals with gang affiliation are residing in the upper middle class neighborhoods, bringing with them their callous disregard for good versus evil. With yet another body on their hands in a city already reeling from monumental increases in crime, Detective David Storm and his loosely put together team of investigators struggle to solve the bizarre murder of one of their own.